A
BITTERSWEET
SURPRISE

ALSO BY CYNTHIA ELLINGSEN

Starlight Cove Novels

The Lighthouse Keeper
The Winemaker's Secret

Additional Novels

The Whole Package
Marriage Matters

Middle-Grade Novel

The Girls of Firefly Cabin

A
BITTERSWEET
SURPRISE

CYNTHIA ELLINGSEN

LAKE UNION
PUBLISHING

Published by Lake Union Publishing, Seattle
www.apub.com

Amazon, the Amazon logo, and Lake Union Publishing are trademarks of Amazon.com, Inc., or its affiliates.

ISBN-13: 9781542094245
ISBN-10: 1542094240

Cover design by Caroline Teagle Johnson

Printed in the United States of America

To John Rice, for the writing times, the writing talks, and the donuts at Bud's

Chapter One

Summer sunlight illuminated the painting on the wall of the Starlight Cove Sweetery, making it glow in the early afternoon. *The Girl with the Butterscotch Hair* was the centerpiece of the candy shop and had been there for twenty-seven years now, ever since I was five years old. It wasn't an important work by a famous artist or anything, just a friend of my father's, but it was important to me.

The painting captured the exterior of the Starlight Cove Sweetery at Christmas, the white lights shining from the edges of the windows and the black-painted sills dusted with winter snow. Inside, the shop's display cases gleamed with trays of chocolates and brightly colored candies. A little girl in a frilly dress sat at a table in the corner, beaming as she sipped on a hot chocolate.

It was hard to believe that little girl was me.

So much has changed. And yet, so much has stayed the same.

With a rueful grin, I stirred my hot cocoa. The hard dollop of chocolate on the wooden spoon melted into the cup of cream, releasing its rich aroma. The Chocolate Dream, as my father had named it, had been a staple of the Sweetery ever since he'd opened the doors just over thirty years ago. It was served on a tray alongside a small plate of whipped cream and three shortbread biscuits. I drank it like coffee, the chocolate as warm and comforting as a hug.

Today, that comfort evaporated like steam when my cell phone chimed with a text alert from my stepmother, Gillian.

Emma—dinner at six. Harbor Resort. Big news!!!

So much for a relaxing night.

Back when I was little, I'd loved everything about Gillian. I thought her job as a newscaster was so glamorous, and I adored her perfectly done hair, her makeup, and the outfits she wore on television. She was charming and funny, and I wanted to be just like her. That is, until my father died, and she dumped me on my grandmother to raise. The rejection had crushed me. Gillian was the only mother I'd ever had. The fact that she'd abandoned me at the time I'd needed her most was something I had never understood. Of course she'd tried to spin it, telling everyone she'd wanted to give my grandmother purpose after the loss of her son. True or not, I'd never shaken the feeling that Gillian had wanted me to prove my value, and I'd fallen short. It was my issue, not hers, but that didn't make spending time with her any easier. It also didn't help that I'd now put myself in a position of servitude to her, working as her employee at the Sweetery for the past few years.

Maybe that was what the dinner meeting was about. Sales had been sky high, and—with the exception of the two o'clock lull—the Sweetery was always busy. A few weeks ago, I'd asked her for a raise but had never gotten a real answer. Feeling hopeful, I texted her back.

Good news?

The response bubble popped up, and I held my breath.

You'll be excited!!! See you then.

Oh, it had to be about the raise. Thank goodness. The extra money would go a long way. My grandmother's assisted living insurance was slated to switch from full coverage to partial coverage at the end of the year. If I could make a little more each month and cut some corners elsewhere, I could use what I had in savings to make it work. Gillian certainly wasn't going to pick up the slack. She and my grandmother weren't close anymore, mainly because Gillian had pulled away from my grandmother too.

After setting down my phone, I headed to the front window to see if foot traffic had increased. Starlight Cove was in the middle of a rare heat wave, so the tourists were hiding indoors. I didn't blame them. Our air-conditioning was always on high to protect the chocolates, but today, it was so hot and muggy that the room was barely cold.

Outside, the pastel buildings on Main Street nearly looked white in the bright sunlight. Lake Michigan glimmered like a cool oasis behind the shops across the street, but the small sections of the beach I could see were empty, even by the lighthouse.

My father had often said few places compared to Bruges, where he had apprenticed, but the sense of charm and community Starlight Cove offered gave that same vibe, of a place that people wanted to visit again and again. It was a fairy tale–like setting. There were thousands of pictures on social media of our storefronts with the lighthouse somewhere in the background.

I was about to turn away from the window when I noticed the car again, a wood-paneled station wagon that was rusted on the bottom and packed full of stuff, like the occupants had left somewhere in a hurry. It was the third time this week it had limped back and forth in front of the shops, smoke billowing out of its tailpipe, without anyone stopping to shop or grab food or anything. The driver was a woman, about midthirties, and she kept peering into the windows like she was looking for something. Or someone.

Why was she back? I chewed my lip as she pulled into an empty spot in front of Henderson Hardware. The phone rang behind the counter, and quickly I moved to answer it.

"There's that car again." It was Jenny, the owner of Chill Out, a popular coffee shop across the way. "I'm telling you, Emma, it's up to no good."

"The car's up to no good?" I teased. "Or the woman inside of it?"

"I'm serious. It's freaking me out."

"Jenny, it's fine. At least, I think it is." There had to be a logical explanation. "Why are we being so suspicious?"

"Because of the world we live in," Jenny said. "Well, except maybe you. You're in your candy-coated heaven over there. I guess being on a constant sugar high would make it easy to believe the world's a good place."

I laughed. "It *is* a good place."

I had to believe that; otherwise, how would it be possible to get out of bed each morning?

My father had taught me that the quickest way to stop a bad day was to make someone else's easier. He had always done that at the candy shop by giving out extra treats, and he'd done it in his daily life too. I'd seen him hand over his last dollar to pay someone's electric bill and shovel the driveway for our elderly neighbor while he'd had the flu. Little stuff, but it all added up.

Besides, I knew from experience how painful it could be to feel alone in the world. The smallest act of kindness could make all the difference. Back when my father died and Gillian ditched me, the woman who lived next door baked me a batch of cookies every Friday, for six months straight. Those cookies meant everything to me, because someone saw my pain and took the time to help me move through it.

"There are more good people than bad," I told Jenny, wiping down the candy counter. "It's a proven fact."

"I'll take your word for it," she said. "You've got a customer."

We hung up as the bell on the door jingled and a man walked in. He was middle aged with glasses, and his lime-colored golf shirt was damp with sweat. I hoped he hadn't actually played golf in this heat. I reached under the counter, pulled out a bottle of water, and walked it over to him.

"Hi," I said as he unscrewed the cap and took a grateful sip. "Welcome to the Starlight Cove Sweetery. Take a look around, and let me know how I can help."

The man browsed, and I peeked out the window again at the car. The driver still sat inside. It looked like she was fiddling with her hair in the rearview mirror.

"This is remarkable," my customer said.

I turned, fully expecting to find him snacking on the chocolate-covered cherries I'd set out. Instead, he was studying *The Girl with the Butterscotch Hair*. I walked over and stood next to him like we were at a gallery.

"Thanks," I said. "It was painted by an artist named Montee in the early nineties, and he gave it to my father."

Montee had come to Starlight Cove for the winter to do a study of light on snow and had befriended my father at the local pub. They'd spent days hanging out at the Sweetery, laughing and swapping stories. I'd always looked forward to seeing Montee, because he'd encouraged me to play with his paints and paintbrushes, no matter how many times my father had told me not to.

"Is he well known?" the man asked.

"No, surprisingly. I've googled him several times, but nothing ever comes up. I've always wondered what happened to him. He was talented."

"I'd say so." The man adjusted his glasses. "My wife is an art professor downstate, and she's dragged me to countless exhibits. She'd kill me for saying this, but this is one of the best pieces I've ever seen."

"High praise. But yes, I do love it."

5

He gave me a sidelong look. "Do you think your father would sell it?"

The question surprised me. Not just because he assumed my father was alive, which hadn't happened for a while, but because the man liked the painting enough to ask. It filled me with a sense of pride, because other than the engagement ring from Joe, it was the only thing I owned that really meant something to me.

"It's actually mine now," I told the man. "I'm sorry, but I'm not interested in selling. It's too sentimental."

He looked disappointed. "Well, then, I guess I'll take the consolation prize." He indicated the assorted chocolates and chocolate popcorn he'd set by the register.

Since the candy was most likely for his wife and kids, I threw in a small bag of chocolate-covered potato chips for him. "Eat them fast. They'll melt like ice cream out there."

On the way to the door, he pointed at the painting once again. "It really is a work of art."

The moment the door chimes signaled his exit, the rusty old station wagon eased into a spot in front of the Sweetery. Was the driver going to come in? That would make the day more exciting. I half hid behind the wall and peered out the window to get a good look at her.

The woman was pretty, in a weathered sort of way, with high cheekbones and long red hair pulled back into a sloppy ponytail. Instead of getting out, though, she leaned back against the front seat as if to take a nap.

It was much too hot to fall asleep in the car. The shade beneath the tree was sparse, and besides, it would move with the sun. Suddenly, I stood up straight.

She's not alone.

For the first time, I spotted a small head in the back, in the midst of all the junk. A boy who could not have been more than ten. He was fast asleep.

He'll overheat in there. They both will.

I had to do something, but that little warning voice, the one that knew all too well the dangers of getting involved in other people's business, warned me to back off. I'd been burned before. Something was wrong, though, and it only felt right to try and help. Letting out a breath, I headed outside.

The humidity instantly dampened my silk sheath dress. It was shapeless enough to hide the extra fifteen pounds I kept trying to shed from my thighs and midsection, but it wasn't made for days like this. Tugging at the turquoise fabric, I walked past the old-fashioned gas lamps out front and approached the car.

The stale breeze caught the scent of fast food, burned motor oil, and berry-scented air freshener wafting from the window. The laundry baskets in the back were packed with clothes, dishes, toys, and old bedding. The boy wore a faded blue T-shirt with a comic book print, and he had a dirty face beneath a mop of thick black hair.

The woman looked a little older than me and wore a saggy cotton tank top. Her makeup was carefully done, but the caked-on foundation did little to hide the large bruise that bloomed yellow and purple on her cheekbone.

I tensed.

That would explain the hasty packing job.

The person who'd given her that bruise could still be out there. Maybe even close by. Still, I couldn't bring myself to walk away.

"Excuse me," I said.

Her eyes flew open. The car sputtered to life as she started the ignition, kicking a foul-smelling smoke across the sidewalk.

"Wait! Will you let me help you?"

The woman's hand paused on the gearshift. She glanced at her sleeping son, then back at me. "Our reservation at the campground ran out, and now they're full. We can't afford anything else. I need a shelter." Her voice was raspy, like she had a cold. "The one listed in the phone book is a store."

The Shelter in Starlight Cove was an upscale camping shop. It was at the end of Main Street and very popular with the tourists. The fact that the woman actually needed a shelter made me feel embarrassed, somehow, for our town.

My gaze landed on the bruise. "Is the person who did that to you close by? I can't put anyone at risk."

Her hand flew up to cover her cheek. "It's not what you think. That's not my life." Ducking her head, she said, "Not anymore."

"You're sure?" I pressed.

She took the car out of park. "This was a mistake."

"I'm not trying to upset you," I said. "I just want to make sure that you're—we're—safe."

She held my gaze. "It's fine."

"Good." I brushed off my hands as if wiping away the topic. "I have a friend who owns a hotel. I'm sure they would give you a complimentary room for the night. It's a bed and breakfast, so there would be meals too."

Her voice wavered. "That's probably not the best idea."

Why would she say no? Is she lying about the person who hurt her?

It was hard to tell for sure, but something felt off.

I was just about to retract the offer when she said, "You know what? That would really help. Thank you."

"Let me shut down the shop," I said, before I could change my mind. "We'll head over together."

Indoors, the sudden burst of air-conditioning made me shiver. Resting my hand on a cool marble table, I wondered if helping her was the right move.

But if I don't, who will?

The phone rang, and I jumped.

"They look harmless," Jenny mused. "I didn't know there was a kid."

Out the window, I saw the woman's son was awake now. The two of them stood outside the car, her hand resting on his shoulder. They looked exhausted but grateful for the help.

"I'm getting them set up at Melodic Winds," I told her. "They need a place to stay."

"You know, Emma, the world isn't all bad when there are people like you," Jenny said. "Let me know if I can do anything to help."

It was a nice thing to say. It also made me feel a lot less anxious about the situation.

After posting the sign with the little clock on it in the door, turning the red hands to indicate I'd be back in an hour, I headed down the steps and gave the woman and her son each a small box of chocolates. The boy's eyes went huge as I offered him the candy. He looked at his mother as if for permission. She nodded, and his face crinkled into a smile.

"What do you say?" she said softly.

His expression went shy. "Thank you, ma'am."

"You're very welcome," I told him. "Hey, what's your name?"

There was a beat. Then his mother said, "Jamal. I'm Lydia."

"Emma." The sun was boiling, and I nodded at their car. "Mind if we drive there? It's only two blocks over, but it would be better than carrying a bunch of stuff in this heat."

Lydia worked quickly to make me a spot in the front seat, and I got in. It felt a little risky getting into a strange car, but the kid was eating chocolates in the back, and Lydia kept apologizing for the mess, so it didn't feel like walking into danger. At least, not until Lydia rolled up the windows and hit the power locks.

She gave me a searching look. "You've really helped us. Thank you."

The haunted expression in her eyes made me sad for her. It was clear she and her son had been through a lot, and I had no business being suspicious.

"I'm happy to do it." I waved at Jenny, who watched from the window of Chill Out. "Head down the block, and turn right at the corner."

Lydia took the car out of park. The steering wheel groaned as she pulled onto Main Street.

We made it to the hotel without incident, but I did breathe a little easier when the locks clicked open and I could get out of the car.

"We're going to stay here?" the little boy said, climbing out of the back seat and looking up at the wisteria-covered house.

"Yes," I told him. "They even have free cookies."

He grinned, and Lydia gave me a grateful smile.

I smiled back, happy to be in a position to help someone. Things would still be bad for Lydia and her son in the morning; I knew that much. But at least they'd have a good night's sleep. For now, that was the best I could do.

Chapter Two

Milly, the owner of the bed and breakfast and one of my grandmother's good friends, was happy to help. She fussed over Lydia and her son, complimenting Lydia's red hair and saying how nice it would be to have a child at the dinner table. Once she got them settled in their room, she called her son, who owned the local auto repair shop, and set up an emergency repair session for Lydia's car.

Milly settled into the chair at her desk and shook her gray curls. "That poor woman's been through it. Where's she headed?"

"Pennsylvania. She said she has family there."

"Mercy me." Milly frowned. "Did she really think that car would make it?"

"I don't know that she was thinking about much of anything but survival," I admitted, wondering if Milly had noticed the bruise.

Probably. Milly didn't miss much.

"Well, I'm glad we had the space." She studied the computer screen over a pair of reading glasses and shook her head. "We're all booked up again tomorrow. I'll tell Garrett to work fast on her car. What else do you think she needs?"

Milly and I decided to place an order with the local grocery store to stock the car with bottled water, a first-aid kit, and nonperishable foods. We also set up a plan to swipe the stack of dirty clothes from the back so Milly could put them through the wash. Since Lydia and her son had stayed at the local campground, everything would be full of grime, dirt, and woodsmoke.

"That should make their life easier," Milly finally said, pushing her chair back from the desk. "You get her keys. I have to get prepped for happy hour."

Waving off my praise, she headed to the kitchen to set up the wine and cheese she served each afternoon at four. I called up to Lydia's room, and even though she sounded embarrassed, she agreed.

I waited for her in the sitting room. It was a quiet space, small and cozy, with a sofa, magazines, and a do-it-yourself coffee machine. She accepted the freshly brewed cup I handed her in exchange for her keys, and the scent of vanilla hung thick in the air.

"Okay." I gave her a big smile. "The mechanic will bring your car by first thing in the morning and leave the keys with the front desk. Milly's going to do your laundry. Get some rest, and you should be all set to travel safely tomorrow. There is no charge for any of this. It's just stuff we'd like to do to help you out."

Lydia held her coffee tight. "I don't even know what to say. Emma, I didn't come to Starlight Cove to get help. I . . ." Her gaze dropped to her coffee, and her eyes filled with tears.

Handing over a tissue from the nearby table, I said, "Lydia, we're happy to help you."

She blew her nose. "You wouldn't be, though. Not if you knew."

"Knew what?"

The worry I'd felt on the drive over came back, but it wasn't like her answer would change anything. Milly wouldn't send her away, no matter what she'd done. This was a woman on her last resource, clearly exhausted. Besides, whatever she was hiding couldn't be that bad.

Could it?

"Look, I don't need to know," I said quickly. "The fact that you and your son are safe is the only thing that matters to me. Get some rest. I have to go back to work."

Lydia stared down into her coffee cup. "Thank you," she mumbled.

I headed for the door, giving her one last smile before walking outside.

Standing in the sunshine, I paused in front of the window. Lydia hadn't moved. She stood in silence, shoulders shaking, as she cried into her paper cup of coffee.

~

Lydia and her son stayed in my thoughts all afternoon, even as I moved on to my own worries and headed to the Harbor Resort to meet my stepmother for dinner. The outdoor dining deck left me struck, as always, with its beauty. The resort was a grand hotel right on the water and had been in business for over a hundred years. The restaurant was a local staple and managed by my best friend's father, so I ate there quite a bit. It was always a treat, because the ambience was great and the food even better.

The host guided me to a secluded table. It was beneath the trellis, which created a shady oasis that, if not cool, would be comfortable in spite of the heat. Piano music tinkled softly in the background. I settled in, pulling the starched white napkin into my lap.

"Bonjour, bonjour." Gillian waltzed up, flashing a million-watt smile. Her honey-blonde hair was perfectly in place, like always, and the pink pattern of her dress was as bright as the filling in our raspberry truffles. More than one set of eyes followed her as she took a seat at the table.

It wasn't anything new. Gillian's role on the news made her a local celebrity. She wasn't exactly attractive, but she was so put together that she always turned heads. Her face was long and thin, with prominent cheekbones, and her dark eyes were constantly searching for the next story.

"Hi." I half rose, and we air-kissed. Her phone chimed, and she slid back into her chair, then tapped out a response.

"Two seconds," she murmured. "There." She set the phone on the table where she could keep one eye on it, then flagged down the waiter.

After ordering two sparkling cherry wines, she gave me full focus. "I'm telling you, Emma, this heat has boiled the crazies up and out of the center of the earth. Listen to what I reported on today."

Gillian launched into a story about a family two towns over who earned their living from a live circus made entirely of cats. She had me laughing until I had tears in my eyes, which was one of the things I loved about her. She knew how to entertain.

The waiter left with our salad orders just as Gillian's cell rang with an urgent work call. She stepped away from the table, and I gazed out at the water, grateful she seemed in a good mood. I sincerely hoped she had brought me to dinner to talk about a raise. It would mean so much to my grandmother to stay in the assisted living facility because in the past few years, it had become her home.

Gillian swept back to the table as the food arrived. "Sorry. This looks wonderful."

I'd ordered the southwest chicken salad. Its mixed greens were blended with a creamy avocado-lime dressing, black beans, sweet corn, and avocado, but the best part was that it was topped with fried chicken.

I'd had it the last time my best friend and I had had dinner at the resort, and its crispy fried goodness made the salad. I waited for Gillian to take a bite of her ahi tuna. Once she did, I lifted my fork to dive in.

"Wait!" Gillian drew back, as if she'd spotted a bug. "They put fried chicken on your salad. I'll get the waiter back for you."

"No, no, I ordered it fried." I breathed in the oily scent. "It's delicious."

"Not grilled?" Gillian looked genuinely puzzled. "I thought you were trying to lose weight."

"No." My cheeks heated. "I mean, not lately."

"Well, that's good news, because it won't happen with fried chicken. I swear, I gained ten pounds just looking at it."

I gave a weak smile. "Probably true."

Was it that obvious that I needed to slim down? I mean, I struggled with those extra fifteen pounds, but I thought I looked okay. Still, Gillian's comment made me lose my appetite.

"Well." She lifted her drink. "I have exciting news. I think you'll be happy to hear it."

Forcing aside the hurt I'd felt, I picked up my glass. "Yes. I can't wait."

"You have done a fantastic job managing the Sweetery." She smiled at me. "Sales have increased, we've received countless mentions on the local travel blogs and social media, and I'm really impressed with what you've done."

Wow. I hadn't expected this type of praise. Embarrassed, I watched the bubbles rise to the top in the cherry drink. Gillian's approval meant more to me than it probably should have, maybe because it didn't come my way that often.

"Since you have done such a spectacular job . . ."

My grandmother's smiling face flashed through my mind. This year, on her eighty-fifth birthday, the assisted living center threw her a party, and she was as excited as a child. Everyone from the nurses to the grumpy man who always slept in a chair by the chessboard sang "Happy Birthday," and she ate every bite of a piece of chocolate cake, which was a big deal, considering she struggled to keep an appetite.

Gillian clinked her glass against mine. "I am pleased to announce that Talbaccis has presented an offer to buy the Sweetery. I plan to sell at the end of the month."

The piano music and the laughter of the other patrons faded into the background.

Sell the candy shop?

I set down my drink. "Gillian." The word felt thick, like a piece of caramel stuck in my throat. "What—?"

This is all a charade.

The realization made my heart sink. Everything from the text where Gillian acted like she thought I'd be so excited, to the way she presented the news. It was all a setup, designed to guilt me into going along with it, because she knew exactly how I felt about selling my father's store.

"Emma, you should be really proud." Her eyes flitted to mine before she stabbed at a piece of tuna with her fork. "This is *Talbaccis* we're talking about. It's a big deal."

Talbaccis was a chocolate company popular with vacation resorts and high-end golf clubs. Wildly successful, it had been family owned and operated for nearly a century. In fact, it was one of the few brand names that might actually get approval from the city council to buy out a business on Main Street.

The music switched from piano to a swinging jazz. The low pulse of the bass felt frenetic, like the sudden panic in my heart.

"The sale will give me the resources to winter in Florida," Gillian said, taking a big drink of wine. "Your father would be proud."

"No." I finally found my voice. "No, he would not. My father would not have wanted to see you sell the shop right out from under me."

There was a time when my father had dreamed that he and I would run the Sweetery together. Of course, that had changed when he died. It had been completely unexpected, and he hadn't had a will, so the Sweetery had transferred to Gillian. She'd had no interest in working in the shop, so she'd put a management company in charge. I'd never had the option to be a part of it until three years ago, when the woman from the management company had retired. Gillian had almost sold the store then, but I'd convinced her to let me run it instead.

"Emma, that is the most ridiculous thing I have ever heard." Gillian waved her fork at me. "I am not selling the shop out from under you. If you wanted it, you could have made me an offer. You haven't done that."

"Make you an offer to buy the store?" I was baffled. "Gillian, with *what*?"

It wasn't like I had money to spare. Before managing the candy shop, I'd worked for a nonprofit program for nearly a decade. It provided transportation for housebound patients to make it to church, the grocery store, and social activities. It was a worthwhile cause, but it had never paid enough to allow me to build up any sort of savings, let alone buy a business.

Gillian lifted a well-shaped eyebrow. "You could have applied for a small business loan from the bank."

Anger cut through me. "You know they would have turned me down."

Gillian shrugged. "So, you've made some bad decisions. Maybe that means you're not meant to be a business owner. Not everyone is, and that's okay. But that fact shouldn't have to hold me back."

She reached for my hand, but I pulled away. With a practiced smile, she picked up her fork and continued eating. "Either way, the deal will close in thirty days, so you'll need to look for a new job."

I shook my head, feeling numb. "This all feels pretty rotten, to be honest. Especially the part where you tried to act like you thought this would make me happy."

Gillian dared to look insulted. "Emma, you're always so gung ho about making sure other people are happy. I figured you'd be delighted to know this is the right thing for me."

My eyes blurred, and I looked down at my salad. The bright green of the avocado and lettuce, the colorful tomatoes, and the bright-yellow corn blended together. For some reason, the vibrant colors made me think of the painting. If Gillian sold the candy shop, the painting would be the only place it would still remain, like a family photo from an era long past.

"Please don't be upset." She gestured at my salad. "Eat."

"The chicken is fried," I managed to say. "Better not risk it."

Somehow, I kept it together as I stood and walked across the roof deck, the evening sun warm on my cheeks. Gillian called after me, but I ignored her. Instead, I gave a brave nod at a group of locals celebrating a birthday and even smiled at the busboy balancing a tray of waters. But when I saw my best friend's father at the exit, my eyes started to sting.

"Emma! How are you?" his jovial voice boomed.

My face crumpled. Quickly, I rushed down the white wooden steps and escaped into the lobby of the Harbor Resort Hotel.

The dim opulence allowed me to slip unnoticed into the lobby bathroom. It was empty, just as I'd hoped. The lock on the stall clicked beneath my fingertips. Then I sat on the lid of the toilet seat and burst into tears.

Chapter Three

"Emma!" A hushed whisper echoed in the bathroom. "Where are you?"

It was Kailyn, my best friend since elementary school. Her father must have texted her.

I pushed open the stall door. The wood was heavy and reached all the way to the floor. "Here."

Kailyn rushed over in a waft of apple-scented perfume and winced, probably at the sight of my puffy, tear-streaked face. "Here." She guided me to the sink. "Wash your face, Em."

I glanced in the mirror. My hair was limp from the heat, the turned-up tip of my nose red from crying, and my blue eyes so dejected they practically looked gray. I took a deep breath and splashed water on my cheeks. The cold stung.

Kailyn handed me one of the soft towels that rested on the counter in a woven basket. "Let's get some air."

We walked in silence, the heels of Kailyn's designer sandals clicking across the tiled floor of the hotel lobby. She slid open the patio door, and we settled into some ridiculously comfortable lawn chairs overlooking the water. The attendant came right over, and Kailyn ordered a cheese plate and two shots of whiskey.

"Trust me on this one," she said when I tried to protest. "I haven't seen you this upset in ages. What happened?"

The cheese plate had arrived by the time I'd finished the story. I was grateful for it, because in spite of my anger, I was hungry.

Kailyn sliced us each a piece of brie and shook her head. "You know, I'd love to be surprised by all this, but Gillian is pretty clueless."

"She told me it was time to start looking for a new job. Like jobs are growing on trees around here."

Starlight Cove was an idyllic place to live, but it wasn't booming with opportunity. The majority of the people who lived here had old money. Their houses had been passed down over the years, and those same families owned the shops and the real estate. The jobs that were available were typically low-paid, seasonal employment perfect for college kids looking to make an extra buck. Not to say that there weren't any jobs. It was just that the good ones were few and far between. Kailyn had spent years carving out a successful career as a real estate agent. It was not likely I'd find something anytime soon that could keep my grandmother in her care facility.

Depressed, I stared out at the water. Lake Michigan was a deep blue in the evening light. The wind made whitecaps on the surface, and the view was serene but melancholy.

"The thing that really gets me is that she acted like I should have stepped in to buy the store," I said. "Two seconds later, she's telling me not everyone is meant to own a business."

"Has she closed the deal?" Kailyn asked.

"It closes in thirty days."

"Then, maybe you *could* still buy the store."

"Hey, guys!" Sheila, from Search and Rescue, waved from across the lawn.

Sheila was in her midfifties and into everyone's business, but in the sweetest possible way. Each month, she came into the store and treated herself to a box of vanilla creams. I always threw in an extra bag of caramels because she made me laugh.

"I heard all about that woman sleeping in her car," Sheila said, squeezing her perfectly painted nails into my arm. "Thank goodness you were there to help."

"Help with what?" Kailyn asked. Her mouth dropped open when she heard the story. "Emma, you should have sent them to the police station for help! You don't know the first thing about her."

Sheila waved her hand. "Our police chief is not exactly the most compassionate man on the planet. He would have found something to cite them for, then sent them on their way." She turned to me. "We do have spare beds at Search and Rescue. The woman and her son would be very welcome to stay with us for a few nights, and Captain Ahab would be happy to have a little one to play with. Oh, there's Carl."

Sheila's husband waved at her from the awning by the lobby. She darted off to meet him, stretching up for a quick kiss as if they were newly married. The gesture made me think of Joe and wonder what our life would have been like. We'd be far past the newlywed stage by now. Maybe we'd even have a family. I'd always wanted kids, and the thought that I might never get the chance to have them made me push the topic out of my brain altogether.

Kailyn shook her head. "Everything about that story with the woman freaks me out." Her green eyes were serious. "You can't step in the middle of a domestic dispute. You, of all people, should know that."

My stomach tightened. "I also know better than to leave a woman sleeping in her car with her kid. Sorry, but I can't just sit by and watch that happen."

"Her husband or boyfriend or whatever could still be out there."

"He's not." The sun had started to set, and the sky was a deep red. "That's what she said."

"Oh, okay. Then, I believe her." Kailyn's voice was thick with sarcasm. "Emma, I'm only going to say this once because I love you: I appreciate it that you want to save the world, but you won't be able to help other people if you can't help yourself."

"I'm not trying to save the world. I'm just trying to help someone who needs it. I get it that bad things happen—*trust* me; I get that—but there are times it's worth the risk. This is one of them."

"But what about—"

"Please. Let it go."

The silence hung heavy between us. Finally, Kailyn stretched out on the chair, one arm behind her head.

"Sorry," I mumbled. "It's been a long day. How's everything with you?"

"Fine." Kailyn paused. "I mean, I don't know. The funniest thing happened today. Dana Simpson from the chamber of commerce reached out to me. She said there's a seat opening up on the board of directors and asked if she could submit my name for consideration."

My heart leapt. "Kailyn, that's a big deal."

The chamber of commerce was an important part of our city. The group was dedicated to protecting the best interests of the local businesses and helping Starlight Cove to maintain the old-fashioned charm that made our tourism industry successful. I was proud of Kailyn, as it was no small feat to receive an invitation like that one.

"*Pfft.* I told Dana she must have dialed the wrong number." Kailyn fiddled with her bangle bracelets. "There are a few weeks until they need an answer one way or another, but I think I'm going to tell her no."

"Why on earth would you do that?" I said.

Kailyn waved her hand, her bracelets clinking with the effort. "I'm too busy with work."

It was true that Kailyn's job as a real estate agent kept her running all hours of the day, but that couldn't be the reason. She'd always made a point of being involved with the community. This would put her in the center of everything.

"That doesn't make sense." I squinted at her. "Is there something else stopping you?"

"I mean . . ." She bit her lip. "It's nice to be asked, but there's not a chance they would pick me. That would be embarrassing once the word got out, don't you think?"

"Kailyn." I couldn't believe what I was hearing. "They wouldn't have asked if they didn't think you were a good candidate. You'd be great."

"Nah. I just thought the whole thing was kind of funny, you know?" Pushing back her dark hair, she sat up. "Either way, I see you trying to switch the focus to me, but we need to get this thing with the Sweetery figured out. I vote you talk to Gillian tomorrow. Tell her you're going to meet with the banks and make a bid."

I paused. Kailyn didn't know about my credit history, and as close as we were, I couldn't bring myself to tell her. It would only back up her theory that I spent too much time helping other people and too little time helping myself.

"It might not be the best idea." I tried to keep my voice casual. "The bank could turn me down."

"No way. The Sweetery has been profitable for over thirty years. There's not a bank in the world that would turn that down. Put together the numbers, show them to the loan officer, and voilà. You'll have your loan."

What if it really could be that simple?

It had been a while since the fiasco with my credit. Maybe that, coupled with the strength of the store's profitability, actually could be enough. Still, the very idea of asking for a loan was intimidating.

"The whole thing scares me," I admitted. "Besides, what if they said yes?"

Kailyn laughed. "Isn't that the goal?"

I nibbled at a piece of smoked cheddar, looking out at the horizon. The sun was down, and the sky had turned gold. The light reflected off the water, and it was so beautiful my heart ached.

"What if Gillian's right?" I asked. "Not everyone's meant to run a business. I've done just fine for the past few years, but what if I panicked when it was actually mine? It wouldn't take much to drive it into the ground, and everyone would know I destroyed my father's legacy."

"Emma, that's not going to happen. You've told me all these great ideas you've had, like the e-commerce site—"

"Which Gillian would not let me do."

"And the animal chocolate truffles, like the ones in the painting—"

"Which Gillian would not let me do."

"Not to mention a hundred other brilliant ideas that could bring in a profit during the off-season."

Starlight Cove was a tourist town, but we were only attractive to tourists in the summer and the fall. If a small business couldn't make the money necessary to survive October to May, it wouldn't last. The Sweetery had gotten lucky, simply because it had been in business for so long that we had a built-in customer base.

But it was never a good idea to coast, and I had brainstormed many ways to monetize our products well past the season. One example was setting up an online store, not that I had the first clue how to go about doing that. I knew it would be worth it to figure it out, though, which was something I'd been trying to convince Gillian to do for ages.

"You know, she kept telling me she didn't want to set up an online store because the initial investment would cost too much," I mused. "That never made sense to me, considering the money it would have brought in long term. But Gillian wasn't planning to be there long term."

Kailyn gave an eager nod. "There's plenty of room to grow. So, make it happen."

Her enthusiasm was contagious, along with her belief that I could pull it off. We ordered dessert to celebrate, a giant piece of molten chocolate cake. Its rich scent took me right back to the candy shop, and I realized it was hard to imagine life without the Sweetery. It was impossible, actually, which was why I had to figure out how to make this work.

Chapter Four

When I woke up the next morning, my grandmother was the first image that popped into my head. I needed to find a solution for her care facility, because as much as I wanted to buy the store, there was still a big chance it might not work out. My phone already had a text from Gillian.

Should I expect you to be at work today or will Ashley be in charge?

Ashley was our college-age helper. I'd hired her when I took over, because the store was too busy for one person to handle. It had been a good move, decreasing our wait time and increasing the amount of money we brought in, in spite of her hourly rate.

I was half tempted to text Gillian, "Nope. I quit," but that wouldn't have been smart. Even if I only ended up working for another month, I needed the money. So, with a heavy sigh, I texted her back.

I'll be there. Sorry about last night.

It wasn't how I felt, but I didn't like fighting with anyone. It made me feel guilty. Besides, it would be easier to approach her about buying the Sweetery if the argument from last night wasn't hanging over us.

The shop had been so slow the day before that I didn't need to go in early to make the chocolates. Instead, I decided to head over to Morning Lark to talk to the business office. I whipped up a quick breakfast of eggs and homemade chocolate muffins before heading out with the neatly wrapped muffins in my backpack. The streets whizzed by in a blur from my mint-green bike.

Bike rides had been a part of my lifestyle ever since I was old enough to ride. When my father had served his apprenticeship in Bruges, his bicycle had been his closest friend. He'd returned to Starlight Cove with a need to recreate that life, and he'd had me riding before I could even walk.

The memory of my father's bike always made me smile. He'd added flare to nearly everything he did, and his bicycle was no exception. It was electric blue with a sparkle finish and colorful ribbons woven through the spokes of the wheels, as though he was in a parade. The effect was a swirling kaleidoscope, which I'd always loved.

He'd also been one of the few who dared to ride a bicycle in the freezing cold. He only put away his bike when the snowdrifts interfered, but the moment they became slush, he was back at it. More than one of the concerned women in our town had liked to say that my father's demise would happen on a bike ride, since he'd pooh-poohed the idea of wearing a helmet. He'd showed them by dying of a heart attack instead, so he'd gotten the last laugh.

The bike ride to the care facility calmed me down. The weather was still a little humid, but it had rained the night before, and the lake breeze made it a perfect summer day. The scent of fresh grass and blooming flowers was heavy in the air, and a bright-blue glimpse of the water flashed through the trees.

Morning Lark was in the residential business center right off Main Street. Made from stately brick, it reminded me of a well-heeled dormitory. The check-in desk was patrolled by the desk matron, and I waved at her before heading into the main room.

The space was bright and lovely, with blue carpet, yellow window treatments, and cozy blue couches positioned in a half square to create a shared sense of community. There were also several small tables with reading lamps, as well as a grand piano that rested in the corner. Tuesdays and Fridays, a musical troupe came in to provide entertainment, and if my grandmother was in her right mind, she clapped, sang along, and couldn't stop talking about the visit until the next one.

There were always people in the lobby, white heads of hair playing cards, reading books, or staring off into space. One woman, Delores, had my heart because she never stopped knitting afghans and had sent me home with at least five to pass on to friends in need. Sure enough, even though it was only eight o'clock in the morning, she was already hard at work knitting a lattice pattern with bright-purple yarn.

"Your grandmother is still in bed, darling," Delores called in her wavery voice. "She loves her beauty sleep."

My grandmother typically stayed up until three in the morning watching sitcoms from the eighties and slept until eleven. It made her happy, but there was only a small window of time to spend with her, because recently she'd started getting confused somewhere around dinnertime.

"Well, be sure to tell her I brought muffins," I said. "Have a great day."

I put a chocolate muffin on the end table next to Delores, who grinned, and set out the rest in the dining room before heading to the business office. It had just opened, and Mary, the accountant, beckoned me in.

"It's good to see you, Emma." She patted her trusty computer. "This thing is just getting fired up, so you might have to bear with me. What can I help you with?"

I explained about the insurance. "Full coverage runs out at the end of the year, so I need to talk to you about options."

"Oh, goodness." Mary glanced around the office as if someone might be listening. "The owners are so mercenary. They'll knock ten percent off the price if your insurance won't cover it all, but that's it. Trust me—I've tried before." She tapped her computer. "Let me look at your account."

A cherry tree bloomed just outside the window, its branches scraping the pane in the early-morning breeze. The business office was neat and tidy, like everything in the care facility, and I hoped with all my heart that Mary could come up with a solution.

"This is troubling." She slid on a pair of reading glasses and peered at the screen. Turning it toward me, she pointed. "Your grandmother's insurance paid out at the beginning of the year. So, if the insurance is only covering half, you'll have to pay out the remainder for the entire year up front if you want to keep the same rate." She slipped off her glasses. "It's nearly fifteen grand in one lump sum. Can you afford that?"

My stomach dropped. "No. I . . . I can't do a payment plan? Month to month?"

That would make sense, given the age of the residents, but Mary shook her head. "The only way to grandfather her in at the same rate—or grandmother her in, as it were—" Mary smiled, but when I didn't, she got serious again. "The only way to get that same price point is to pay up front. Month to month would be a significant increase."

"How significant?"

She pointed at the latest brochure. The cost was nearly 20 percent more. It would be impossible to cover unless I could buy the store and pay myself a much higher salary.

I slid the paper back to her. "This is not the news I was hoping for."

Mary gave the brochure a sorrowful look, as if it had let her down. "I'm so sorry. But at least you have a few months to figure it out."

That sounded well and good, but in reality, a few months was hardly any time at all. I had to find a solution, and fast.

~

There was a message waiting for me when I stepped back outside. I pressed play right before climbing onto my bike, and the familiar voice made me adjust my Bluetooth.

"Good morning, Emma. It's Kelly Phillips."

The air left my lungs. It was Joe's mother. I stared at a small section of purple geraniums planted along the sidewalk, my breath suddenly tight.

"It's been a while, but I was hoping to catch you." She paused. "The ten-year anniversary of Joe's death is coming up, as I'm sure you know, and we're planning to host a remembrance ceremony. It would be lovely if you could make it, or if you would be willing to say a few words . . ."

I ended the message before it was finished. It was hard to believe ten years had passed. In some ways, it felt like yesterday that I'd lost him, but in others, every second of the decade that had passed weighed on me.

A remembrance.

Was that really something I could do? I certainly didn't feel equipped to handle it at the moment. My emotions were at an all-time high, and this did not help. I decided to take some time to sit with the idea before calling back. There was a time Kelly and I had spoken on the phone every day, but it had been a while, and I was sure she'd understand.

As I pedaled down the paved drive, I forced my thoughts back to my grandmother and what it would take to keep her in the facility. Mary had said *thousands* of dollars, which was an impossible amount. My cell phone was the only bill that still had corners left to cut. It wouldn't be enough.

She'll have to move.

The thought made the sky seem a little less blue. My grandmother would be crushed. I would be too. She had given me so much. It would be terrible not to be able to repay her at the time it mattered the most.

There must be something I can do.

I pedaled faster, then coasted down a hill, desperate to find a solution. The only possibility was buying the candy shop. It all kept coming back to that. Then I could afford to pay the monthly fee or even take an advance on my salary to pay up front.

I need to talk to Gillian. Get this figured out.

It meant stepping outside of my comfort zone, but I had to do it. Otherwise, I wouldn't be the only one losing something I loved.

Chapter Five

Since the heat wave had passed, the Sweetery was busy from the moment I opened the doors until right before lunch. The second there was a brief lull, I brought out a tray of chocolates to replenish the assorted chocolates in the display case. The bells on the door jingled, and the man who'd had such kind words for my painting walked in.

"You're back." This time, his wife was with him, a fit blonde with appraising eyes.

Hooking a thumb in her direction, he said, "I wanted her to see the painting. Figure out a fair offer so we could take home a memento."

My good cheer faded. The man had been serious when he'd asked if I wanted to sell, and I'd been serious when I'd said no. It was insulting to think he'd try and talk me out of my most-prized possession simply because he wanted a souvenir.

"Take a look." I kept my tone light. "But it's still not for sale."

The busy morning continued, and as I helped other customers, I kept one eye on the couple. At one point, they compared the painting to something on the woman's phone. They seemed excited and kept stealing looks at me. Finally, curiosity got the best of me.

"So, what do you think, Mrs.—?" I asked, walking back over to them.

"Call me Margot." The woman stuck out a thin hand and shook mine. Her skin was cool and well moisturized, and she wore several artsy rings twisted from platinum. "This is truly special. What can you tell me about the artist?"

It would have been nice to give her something factual since she was an academic, but I knew very little.

"His name was Montee, and he spent a winter in Starlight Cove in the early nineties. I was little, so I don't remember much."

I had been semiaware of Montee in that way that kids notice things that have little to do with them. He'd been in the candy shop a lot, playing cards with my father as they drank something that smelled like the doctor's office. They'd laughed and told stories, but I'd never paid any attention because it was grown-up talk and therefore superboring.

"How old was he?" Margot asked. "When he was in town?"

I drummed my fingers against my lips. "Probably in his thirties. He seemed close to my father's age."

Her eyes went bright with interest. "What was he like?"

The candy shop was busy, but a quick look assured me that Ashley had everything under control, so I shared one of my favorite anecdotes.

"My grandmother liked to say all the women in town were acting a fool for Montee. I didn't know what that meant, so I repeated it in front of him. He blushed, and my father laughed. Montee was a good-looking guy. Huge head. Dark hair. To me, though, he just looked like a friendly Saint Bernard."

The wife winked at her husband, and he smiled. The exchange suggested their interest was more personal than they were letting on.

"What's the story?" I asked. "Is he a friend of yours or something?"

Thousands of people visited our town. If they knew him, perhaps Montee had told them that he had painted the Sweetery and asked them to see if it still hung in the shop. That would be pretty cool, actually, to finally learn what had happened to him.

The man leaned back on his heels. "We don't know him. However, we are absolute geeks about art."

A rowdy group walked through the doors. The woman gripped my arm, as if afraid to lose me.

"It's our anniversary." She gave me a hopeful look. "We've been looking for something special to commemorate this trip. I know you're not interested in selling, but we're prepared to make you a substantial offer. Would you let the painting go for five grand?"

"Five thousand dollars?" I echoed.

I did not expect that. Maybe a couple hundred, but five grand? With that boost, I might be able to scrape together the month-to-month payments, at least, to keep my grandmother at Morning Lark, regardless of what happened with the sale of the shop. It still wouldn't solve the problem long term, though, and the painting meant too much to me to let it go.

"Sorry. It's really not for sale."

The man adjusted his glasses. "I told you, Margot. She's tough."

His wife squinted at the painting. "Ten, then. We planned to pay that for that sculpture at the gallery. It's from an unknown artist, as well, so what's the difference?"

Ten thousand dollars? My heart started to pound. That, coupled with my savings, would give me the lump sum I needed to keep the current rate my grandmother was paying.

"Wow, that's tempting."

Ten thousand dollars was a lot of money—probably not to these people, but it was to me—and this was perfect timing. It would solve a lot of problems. But the painting was such an important part of my history, the only real thing I had from my father. My eyes fell on my favorite part, the window display with the truffles shaped like animals. The dog was so cute, with his candy nose low to the ground and his little tail poking straight up. I couldn't let go of it, regardless of how much money was on the table. There had to be another solution.

Besides, it did seem strange that the couple was willing to pay so much. It made me wonder if it was valuable. Maybe it fell into some small-town category that only art experts knew about, and it would serve me to research it. Not that I'd sell, either way, but I couldn't help feeling suspicious at their interest.

"Sorry," I finally said. "I can't do it."

The wife adjusted the strings of the khaki sun hat that hung around her neck. "We'll leave our contact information. That way, if you change your mind . . ."

The bells on the door jingled the arrival of Lydia and Jamal. Jamal was dressed in a shirt and short set most likely gifted from Milly, because the clothes were too clean and too large. He looked like he felt hopelessly out of place. I could relate, considering the conversation I was stuck in.

"Thanks for stopping in," I told the couple. "Enjoy the rest of your vacation."

I headed across the room, waving to Lydia and still trying to process the offer. Ten thousand dollars? That was an outlandish price to pay for a random painting on the wall of a candy shop. There had to be something more behind it, but I couldn't imagine what.

What if Montee had gone on to become a big deal, and I was the only person on the planet who didn't know it? It wasn't likely. I'd searched him online like a hundred times, and he didn't even pop up. It could be what I'd thought earlier, though, that the painting belonged to some special category that mattered and made it valuable.

If it is at all.

Even though I didn't plan to sell it either way, I kind of hoped it was some hidden treasure. It would make me feel better to think the couple was trying to invest in something, instead of throwing their money around because they had too much. Especially when there were people like Lydia who had so little.

Walking up, I gave her a warm smile. "Hi. How are you feeling?"

Lydia looked a lot better, like she had taken a shower and gotten a good night's sleep.

"I wanted to thank you." Her voice was less hoarse today, but she refused to meet my eyes. Maybe she was embarrassed for crying in front of me. "The kindness you and your friends showed us meant a lot. It's been a long time since someone treated us that way."

"It was nothing."

The art-loving couple headed toward the door. The wife slowed as she approached and gave me a big smile like she planned to interrupt. I must have given her a frustrated look, because she held up her hands.

"We're headed out. We won't nag you anymore."

"Not today, at least." The man adjusted his watch. It was fancy, all metal and titanium. "Our contact information is by the register. Let us know when you change your mind."

I ran my tongue over my teeth as they walked out. The exchange irritated me. Probably because he'd said "when," not "if," even though I had made my stance clear.

Turning back to Lydia, I noticed Jamal taking in the shop with awe.

"Jamal, did you try the chocolates I gave you?" I asked.

He nodded and looked down at the floor.

"They're gone." Lydia's voice was full of affection. "I'm sure he'll gobble mine up next." Reaching out, she tried to rub his head. He stepped away, and sadness flared in her eyes. It was obvious there was some sort of rift in their relationship.

"Jamal," I said, my voice bright. "It sounds like your mother is saying you need a bigger supply of candy."

I marched behind the display case and pulled out our largest cellophane bag. Efficiently, I filled it with a bunch of our wrapped, colorful candies—cherry crèmes, saltwater taffy, and, of course, the brickle-brackle butterscotch. He couldn't stop thanking me when I handed it to him.

"Jamal, set that on the table, and go use the bathroom," his mother said. "We have to get on the road." Once we were alone, she said, "I have a lot to say to you, Emma, but it's hard." Her expression was anguished. "I'll send it in a letter."

The very idea embarrassed me. I hadn't done anything extraordinary. I'd just helped her to find a place to stay.

"Please don't do that," I said. "It's not necessary."

The rowdy crowd headed up to the cash register, purchases in hand. Ashley was starting to fall behind, and I knew I'd have to help her soon.

"Is your car all set?" I asked.

Her cheeks colored. "We're going to head on. The mechanic said it needs a few things, but it will take too long for the parts to come in."

"Oh. You can't wait because you don't have a place to stay?" I asked, wanting to make sure I understood the situation.

"Yeah." She looked tired once again. "But the car will be fine. We made it this far."

How frustrating. The whole point of setting Lydia and Jamal up in the bed and breakfast the day before was to keep them safe. I couldn't let them get back on the highway in a car ready to break down. I couldn't do it.

Kailyn's warning that I didn't know anything about this woman rang through my head, but I pushed it aside. It was clear Lydia was having a hard time, and she didn't deserve to feel so alone. No one did.

"Look. This might sound really weird and invasive," I said, "but you should stay and get your car taken care of. My friend at the Search and Rescue facility said they have a few spare beds and you're welcome to stay, but I don't know that it's the best option for your son, because an emergency could come through at any time of night. I was thinking it might be better to stay next door to where I live, in my grandmother's duplex. Now, it's having a lot of small repairs done in the next few weeks because we have a new tenant moving in. The work will be pretty steady, but it's during the day and scheduled. If you don't mind that, you could stay there for free and take the time you need to get things back together."

The duplex belonged to my grandmother, and the rental income from the other half covered part of the mortgage. Thanks to the financial mess I'd walked into a few years back, I could barely pay my rent for a while. My grandmother had talked me into moving in with her. "My house is your inheritance," she'd said. "You might as well enjoy it now."

Once she went into assisted living, I tried to convince her to sell the duplex to offset the cost of the care facility, but she refused. I think a part of her believed that, as long as her home was there, the assisted living facility was still a choice. I also suspected she did not think I was capable of keeping a roof over my head. Embarrassing, considering I was very responsible with money—I'd just fallen into a con a few years back. But I'd been grateful for the help, and now I was happy to offer the same kindness to Lydia.

Her response was a furrowed brow. "Why would you . . . ?"

"Because it's really not a big deal," I said. "My grandmother doesn't like for it to sit vacant, and we don't have a tenant moving in until August. You would be very welcome."

"I don't understand." She reached up and rested her hand on her bruised cheek. "Why are you being so nice to me?"

My stomach twisted as I once again considered the origin of that bruise. But I refused to worry. The next few weeks would be hard dealing with the uncertainty of the candy shop, and helping her would help me.

"It's empty," I said firmly. "Use it, and get your car fixed too."

The line at the register had gotten longer, so I excused myself to help. Once things had quieted down, Lydia approached the counter. Her shoulders were hunched, as if trying to take up as little space as possible. Her son sat at a table by the window, digging into his bag of goodies.

"We'd like to stay," Lydia said in a small voice, smoothing the flyaway grays in her hair. "If that's still okay?"

The idea that she and her son would not be on the road in this heat, in that car, filled me with relief.

"It's more than okay. I'm happy you decided to do that. Here." I pulled the appropriate key off my key chain and handed her my address on a slip of paper. "Make yourself at home. If you need anything, I'll be right next door."

Chapter Six

The end of the day arrived before I could blink. The constant stream of customers kept my mind off the one thing I didn't want to think about. But once Ashley and I had closed out and the doors were locked, I couldn't help but face the possibility of losing the Sweetery forever.

As I looked around the cozy space, it seemed impossible that in one month, it could be stripped bare. There were so many fixtures that had been there forever. The clock my father had bought in Europe hung proudly over the door leading to the kitchen. The old-fashioned photos showcasing the history of Starlight Cove greeted guests by the door. And of course, the burgundy-and-gold-covered chairs that rested by the marble table had sat thousands of customers.

It never failed to amaze me that my father had had the foresight to buy enough fabric to ensure the chairs would always look the same. There was a roll of replacement fabric in the storage unit large enough to cover a football field. The company that sold it had gone out of business years ago, but there still had to be at least ten years of traditional Sweetery chair covers remaining.

Couldn't Gillian have waited until it was gone?

Speaking of . . .

Gillian appeared on the front stoop outside looking as bright and shiny as a penny in the evening light. She wore a short-sleeved navy pantsuit with gold buttons. Her hair looked freshly highlighted, and, as always, the waft of perfume that followed her into the shop was strong enough to cloak the heady scent of chocolate. Spotting me, she stopped halfway across the room.

"I thought you'd be gone." Her voice was friendly, but she seemed on guard.

"It was busy today," I said. "There was a lot to finish up."

Nodding, she walked to the candy counter. "Well, I wanted to drop by the list of items that need to be accomplished prior to the closing date. If you'd like to continue on until the end, I'll need you to focus on these tasks in your downtime."

She handed me a manila folder. It only had two sheets of paper in it, but it felt heavy in my hand.

"I'm glad you stopped by," I said, looking down at the folder. "Gillian, are you definitely selling to Talbaccis?"

"Yes, if I can get a letter of approval from the city to give Talbaccis permission to purchase. You know how they feel about outside businesses coming in." She pursed her lips, clearly irritated at the bureaucracy. "However, they have promised me a letter of approval within the week." She paused. "Why? Have you heard something?"

"No." My eyes took in the shop and settled on the painting. The sight of it gave me the courage, somehow, to say what I needed to say. "Gillian, I'm sorry I got upset last night. It's just that the Sweetery is so special to me. Last night, you said you've been waiting for me to make an offer." I let out a slow breath. "Well, I've decided to put together a proposal and meet with the bank. Tell me what Talbaccis has offered you, and I will pay ten thousand more."

Gillian blinked. "My dear, they'll simply counter."

My mouth dropped open. "Gillian, I'm not trying to start a bidding war for you," I said in disbelief. "I'm asking if you will accept ten thousand dollars more than the money you already have in your hands so that I can keep my father's legacy alive. Is it really that hard to agree to that?"

"Emma." She sounded frustrated. "It's not simply the money. Imagine the support Talbaccis could give the Sweetery. Think of the ways it could grow and develop."

It suddenly hit me: Gillian liked the prestige that came with the brand name. It was much more glamorous than selling the store to her stepdaughter. Unbelievable that that would matter to her more than helping out her own family, but I hadn't been her family for a while now.

I squared my shoulders. "Would you accept that offer or not?"

The pause made the distance between us grow exponentially. Finally, she sighed.

"I suppose it would be the right thing to do."

The Sweetery seemed to bloom from black and white into color. The ray of sun that stretched across the marble table looked brighter, the chocolates in the display case seemed to glisten, and in the painting, the girl at the table beamed. I hadn't realized how much I'd limited my hope that things could actually work out, but now I was so relieved.

"Gillian, thank you," I said, grabbing for her hands.

She took a step back. "Emma, wait. I don't want there to be any confusion. I will assume the deal with Talbaccis is moving forward until I have written documentation from you stating otherwise."

My hope vanished as quickly as it had appeared. It sounded like Gillian had zero confidence that I was capable of getting the loan.

My eyes fell on the glass case to the caramel display. There was a big smudge, probably because a kid had pressed his face against it. I grabbed a paper towel and some cleaner and wiped it up, mainly to hide the hurt on my face.

"Emma, I have to cover my bases." Her tone softened. "I sincerely would like for you to acquire the store. It's what your father would have wanted, but I'm not young. I have to plan for my future." She paused.

"The station has granted me a permanent winter hiatus," she said, her voice suddenly tight, "which I did not anticipate or ask for."

Ouch.

For a split second, I felt sorry for her.

Gillian had always been worried about getting replaced by someone younger or better. The situation had probably sent her into a panic, which explained the sudden need to sell. She had come from nothing and had always lived like she was afraid she'd end up with nothing, regardless of how successful she'd become.

"So, please," she said. "Let's move forward and hope for the best."

"Thank you, Gillian," I said. "I really appreciate it."

Not sure what else to say, I continued to clean up. There were a few stray receipts left by the register. The stack was about to go in the trash when I noticed one was a note. The ornate writing read:

> My husband and I have decided to offer twenty thousand for the piece. It is such a treasure! It could be such a fond, delightful reminder of our time in Starlight Cove. Our contact information is listed below.
>
> —Margot Del Rey

Gillian had come behind the counter to open the safe. I must have looked as stunned as I felt because she squinted at me. "Emma, are you all right? Look, I'm happy to discuss this further, but it would probably be more effective to speak to a bank first so that we can work with the appropriate information."

"Uh . . ." I squeezed the note, the edges of the paper cutting into my hand. "I'm fine. Yes, I'll talk to the bank."

Turning away, I shoved the note into my pocket.

The offer floored me. Twenty thousand dollars? That type of money would not only allow my grandmother to stay at Morning Lark; it would buy me the time to find a good job if I failed to get a loan and buy the store. Or it could even help me secure the loan, having twenty grand in my bank account. I was tempted to pick up the phone right then and agree to sell. But something didn't add up.

The offer was the equivalent of a new car. Yes, it was obvious the couple had money, but they also weren't stupid. The fact that they planned to drop twenty grand on an unknown painting brought me back to my earlier theory that something was up.

Gillian was replying to a text, and I eyed the way her perfectly combed hair fell across her face, wishing I could get her take on the situation. She was much bolder than me. She'd probably pick up the phone and demand the couple tell her exactly why they were interested and even get them to double the price. But I didn't dare tell her. Gillian could easily try and claim the painting as her own, since she had inherited everything when my father died. The only thing I had to prove the painting was mine was a note from the artist, but I had no idea whether or not that was legally binding and could just imagine Gillian spending the next ten years fighting me on it.

"Well, keep me posted," Gillian said, oblivious to my confusion. She slid her phone into her purse and gave me a tight smile. "I'd be happy to sell you the shop if you come up with the money. But like I said, I can't afford to wait forever."

"I know," I said, watching as she walked out the door.

The moment the door jingled her exit, I called Kailyn. The phone rang as I stared out the window, watching the remaining tourists straggle back from the beach, their shadows long on the sidewalk. She didn't pick up, so I left a message about the encounter with the couple.

She called me back as I was locking up. "Sorry. I've been running all over the place today. Hey, will you do me a favor and forget that thing I told you about the chamber? I'm going to tell Dana no. It's not a good fit."

"Kailyn, please don't do that." I stopped on the stoop and looked out across Main Street. It was picture perfect, and a lot of that had to do with the effort the locals put into helping to make our town great. "If you say no now, they might not ask you again. It feels like a once-in-a-lifetime kind of thing, and I really think you should go for it. Give it some more time before you make any big decisions."

"Time won't change my mind."

"Then what about professional opportunity? Think about what it could do for your business. The chamber is a big deal. They do so much for our town, and it's pretty impressive."

Kailyn grunted. "They're impressive. I'm not."

"Stop selling yourself short," I insisted. "You're amazing. You just need to believe in yourself."

The fact that Kailyn had an opportunity to take a seat at the table was such an honor. I didn't want her to miss out on it because she was scared.

"Please tell me you'll think about it," I pleaded.

"Fine," she grumbled. "I'll think about how long I have to wait before saying no. So, listen. That couple you left me a message about? I think they think the painting is worth something."

"I mean, I kind of thought that, but . . ." I stopped at the front window and looked back into the shop, at the painting. It was the perfect complement to the cozy space. "I don't know. I told them the artist wasn't famous."

"Right, but you said she's an art professor," Kailyn pointed out. "Maybe she knows something you don't. What were they looking at on her phone?"

"Don't know." I'd been busy talking to Lydia at the time. "I was helping another customer."

It would be a good time to tell Kailyn that I'd invited Lydia to stay in my grandmother's duplex, but I couldn't do it. She would panic and bring up what had happened to my former fiancé. I wasn't in the mood for that right now, considering I planned to return his mother's call when I got home.

"Check the security cameras," Kailyn was saying. "If you know about what time they were there and all that, maybe you could see what they were looking at."

The security system set up in the store had four different cameras. Each one covered a section of the shop, so the moment would have been captured. Would I be able to see the woman's phone well enough to know what she and her husband were looking at?

You're being ridiculous.

It was probably a text from their accountant, trying to talk them out of making such a ridiculous purchase.

"Kailyn, I can't do that." I grabbed my bike from the rack and stood off to the side under a tree. "It's invasive. Besides, I think they probably have a lot of money and don't know how to spend it. I'm sure it's nothing."

"*Pfft.* Tell me that when you see them on *Good Morning America*, bragging about how they duped you out of millions of dollars. Look, I'm just saying they're offering you twenty thousand dollars because that professor thinks she knows something about something. Find out what they were looking at on the phone. I've gotta run. I'm headed into a showing."

Once we hung up, I fiddled with the bell on my bike. Could Kailyn be right? Could the piece be some important work that could change the art world forever?

Yeah, right.

Sure, it was beautiful. The way the light fell around the shop with the Christmas lights, and the gold illumination from the indoor wall sconces made it sing. The colors were captivating, with the juxtaposition of the dark chocolates, the details in the animal truffles, and the pink shimmer of my dress. Still, I had to be realistic.

The painting had been here for a quarter of a century. If it was really some lost *Antiques Roadshow*–type find, someone would have noticed it a long time ago. The couple probably just wanted an anniversary memento and thought they could convince me to change my mind with their wealth. Maybe they even had a candy-shop art collection.

Instead of snooping around in our security footage, I needed to focus on what mattered: putting together a proposal to take to the bank. Otherwise, the painting would be the only place where the Sweetery would still exist.

Chapter Seven

I returned home determined to gather the information I needed to take out a small business loan, but before I could focus on that, I wanted to return the phone call from Joe's mother. Settling into my grandmother's sofa, I pulled an embroidered pillow close to my chest and dialed the once-familiar number.

His mother must have still had my number in her phone, because when she picked up, she said, "Emma. I have been hoping to hear from you." The sound of her voice took me back ten years, and we spent nearly a half hour on the phone, catching up.

"It makes me so happy to hear you're doing so well," she finally said. "Now, what about men? Is there anyone special?"

I stared out the window at the yard, debating my answer. Years ago, Joe's mother had been the one to put a stop to our daily phone calls, because she wanted me to free up my heart so that I could move on. It was embarrassing to admit I hadn't been successful in that area.

"No one yet." I tried to keep the tone light. "He left behind big shoes, you know."

"It's not about replacing him," she said gently. "Give yourself permission to move on, Emma. It's been ten years. I'd like to see you at the memorial, but if it's going to be too hard, skip it. Life is meant for living."

The words stayed with me long after we hung up.

It wasn't that I hadn't tried to move on. It was just that spending time with my grandmother, working at the candy shop, and helping out my friends felt more important than going on dates that went nowhere. I'd put in a good effort and had even dated a few guys for a month or two at a time, but nothing had clicked. Not like it had with Joe.

Joe and I had met in college at a house party, the second month of the first semester. I'd stepped onto the balcony to enjoy the brightness of the stars. It was quiet, other than muffled music coming from behind the sliding-glass door. Suddenly, someone spoke from the shadows at the end of the porch.

"There's something about the fall that feels like pure nostalgia."

Even though the college I attended was small and still in Michigan, it had been an adjustment for me to leave Starlight Cove. Our winter population hovered at forty-five hundred, so conversations with people typically started in the middle, because we all knew each other. It delighted me to find a stranger who jumped right into the middle of a topic, because it felt like home.

I walked over to him. "I feel that way every year. It's the smell of the leaves, that crispness in the air, and the sense that something is beginning. School, maybe."

He turned, and our eyes met. "Maybe."

I took in the close cut of his sandy-brown hair, the collared shirt layered with a sweatshirt, and the hint of a smile at the corner of his lips. He lifted his beer and touched it to mine. "To new beginnings."

Later, when we had that talk about who was attracted to whom when, we admitted it happened right then. Still, it took about two weeks for him to work up the nerve to ask me out. He finally did, fumbling through an invitation to a romantic comedy that was at the college theater.

The night was perfect. We shared a large Coke and a huge bucket of popcorn with real butter and spent the movie talking quietly in the back. We were still talking as the credits rolled and a girl from our sociology class stopped off at our aisle.

"Normally, I have no problem shushing people who disrupt a movie." She looked tired, like the movie was her one break from studying. I was just about to apologize when she held up her hand. "Each time I turned to shush you, though, I thought you guys were cuter than the couple in the movie. So, rock on." She gave us a thumbs-up and headed out.

Joe turned to me. "Do you think they sell gift cards here? I could get her one."

"You are the nicest person," I said, startled that we were thinking the same thing.

"Nah." He shrugged. "I just try to treat others the way I'd like to be treated."

By then, the theater had emptied, and the movie reel was making that clicking sound it did at the end of a film. We had looked at each other. Then, he had brushed his finger across my cheek, gently moved my chin forward with his thumb, and kissed me.

That moment, that kiss, played again and again in my mind the night I learned that he had been killed.

It happened three years after we'd been together, during finals week. Joe had graduated the year before me and had a job with a sales company that required him to travel. The travel was frequent, but it was still within the state. We were thrilled, because he was eager to make money to help pay for our wedding, which was booked for the following summer.

That night, I was studying at the local coffee shop, an old schoolhouse that made me think of the buildings on Main Street back home. The scent of steamed milk and vanilla was strong in the air. I had just packed up my books, feeling confident I'd do well on my last exam, when my cell phone rang.

From there, the memories are a blur: Friends driving me to Joe's hometown to be with his parents. The feeling of the wool blanket in his bed, where I'd slept, the fabric scratchy against my wet cheek. The horror of learning the details.

Joe had died on a business trip. He'd stopped at a bar and grill to pick up dinner. There, a man was screaming at a woman as she cowered in the corner. Joe rushed forward just as the man made a move to smash a bottle over the woman's head, and the bottle hit him instead.

Stunned, Joe fled to the safety of his car with pieces of glass embedded in his forehead. He tried to drive to the hospital, passed out at the wheel, and crashed into a tree. He died instantly.

Losing him was the worst thing I'd ever experienced. It took me nearly a year to accept the fact that he was gone. Then, I mourned him deeply, thoroughly, and in a way that left me with the choice to give up or go on.

I remember the night I made that choice. It was late October, nearly two years after he died. The air was crisp, the stars bright, and the smell of leaves was strong in the air.

There's something about fall that feels like pure nostalgia.

Pulling my arms close to my chest, I had stared up at the stars. Their reach was beyond the edge of the horizon, past the edge of memory, and somewhere close to forgiveness.

I walked along the edge of the water for hours, thinking of him and each moment we'd shared. The beam from the lighthouse panned across the water, and mist swirled around me like a ghost. When the cold was too much to bear, I finally headed for the warmth of home, the tiny pinpoints of starlight shining through the night sky.

To new beginnings.

The words had echoed through my ears on the cold, lonely walk back home. I knew it could take years to fall in love again, or even to date anyone, but for the first time, I felt I could survive.

It was so long ago, and I thought I'd moved on, but the talk with Joe's mother made me wonder about that. I hadn't exactly pressed forward.

It takes time. One day, it will happen.

Setting aside my phone, I wandered into the kitchen and stood in silence for a few moments. It was still early, only just after six. To get my head straight, I decided to make chicken orzo soup for dinner and drop some off as a welcome for Lydia and her son.

Once it was ready, I walked across the front porch to their front door. I hoped they were home, because I didn't want to spend another second wallowing in my memories.

Lydia answered the door, her face damp with sweat and pieces of her hair loose from a ponytail. "Emma, hi!"

"I brought dinner," I said, holding up the large pot. "It's lemon orzo soup."

"Oh my gosh." Lydia's eyes went big. "Thank you!"

She ushered me into the living room. Unlike my grandmother's home, this half of the duplex hadn't been remodeled, but it was nice enough. The living room was a large space that led into an open kitchen. It was carpeted, the curtains were floral patterned, and the well-loved furniture gave the space a cozy, familiar feeling. There was also a large patio door that led out to the backyard, which was one of my favorite places to sit and relax during the summer.

The only drawback was that the prior tenant had been an older gentleman who'd left it smelling of mildew and mothballs. Now it smelled like cleaning products.

"It looks great in here," I said, looking around in amazement.

"You think so?" Lydia smoothed her hair, her expression tired but hopeful. "Good. I didn't know if I was overstepping my bounds, but I love to clean."

"Are you kidding? I really appreciate it." Cleaning was on my to-do list, because there had been so many areas that needed work, like the fridge. The former tenant had left it filled with crumbs and stains. Now, it was bright white again and smelled brand new. "You have made my day," I said, shutting it with delight. "I have been dreading this fridge."

In fact, everything looked clean, bright, and inviting.

Lydia grabbed a washcloth from the sink and began wiping down the exterior of the cupboards. "Well, I'm happy to help. I've always enjoyed cleaning. It helps me to think."

"Me too," I said. "It helps me think how much I hate cleaning."

We laughed like friends, but her comments inspired me. There weren't many cleaning services in town, so many of the shopkeepers needed help. It might be a good idea to set Lydia up with some cleaning jobs to help her earn some extra cash, if she wanted to do it. I made a mental note to ask around and see what I could find.

Lydia had already pulled out some dishes for the soup and was busy setting the table. I'd bought some bread at the local bakery, and it hit me that I should have brought it over. Once I returned with the loaf, Lydia insisted I stay to eat with them, so I finally agreed.

"Thank you for the invitation. I really didn't plan to intrude." I settled in at the table. "I actually have quite a bit of work to do, so I'll have to eat and run."

"What are you working on?" Lydia's voice was shy. "Inventing a new piece of candy for your shop?" Her cheeks colored. "I probably sound so stupid. I don't know how it works."

"You don't sound stupid. Yes, we produce our own candy. I make it fresh the mornings that we're running low. My father was the one who came up with all the recipes. He died years ago, but to this day, his recipes are still the only ones we use."

If I failed at acquiring a loan and Talbaccis bought the shop, the sale would most likely include the rights to my father's recipes, so they could continue making what had attracted customers to the Sweetery in the first place. The thought made me bang at my soup bowl with a bit more force than necessary.

Jamal had been sitting in silence, staring down at the table, and he jumped.

"Sorry," I said. "Sometimes I don't know my own strength."

"I'm sorry to hear about your father," Lydia said, after taking a careful bite of bread. "What happened?"

"Heart attack." The tartness of the lemon sat on my tongue. "He was active and had even run a marathon the week before he died. I was only seven at the time, so I didn't really understand any of it."

"That's awful," Lydia said. "Who raised you?" She glanced at her son. "Honey, take slow bites."

It was obvious Jamal liked the soup. His spoon struck the side of the bowl with every quick bite. It hit me that they probably hadn't eaten much other than candy, and I made a mental note to drop off some real groceries in the morning, not the granola bars and portable rations we'd ordered to stock Lydia's car.

"My grandmother raised me," I said, bringing my focus back to Lydia. "Talk about a lifestyle change for her. She went from living the quiet life of a widow to desperately trying to figure out how to entertain a self-conscious, sad kid. I spent a lot of time at bingo and bridge."

I actually did have great memories of that time, thanks to my grandmother's friends. They'd been quick to make sure I had a full glass of lemonade and as many homemade brownies as I could eat. Eventually, I'd earned the privilege of calling the bingo games. It had been a ton of fun, because I'd known just how to rig it to let the old folks who needed a win take home the prizes.

"That was kind of your grandmother to take you in." Her eyes flitted to Jamal. The comment seemed to anger him, because he went back to banging his spoon against the bowl.

"We had fun together."

There wasn't butter for the bread, so I dipped it into my soup. Jamal noticed and did the same to soak up the last bits.

"This is so good," Lydia said, after a moment of silence. "I could never cook anything like it." She looked into her bowl. "I love lemon."

She had only taken a few bites, and I realized that she probably planned to give the soup to Jamal the second I left. Not because she didn't like it, but because he needed it. Feeling guilty, I drank the rest of mine and got to my feet. I wanted to spend more time getting to know Lydia and better understand what was going on with her, but it was more important to give her son a chance to eat.

"I should get to work," I said. "Thanks for letting me stay."

Lydia gave a quick nod and walked me to the door. Evening had started to fall, and outside, the air smelled rich with the scent of freshly mowed grass and cherry blossoms. The lightning bugs flitted across the yard, brightening the evening light.

"We don't plan to stay here long." Her voice was hushed. "But I really do appreciate all this."

"I'm happy to have you," I said. "Truly. Thanks again for cleaning, and I'll check in with you tomorrow."

Lydia locked the door the second she shut it. It reminded me of my earlier fears about the origin of her bruise, but maybe she was just cautious. Yes, Jamal had jumped when my spoon made a sudden noise, but it wasn't like they were looking over their shoulders. Lydia just seemed hopelessly insecure, like her confidence had taken a beating.

Back in my place, I made a cup of tea and settled in at the desk, determined to finally focus on the task I'd been dreading, figuring out how to get a loan. Earlier, I'd printed some facts and figures from the financial database of the computer, but I had no idea how to present them to a bank. I pulled the information out of my bag and stumbled across the folder Gillian had given me with the list of things that needed to be completed prior to the sale of the store.

I skimmed through the items, and a cold feeling of dread crept through me. Quickly, I slid the list back in the folder.

It was easy to find a mind-numbing series of videos about the topic on YouTube. Basically, I learned I needed to put together a presentation that would convince the bank to take me seriously, including professional-looking charts that could showcase the fiscal information of the store. It sounded great in theory, but for me, it was a whole new experience.

First, I needed to understand Excel. It looked simple in the video tutorial, but the host forgot to mention that it would be impossible to accomplish anything based on one quick video. Two minutes into trying to build a chart, I was completely lost. I didn't have the first clue how to put together columns or graphs or any of the so-called "easy formulas." It would take weeks, if not months, to learn how to do any of it, and I didn't have that kind of time.

My phone rang during the height of my frustration. Kailyn.

"Did you look at the security cameras or what?" she demanded.

Right. The painting, the couple, and their outrageous offer.

"Sorry, not yet." I knew she'd be disappointed. "I had some things to take care of. Like this darn loan."

"Is it ready to go?" she asked eagerly. "I have a friend at Starlight Cove Central. He could get you in tomorrow."

"It's not." Embarrassed, I admitted to my complete inexperience with any type of professional computer program.

"Wait. You had a real job for ten years." Kailyn sounded baffled. "You really never learned that stuff?"

I stared down at the glowing white light of my computer screen and finally shut it in frustration.

"Nope." Getting to my feet, I pulled a pair of pajamas out of the drawer. "I was in charge of people and events. Not graphs and numbers."

The nonprofit where I used to work had a nice lady named Samantha who handled all the clerical work. Even though I was always busy, it never involved sitting in front of the computer. Now, I regretted not taking the time to learn when I could have.

"You need help, then." Kailyn's voice was brisk. "It's way too important. Let me call Kip. He'll help you put together an entire presentation for the bank."

If only I could afford to do that.

Kip Whittaker was a friend from back in school and probably one of the nicest people on the planet. He owned a successful consulting firm and would be a great resource for this, but his rate would be out of reach. Kailyn scoffed when I said as much.

"He's engaged to one of my best friends," she said. "He'll do it for free as a favor to me."

"I don't feel comfortable with that," I said automatically.

The last thing I wanted to do was have him take time out of his day to work with me for free.

"Emma, come on," Kailyn complained. "For once in your life, let me help you."

I had been about to pull my nightshirt over my head but stopped and held it close, like a blanket. "What do you mean?"

"I tried to tell you this last night, and you refused to hear me," she said. "It's like you're always so busy helping other people that you won't let anyone help you. You know, sometimes . . ."

Her voice trailed off.

My shoulders tensed. "What?"

She sighed. "Sometimes, I think you're afraid to ask for anything, because you're afraid of being difficult or you don't think you're worth it. Or you're afraid that someone will leave you. I'm here to tell you, honey, you are worth it. You're my best friend, and I would never walk away."

The lump that formed in my throat caught me off guard. That wasn't the reason I didn't ask for help. It was because . . . well, I didn't quite know, exactly.

"So, please," Kailyn continued. "Will you let me call Kip? If anyone can coach you on how to put together a decent presentation that the banks will respond to, it's him."

The strength of her words made me nod. "Okay. Thank you."

"Great." She sounded relieved. "We need to get this done."

Once we hung up, I pulled on my nightshirt and headed to the bathroom. The smell of my lavender exfoliating wash and mint toothpaste soothed me. The second I went to dry my face with the towel, though, my eyes filled with tears.

Not a huge surprise, really, since a lot of things I didn't like to think about were suddenly front and center.

Maybe Kailyn's words were true. I'd always preferred helping people to asking for help. It had never occurred to me that deep down, maybe I was worried it would make me seem difficult and therefore unlovable.

Back when Gillian had left me with my grandmother, I'd spent so many nights wondering what I had done to make her mad enough to leave me. I'd retraced that morning and the days before a thousand times in my head, and in my seven-year-old brain, landed on a few things. I decided she was angry because I'd woken her up too many nights after my dad's death, begging her to hold me as I cried myself to sleep. Angry because I hadn't bothered to say thank you for the chocolate chip pancakes she'd made me but instead complained that we didn't have sausage too. Angry because I'd taken up too much space in her world. I'd been certain that if I hadn't needed so much, she would have let me stay.

Now that I was older, I understood that Gillian's decision probably had very little to do with me. Still, it made sense to think it could have affected the choices I had made in my life. I'd never given much thought as to why I felt uncomfortable asking for help, but if that was the reason, I needed to step outside my comfort zone. It would be impossible for me to get this loan without help, and Kip was definitely the perfect person to ask.

Pulling my feather pillows close, I shut my eyes, determined to stop thinking about the past and to get some rest. Still, images of the day flashed through my mind: Jamal's smile when I gave him more candy, my battle with the impossible spreadsheet, my talk with that couple about the painting . . .

The woman winked at her husband when I described Montee.

The sudden thought jolted me out of a half sleep. I sat straight up. In the moment, the wink had seemed like camaraderie between a happy couple. But in that space between awareness and sleep, it suddenly felt like so much more. Like my physical description confirmed something they'd already suspected and helped resolve some mystery about the painting.

I'd commented on it at the time, asking if Montee was a friend of theirs, but at that point, it hadn't occurred to me that something more had prompted their questions.

Goose bumps prickled my arms.

That professor thinks she knows something.

Staring out the window at the starry night, I chewed on my lip. It was unlikely that my painting was more than just a memory on the wall of the candy shop. There was no reason to sit up like the house was on fire.

On the other hand . . .

The woman was a university professor, and art was her specialty. There were plenty of galleries in Starlight Cove where she and her husband could have bought a souvenir. There was even an antique shop with finds from all over the world. Why would they offer so much for my painting?

I needed to get to bed. But no matter how hard I tried to convince myself to go to sleep, the nagging feeling in my gut wouldn't go away.

If the couple knew something, I wanted to know it too. There had to be something special about the painting that had prompted them to offer $20,000.

The question was, what?

Chapter Eight

For once, Main Street was empty of both cars and people. The moment I approached the candy shop and saw the gaslights flickering in the night, I felt excited, like there was something big waiting for me behind the doors. The suspicion had been enough to drag me out of bed and to the Sweetery this late at night, instead of waiting until morning, and I was sure I'd discover something life changing.

In spite of the warm evening, a chill rushed through me at the sudden blast of air-conditioning when I keyed into the store. The space was dark, and the scent of chocolate was incredible, like the night had increased the intensity of its sweetness. Taking in a breath, I looked around, noting the long shadows stretched across the floor.

The painting rested in the dark, and I shined my flashlight on it. Like always, I studied it intently, trying to figure out what it was that made it so captivating. The use of lighting was compelling, but it was also the sense of Americana—that the artist had captured a picture-perfect moment in a small-town shop. But no matter how much I loved it, I couldn't figure out how it could possibly be worth $20,000.

Even though I'd come to the store with hopes of discovering something big, I returned to the idea that the couple had a collection of some sort and money to spare, which made me feel silly for thinking

I was about to solve some big mystery. What did I really think I was going to find?

Don't make it a wasted trip. Go look at the security footage.

I didn't feel right about that, but at the same time, it was the only opportunity I had to discover anything new. The video monitors were set up in the confectioner's kitchen and linked to Gillian's phone. I hoped that by checking them, it wouldn't send her an alert or anything. It would be awkward to try and explain my way around this. Gillian had never been a fan of the painting to begin with, probably because it belonged to me.

My grandmother had shared that information with me when I was a teenager. She gave me a file my father had kept, neatly labeled "Emma." It held my social security card, birth certificate, and similar papers, as well as the first piece of art I'd done in kindergarten. There was also a note from Montee. It was on a small plain piece of stationery and penned in the artist's careful hand:

"The Girl with the Butterscotch Hair," 1992. Gifted to Gilroy Laurent with the understanding that it will pass down to the subject, Emma Laurent, with much affection.

— Montee

"The painting should stay in the candy shop," my grandmother had told me, "because that's where your father wanted it. But one day, you will have every right to put it in your home, if that's what you decide to do."

The idea that I owned an actual piece of art felt so weighty. I spent a lot of time brooding about the painting, wondering why Montee had left it to me, instead of my father. I finally decided that he'd gifted it to me because I'd helped him find his way out of an artistic slump, even though it had happened completely by accident.

Montee had arrived at the shop to drink with my father one blustery winter afternoon, which was not uncommon. It had been snowing nonstop, and I was tired of being indoors. I was delighted to see that Montee had brought me several sheets of heavy paper along with a paper plate that had dabs of red, blue, and yellow paint on it, and a collection of brushes. He clipped the paper to his easel and let me play while he and my father tried to top one another's stories.

With sloppy, halting jerks, I painted the candies that were in the case nearby. They didn't look that great, so I put cat ears on a truffle to try and jazz them up. It got late, and Montee gathered up his stuff to go. When he reached the easel, he stopped and stared at my sloppy work. "Cats for truffles," he said quietly. "Of course."

It was as if my drawing were a key that had unlocked the whimsy he had been trying to find. The next morning, he'd been at the shop first thing, working intently on a menagerie of animals in the window.

Now, I crept into the kitchen at the candy shop, wishing I could whip up some of those animal truffles I'd always longed to sell. Instead, I logged onto the computer. The black-and-white images of the security cameras sprang to life, and I scrolled through the frames during the time the couple had been here until I finally spotted them.

Quickly, I guided the cursor through our polite exchange to the moment where I walked away to speak to Lydia. Then I pressed play. The video did not have audio, and I could not read lips, but it was startling to see the intensity of the couple's conversation. They leaned close to each other, whispering, and every so often, sneaked a look over at me. Then the professor pulled out her phone.

Here it is.

I paused it, debating whether or not to continue. Trying to get a look at the woman's phone felt invasive. Yes, there were signs all over the store warning customers that they were on camera, but still. On the other hand, it was pretty clear that something strange was going on, and this was the only way I had to get to the bottom of it.

After clicking on the space bar, I zoomed in. The angle of the camera was such that I could, indeed, see the screen of the woman's phone. Squinting, I leaned in.

There were lots of colors on the screen, but it was hard to tell what they were. I rewound the feed and tried again and again, zooming closer each time. The heading on the website read . . .

It was too pixilated. I couldn't see it.

Maybe if I printed it. The shop had a professional printer, so it was worth a shot. After saving the image, I printed it out at the highest quality possible. Then I grabbed Gillian's spare set of reading glasses out of the drawer and slid them on, shining my phone's flashlight at the printout for good measure.

The words were too blurry to make out.

Buzz. Buzz.

My phone vibrated in my hand. Startled, I dropped it with a clatter. Gillian.

"Emma, are you back at the shop?" She sounded worried. "I got an alert that someone logged into the security cameras."

My cheeks flushed. "Yes, sorry. I . . ." Lying was definitely not in my skill set. So, I decided to go with a watered-down version of the truth. "There was a couple that was acting weird earlier today. I decided to watch the security feed to get a better idea of what they were up to."

"Oh." Gillian paused. "What was the issue?"

"Nothing, really. Turns out they just wanted something to commemorate their trip to Starlight Cove."

"What do you mean, something?" Gillian asked. "A piece of chocolate?"

I stared down at the picture in my hands, debating how much to tell her.

"They learned I was in the painting and wanted to buy it."

Gillian laughed. "Well, I suppose you should be flattered. Okay, just wanted to make sure it was you. Lock up when you go. I've got to run."

The second we hung up, I shut down the computer, shoved the printout into my purse, and scurried back into the candy shop.

The fact that Gillian had caught me snooping in the security camera footage made me nervous. She had worked in the news business for years and was an expert at sniffing out stories. If she discovered that there was more to what I was telling her, that the couple had offered me twenty thousand dollars for the painting, I wondered if she would try and claim it as her own.

She wouldn't do that. Would she?

If she was worried about money, she might. The painting had hung in the shop for a lifetime, and the shop belonged to her. That right there might make her feel a sense of ownership, which was understandable. Still, I was not about to let her have it.

The painting was a big part of my history, but it could also solve a lot of problems. I didn't know what was motivating the couple, but if the loan for the store fell through, I could sell the painting to them and use that money to help my grandmother. It was an option I didn't want to lose. Pulling my sweatshirt close, I headed back out into the summer night, hoping that Gillian wouldn't give the security cameras another thought.

Otherwise, I might have to sell the painting before I was ready, so that she didn't beat me to it.

Chapter Nine

The next morning, I opened the kitchen window for some fresh air and spotted Lydia. She sat on the bench under the lilac tree. Pleased at the opportunity to continue our conversation, I poured two cups of coffee and headed out to join her.

I didn't want to scare her by sneaking up, so I called, "Lydia? I brought you some coffee; I thought you'd like it."

Lydia sat up straight and wiped at her eyes.

Shoot. She's crying.

I wouldn't have bothered her if I'd realized that, but now it was too late. By the time I'd made it to the bench, her eyes were watery, but she could have passed for someone enjoying the early morning. She accepted the mug of coffee and gave me a weak smile.

"You okay?" I said quietly. "You seem upset."

"Oh, just thinking about all of my bad decisions. Jamal's had such a hard time leaving our home and his friends this summer, no matter how many times I tell him it's temporary. I've been trying for a new start, but it seems like every time I do . . ." She looked down into the mug. "I screw it all up."

It was hard to read between the lines. What was going on with her? I wanted to ask, but I didn't want to push too hard. It seemed that each time Lydia tried to tell her story, it upset her. Maybe, if I gathered just a little bit of information in the most casual way, I could fill in the blanks.

"Are you married?" I tried.

"No." She met my eyes. "I know you think this bruise is from a bad relationship, Emma. It's not."

So much for being casual.

"The truth is," she continued, "I ran out on my lease in the middle of the night. I was trying to move everything out in the dark because my landlord lived on-site, and I bumped my face against the wall. It's not admirable, but it's the truth."

Well, that was a relief. It wasn't great to learn that Lydia was, technically, on the run, but at least no one was chasing her. Except maybe an angry landlord.

"I'm glad," I admitted. "In my experience, that type of thing can be dangerous for everyone involved."

"Yes." She paused. "You mentioned you had a bad experience with a man." Her tone was cautious. "What happened?"

It was my turn to stare down into my mug. "My fiancé was killed."

I told her the whole story, my voice flat.

"That's terrible," she whispered. "It's not fair. I can't tell you how sorry I am."

"Yeah." The word was short.

It was one thing to think about my relationship with Joe, but when it came to trying to understand the horror of the event, something inside me still shut off.

"Jamal's father was violent," Lydia said after a moment. "He attacked me several times."

Was the story about the landlord a lie?

"Not recently," she added, as if reading my mind. "He's in jail. He's been there since Jamal was a baby, so it's not like it's changed anything for Jamal. It did for me. There were some things I couldn't face, and I didn't handle it well. I had to leave Jamal with my brother to cope. It wasn't good."

The day Gillian dropped me at my grandmother's house was one of the most painful days of my life. It had started out so great: Gillian had made me my favorite breakfast, pancakes with chocolate chips, and we had gone to the park to go down the slide. But once it was time for lunch, she had announced it was time to go to my grandmother's. I'd thought the suitcase packed full of my stuff was for an overnight visit, but outside my grandmother's house, Gillian had kneeled in front of me and said my father would not have wanted her to be my mommy anymore. Then she had stood quickly, gotten in the car, and driven away. I hadn't seen her in person again for months.

"Why did you leave your son?" I asked Lydia, hoping it didn't sound like an accusation.

Lydia hunched her thin shoulders. "Depression. Two years ago, it looked like my ex-husband had a chance for parole. I was so scared, and I couldn't function, let alone take care of my kid. Jamal has every right to resent me. I haven't been a good mother. Which is terrible, because I love him so much, and he doesn't know it." She tied her hair up into a bun, which made her look young and incredibly lost.

"It's obvious how much you love him," I said. "He has to know."

Lydia shook her head. "He's so angry. Before school let out, he was getting in fights and almost got expelled. He's so smart, but he stopped getting the grades, and . . ." Her voice broke, and she started to cry again. "I don't know what I can do to make it up to him."

I fidgeted with a loose leaf that had fallen on the bench. There were so many times I wondered if Gillian ever regretted the decision she'd made. It was hard to imagine her feeling an ounce of the heartbreak Lydia was showing me now.

Lydia dried her face on her T-shirt. "I know he's hurting. I wish there was something more I could do."

Two dragonflies buzzed across the lawn. I watched them for a moment, then an idea hit. "Cody Henderson, a boy I went to high school with, owns the hardware store. He started a youth outreach program for boys Jamal's age."

Kailyn had told me about it. She knew everything that was going on in town and had raved about the program. From the sound of things, the kids loved it.

"It teaches boys how to build things and work as a team," I said. "Maybe it would help Jamal to participate."

Lydia shook her head. "We won't be here long enough to do that."

"I'm sure some time is better than none," I tried.

Even if Lydia and Jamal only stuck around until her car was repaired, it would probably do Jamal good to be around kids his own age.

"The program is twice a week, and Cody's great. No pressure. Just an idea."

"It might not hurt." Lydia fiddled with her watch. It was old and digital. "At least he'd have something to do. He's on that video game too much. There was a time when he would run and play outside, a time he would smile at me . . . I know I don't deserve to ask for anything, but I wish things were different." She looked embarrassed. "Speaking of, I should check on him. He'll probably be getting up anytime."

"I need to head into work," I said. "I'm making truffles this morning."

Lydia gave a shy smile. "That sounds like a good way to spend a morning."

Back inside, I considered our conversation. She had been through so much, and she seemed to blame herself for everything that had happened with her husband. It was sad to think of the impact that relationship had had on her and her son.

Jamal didn't seem like a particularly happy kid, but I hadn't been around kids enough to know what was normal and what was not. If anyone could help him, though, it would be Cody.

～

I paid a visit to Henderson Hardware during lunch to find out some more information about the outreach program. The store was crowded, like always. Even though most of the women seemed intent on purchasing paintbrushes or finding just the right grade of sandpaper for their projects, the majority seemed overdressed for a hardware shop. Of course, that was the effect of the Henderson brothers.

Ever since we were little, Cody, Carter, and Cameron had a way of taking over a room with their good looks and charm. They were hard workers, polite, and, until recently, totally single. Then, much to my delight, Carter had started dating Kailyn. They were the perfect match, and I'd never seen her so happy with a guy.

"Hi, Carter," I sang. He was at the register, ringing up a young married couple.

It looked like the couple was in the thick of patching their driveway, based on the buckets sitting on the counter. The husband joked about the cost of the materials, and his wife gave him a loving swat on the arm. Once again, Joe and the conversation with his mother flitted through my mind. I still didn't know whether or not I should attend the memorial. It had been a long time since I'd lost him, but this week, it was like all the hurt had come roaring back.

The couple paid and headed out, the husband lugging both buckets, with the wife jokingly lecturing him on the best way to carry them. I let out a breath. Then, I turned back to Carter.

He grinned. "Newlyweds."

"How do you know?" I picked up a pamphlet advertising lawn mowers. There was a photo of a family. Quickly, I set it back down.

"It's a whole theory I have." Carter's freckled face became earnest. "Okay, so, the ones that have been married for a while are focused on the project, right? They work as a well-oiled machine, or they bicker over every last detail, no in between. Newlyweds, on the other hand, act like each home improvement project is some sort of big secret they're sharing, like they can't believe they're lucky enough to play house together."

"I can see that." Then, because Carter was hopelessly shy and fun to tease, I added, "Do you think it will be like that for you and Kailyn?"

Sure enough, his face turned beet red. "So, what brought you in today?" he asked, in a brisk tone.

I laughed. "I need to talk to Cody about something."

"The fact that he needs to stop wearing muscle shirts to work? Good luck." Carter pointed toward the back. "He's in the office, fresh from the gym, so prepare for grunting instead of full syllables."

The office was down the far aisle toward the back. I knocked on the wooden door, and a gruff voice said, "Come in."

The fresh scent of deodorant and Dial soap nearly knocked me down. Cody's head was bent over some work on his desk, and he gripped what looked like a protein shake. As promised, he wore a muscle shirt and a pair of gray jogging shorts that amplified the huge muscles in his legs.

I stopped in the doorway, embarrassed somehow, to walk in.

Cody and I didn't see each other that often now that we were older, but I'd had a few run-ins with him over the years. The most notable one was at a networking event hosted by the chamber of commerce. They hosted several get-togethers throughout the year, and in order to keep a business license, the businesses on Main Street and the heavily trafficked tourist areas were required to send a representative to at least three events per year.

The restrictions seemed a little silly, because the shopkeepers in Starlight Cove hardly needed to network. We all knew each other and had for years. On the other hand, it was a forced opportunity to step away from work to talk about things other than business, which was something we didn't always do.

The chamber had outdone itself during that particular event. They had set up a mock speed-dating situation, designed to allow each business representative to chat with everyone at the party for three minutes. It was fast-paced, fun, and a great idea, because I typically stuck to my group of friends.

When I sat down at the table with Cody, I kicked off our conversation by offering to grab him a piece of chocolate from the dessert table. Since I had started running the Sweetery, there had not been a community event that had not received some form of sponsorship from the candy shop, and the speed-dating event was no exception.

Everyone loved the free chocolates, and it helped to remind the other shop owners to send customers our way. But instead of accepting my offer, Cody crossed his enormous arms and launched into a two-minute lecture about sugar consumption and childhood obesity.

I was completely caught off guard, and once he finished, I said, "That was interesting. Have you also considered how the hardware store might be impacting public health? I mean, most people aren't prepared to combat the stench of paint fumes or the risk of smashing their finger under a hammer while trying to pound in a nail. I would suggest hiring an on-site therapist to deal with the emotional trauma that could affect the customers that don't know how to be safe on project day." The bell rang, and I hopped up. "Have a great day!"

He'd been so surprised that he'd actually cracked a smile as I'd walked away.

Now, I cleared my throat, and he looked up. "Hey, Emma." His dark eyes were intense. "To what do I owe the pleasure?"

He got to his feet. The small space coupled with his size made me blush, which surprised me. It had been a long time since I'd felt thrown off by a guy.

"I was hoping we could talk for a second?" I nodded at the chair across his desk.

"Yeah, sure." He kicked the chair out with his foot and sat back down. "What's up? How's the shop?"

For a second, I considered telling him about my plans to buy the store. Cody and his brothers had started their business from scratch, and Cody had a reputation as a smart businessman. It would be interesting to hear his advice. But we didn't have that type of relationship, and besides, it wasn't the reason I was here.

"Things are great," I lied. "So, listen. I don't know if you heard through the grapevine about the woman who was sleeping in her car the other day—"

He drew back. "Sleeping in her *car*?"

I briefed him on the story but left out the part about where she was staying. Word traveled fast in Starlight Cove, and I wanted to keep that information to myself as long as possible. He gave me a troubled look.

"Where's she at now?"

Shoot.

"If I tell you, can you keep it a secret?"

He rolled his eyes. "No. I'm going to mass text my buddies, because they can't wait to spread it all over town."

I hid a smile. "My grandmother's duplex. The woman really needed the help."

Even though I expected them, there were no words of warning or condemnation. Instead, Cody drained his protein shake.

"The space is just sitting there, vacant for the next few weeks," I continued. "She seems harmless, so . . ."

"Look, you don't have to justify it to me. If anything . . ." He studied me and frowned. "What do you need from me? You canvassing businesses for them or something?"

I chewed on a fingernail. "Hadn't thought of that."

It wasn't a bad idea. Putting together a purse for Lydia would be a big help. That way, she could have enough for emergency lodging if there was an issue on the way to Pennsylvania.

"Actually, I wanted to talk to you about the youth outreach program you're doing." My phone buzzed. "Sorry." I fumbled to turn it off. The text was from Kailyn, telling me that Kip could meet tomorrow about the loan presentation. Heartened, I continued. "So, the woman's son is having a lot of trouble. They won't be in town long, but I figured it could help him to hang out with kids his age and do something productive. Right now, he just sits around and plays video games."

"Yeah, good." Cody cracked his knuckles. "We've been up and running for a few weeks, and some of the kids are forming friendships, but they have to work with someone new each session. He won't be too far on the outside. We meet again tomorrow morning. Send him over."

I let out a breath. "Cody, that's great. I know it could disrupt what you already have in place, but they're nice people who just had a bad break and—"

"Happy to help," he said. "Now, you're not poisoning the kid, are you?"

I wrinkled my brow. "What do you mean?"

"I mean, you're not pumping him full of sugar, are you? He's in a critical stage of physical development. That means fruits, vegetables, whole grains, and protein, not chocolate bars."

I laughed. "Really, Cody? You were one of the Sweetery's best customers when you were his age."

"Yeah, and I was moody, exhausted, and suffered from mental fatigue." He pointed at me, as if to emphasize the point.

I couldn't help but notice that even his fingers looked ridiculously fit. Was it possible to have a muscular finger? It looked like it, from where I sat.

"Don't give that kid a bunch of candy," Cody said. "His outlook on life will improve."

"Hmm. Maybe I should give him more. Thanks for your help." The chair creaked as I got to my feet. Then, because I couldn't help myself, I added, "Oh, and Carter thinks you should stop wearing muscle shirts to work."

I rushed out of the office before he could respond.

"How did it go?" Carter called, as I headed for the front door.

"Great." I stopped at the checkout counter. "Hey, it's your turn to give Cody a message. Tell him to ditch the protein shake and try a milkshake. He seemed a little hangry."

Carter burst out laughing and gave me a high five.

Poisoning the kid with sugar, indeed. I planned to put together a huge box of chocolates and send it to the hardware shop c/o Cody Henderson that very afternoon.

Chapter Ten

By the time I'd closed up shop, Cody still had not responded to the box of chocolates, and I felt a little foolish for sending it. In the moment, the gift had seemed funny, but now, it seemed flirtatious, which was not how I meant it.

The shop was running low on some key chocolates, so I headed back to the kitchen to make more. I hadn't had as much time as I'd wanted to spend in the kitchen that morning, since I'd had coffee with Lydia, and the thought of heading home to an empty house was not appealing. So, I pulled out butter and bags of sugar and chocolate, setting them on the counter next to an assortment of pots and pans.

It took me two hours to make thirty trays of chocolate caramels, creams, and cherries, and I loved every second of it. Making the chocolates felt like creating art. Ever since I was a child, my favorite part of the process was watching the fillings bounce along the conveyor belt as the chocolate rained down. The act of the chocolate folding over the filling was hypnotic, and the low hum of the machine like a symphony. It calmed me in a way that nothing else could.

Once I'd gotten through the basics of what we needed, I decided to experiment. For the past few days, I'd had this image and flavor profile of a chocolate truffle shaped like a star. I imagined it dusted in edible gold powder and the filling like an explosion of light. There were a couple different flavor combinations that might work, so I pulled out a series of small bowls to see which one worked best.

I got to work mixing the ingredients, embracing the sight and smell of the powders and sugar blending in the mixing bowl beneath me. It was quiet, with the exception of the scrape of the spoon and the hum of the fluorescent lights overhead. I mixed and tasted and tried again. Finally, I found it.

The shell of the truffle had to be a deep dark chocolate, at least 80 percent. The taste needed to be almost too sharp. That way, once you bit into the star, the explosion of vanilla-cream champagne was so pure that it heightened the sudden tang of the granulated kernel of sea salt in the center. It was perfect, and the taste sparkled on my tongue.

"Victory," I whispered, and jotted the winning combination in the back of my father's recipe book.

Instead of feeling happy, I felt almost . . . sad. The feeling I'd had in the hardware shop, that moment when I'd thought of Joe, came rushing back.

I missed having a partner. Especially in moments of creation like this, because I didn't want to stand here and eat chocolate alone—I wanted to share the experience with someone. Yes, I had wonderful friends, and Kailyn was like a sister, but I couldn't help feeling that I'd been cheated out of the joy of living life with the man I loved. For a brief moment, I closed my eyes.

Do you really want to think about this?

No. Joe had been my future, one that I still half expected to start those mornings when I had not yet opened my eyes and crossed over from the land of dream to reality. It was well past time to let him go, but something made me hang on.

Maybe it was because there were still pieces of him that seemed to live on forever. The way he'd treated people, for one. Just like my father, he'd always been so quick to jump in, to give people the benefit of the doubt. He'd spent so much time trying to convince me to rebuild a relationship with Gillian, if only for the opportunity to heal.

I'd always felt he would have been proud, in some way, to see me working in the shop for her. It had brought her back into my life, and even if she and I had never had any big heart-to-hearts, it had given us the opportunity to be together. It struck me that, once the shop was sold, she and I would fade out of each other's lives once again.

I didn't know how I felt about that.

Pushing the thought from my mind, I got to work cleaning the kitchen. Once the stainless steel counter was spotless, the machinery sterilized, and the dishes in the industrial dishwasher, I returned to the tray and took another look at my work. The stars seemed to twinkle, and I thought long and hard about who I could share them with. Finally, I decided to give them to my grandmother and her friends. Quietly, I packed them up to drop at the assisted living facility on my way home.

It was a risk showing up so late. My grandmother typically started to get confused around six, and it was already quarter past seven. Still, I wanted her to try the chocolates and, if she had her faculties, talk to her about my plan to buy the store.

I found her in the main room playing a card game, which was a good sign. There was a time when my grandmother was a fierce bridge player. Now, she stuck to simple games, to make certain she could keep up. It looked like the group was playing euchre, based on the setup of the table, and she seemed to be winning.

"Oh, Emma's here." She waved at me. "Hello, dear!"

I said hello to everyone and passed around the chocolate stars, warning the residents about the tiny drop of champagne, in case they couldn't have it with their meds. Then, I settled in next to my grandmother. She was dressed up, which was something Morning Lark encouraged, and I really liked.

The facility pushed the residents to dress up because they wanted them to feel a sense of personal care and purpose each day. They operated under the theory that it kept them feeling young, which I agreed with.

Back when my grandmother was living at home, there were times she had sat around in her pajamas all day, and it had seemed to depress her. Now, she put on makeup each morning, and twice a week she had her hair done at the hair salon on-site. It did seem to make a difference in her disposition.

Today, her white curls were tinted a subtle shade of purple, and she wore a lavender pantsuit with a white shirt. I hugged her, breathing in her familiar scent of drugstore perfume and a vague sense of body odor. Years ago, my grandmother had read an article on the evils of deodorant and had stopped wearing it that very day. It had embarrassed me when I was younger, but now, I was impressed that she had been so determined to stick to such an unconventional decision.

I sat in companionable silence, watching as she played cards. The television blared over in the corner, where two men napped while another watched a program on attic finds. The host approached people out in the middle of nowhere, requested to search their attics, and usually uncovered a valuable treasure that had been sitting ignored for years.

"Euchre," my grandmother cried, setting down a winning trick. "That's game. We win."

Her partner, Betty Anne, cheered. The two had been friends forever, long before they moved into the home. Betty Anne was heavyset like me, with faded blonde hair and a cheerful expression that didn't waver. Her smile became even brighter at the win, and she turned their point cards to ten.

"Pay up," Betty Anne chirped.

Their opponents grumbled, but the thin one with the glasses fished a quarter out of a small dish in the center. She handed it to my grandmother, who crowed with delight, then passed it to Betty Anne. The jar she slipped it into was nearly full.

Betty Anne beamed. "We're saving up for a trip to Hawaii," she said with a straight face.

My grandmother gave an earnest nod. "We almost have enough to fly first class."

"Well, send pictures. Or better yet, take me with you." We all laughed, and as the women made a move to start another game, I nudged my grandmother. "Hey, can we go grab some cookies?"

The assisted living facility set out homemade chocolate chip cookies precisely at eight o'clock each night. I didn't need more chocolate, but I did need an excuse to talk to my grandmother in private. Several of the residents and two of the caretakers were in the dining room, but we found a quiet table in the corner. After biting into a buttery cookie, I gave my grandmother the update on Gillian and the store.

"Oh, Emma. You're really going to buy it?" My grandmother clasped her hands in delight. "Your father would be so pleased."

"Do you think so?" I asked.

"Of course. He always wanted you to run the store." A familiar look of disapproval settled on her face. "That's why it has always amazed me that Gillian never bothered to offer it to you."

"It was hers," I said, because we'd had this conversation a million times. "I was not entitled to it in any way, so you can't be mad at her for that."

My grandmother's disdain for Gillian extended far past any issue she had with the store. I'd never learned the nature of their falling out, because neither of them would say, so I could only assume it had to do with the fact that Gillian had opted out of raising me. Either way, my grandmother was not a fan.

"Well, this is such exciting news," my grandmother said, biting into a cookie.

"I guess." I fiddled with a napkin. "Really, though, I'm scared it might not work out. I don't know anything about applying for a business loan. They might turn me down."

My grandmother frowned. "I doubt that. The Sweetery has been profitable for the past thirty years, because your father knew exactly what he was doing when he set it up. There is absolutely no reason you would not be able to make good on repaying the loan. There's no risk."

The fact that my grandmother was saying the exact same thing Kailyn had said made my heart beat a little faster.

"Do you really think I could do it?" I asked, running my hand over the vinyl tablecloth. The forest-green material made a whooshing sound.

"Of course." My grandmother took my hands. "My darling, you can accomplish anything you put your mind to."

Betty Anne came into the dining room then with a group of their friends. They each had small plates of cookies and were headed our way. My grandmother brightened.

"Hello, dears!" she called, waving. "Come meet my new friend, Emma. Emma, this is Betty Anne. She's my bridge partner, and boy, she's tough."

Betty Anne gave me a sad little smile. The sudden shifts in my grandmother's personality had been hard for her, too, and we'd cried about it together more than once. She held out her hand and shook mine. "Charmed."

"It's nice to meet you, Betty Anne," I said, and my grandmother nodded with approval.

I got to my feet. "Love you, Grandma. I should head out."

I'd found that it was best to leave the moment her confusion started. Even though I would have much preferred to stay with her, the caretakers had told me that it put unnecessary stress on her to have the vague sense that she knew me but to be unable to figure out who I was. Plus, they were trained on how to guide her through these evening spells in a way that made her feel safe and comfortable, and I was not. I'd tried several times before and had only succeeded in upsetting her.

I gave her a big hug. "I will see you again soon."

She adjusted her glasses and bounced right back into our conversation. "Let me know what happens with the candy shop. I love it so."

"I love you so." I squeezed her hand. "I'll see you soon."

Chapter Eleven

The next morning, there was a knock on my door at eight a.m. sharp.

I'd slid a note under Lydia's door with the information about the outreach program and an invitation to stop by for breakfast. The meeting with Kip about the business loan was at nine, and I figured cooking would help calm my nerves. Jamal scowled at me when he walked in but perked up when he smelled the bacon on the stove.

The kitchen opened into the dining room. Jamal hovered between the two rooms, as if unsure where to go or what to do.

"Take a seat; take a seat." I grabbed an oven mitt. "It should be ready in just a second."

"You didn't have to go to all of this trouble for us," Lydia said, looking embarrassed.

"I need the company. It gets lonely rattling around here all by myself."

This morning, Lydia wore a pale-blue shirt, and her hair was damp but pulled back, showcasing her high cheekbones. The bruise was yellowed and had started to fade. She bustled around, helping set the table and pour the coffee. Still, her actions were careful, like she was afraid to make a mistake.

The heat of the oven made me wince as I pulled out a batch of baked french toast. It looked and smelled delicious, with a hardened crème brûlée glaze. Sugary steam rose up as I set it on the table.

"Whoa." Jamal scrambled into a chair. "I can eat that?" He started to reach for a piece, but his mother blocked his hand.

"Be careful; it's boiling hot." She gave him an affectionate look. "I swear, it's like there's a bottomless pit in your leg."

"Jamal, it will take a minute to cool," I said, using tongs to put it on his plate. "Let me grab you some bacon too."

The french toast was a hit. It was the perfect combination of smoky and sticky, and it probably had more carbs than anything we served at the candy shop. Jamal had three helpings, and I couldn't help but smile at the thought of what Cody would have to say about that. Once we'd finished, Lydia tried to help clean up the breakfast dishes, but I shooed her away.

"I'll take care of it. I don't want you to be late." The kitchen window was open, and the early-morning breeze brought in a gust of fresh air. "It's a beautiful day. Jamal, have fun. Let me know what happens."

The pans needed time to soak, so I put everything in the sink. We all headed out, and both looking a little nervous, Lydia and Jamal went in the direction of the hardware shop. I headed the opposite direction to meet Kailyn at the beach. Our meeting with Kip was early so that I'd have plenty of time to make it to work.

Kailyn waited for me on the boardwalk, hard at work on her phone. Sliding it into her purse, she beamed.

"This is awesome," she said. "Kip's the best."

"The best is that he's meeting with us in the lighthouse."

The lighthouse was located on the beach just off Main Street and rested at the edge of the shore, like a warm and friendly warrior guarding our beach. It was dazzling white with a black iron gallery at the top and a charming red door down below. It had always served as an important centerpiece to Starlight Cove, and nearly everyone had a special memory associated with it.

Mine was the tradition I'd had with my father. Every Fourth of July, he took a picture of us standing in front of the lighthouse. He liked to wait until dark and then, while fireworks rained down on the lakefront behind us, he'd ask someone to get the shot. The flash was blinding but the end result, beautiful. The photo gallery of our lighthouse Fourth of July photos hung in my front hallway. In the last photograph, my skinny arms were wrapped tightly around his neck, like I somehow knew that I needed to hang on before he could slip away.

Today, the lighthouse was owned by Kip Whittaker's fiancée, Dawn Conners. The two were slated to get married next year at a local vineyard. Before they'd met, Dawn had purchased the lighthouse at a government auction. She'd spent the year restoring it, and the interior was rumored to be as magnificent as the outside. I couldn't wait to see it.

The boardwalk slapped against my shoes as Kailyn and I made our way down to the water. Shielding my eyes against the sun, I looked up. The lighthouse was always a thing of beauty, but its magnificence was chilling this close. I couldn't even imagine what it would be like to live in there.

"I am getting darn good at climbing this ladder," Kailyn told me, adjusting her romper. "Watch this."

Like a champion, she scaled the iron ladder and made a big deal out of ringing the large bell that hung next to the door. A window scraped open, and Dawn poked her head out. Her blonde hair was pulled up in a casual chignon, and her eyes were as deep blue as the lake.

"Hi, guys," she called. "Come on up!"

I followed Kailyn up the ladder. The iron rungs were cold in the early-morning sun and made my hands smell like metal. I climbed up over the top rung and into the main entrance of the lighthouse, waited for my eyes to adjust to the dim light, then let out a delighted squeak.

"Dawn, this is so beautiful." I looked around, drinking in each detail.

The main room was about fifteen feet wide. The sunlight filtered in through the windows, showcasing a stunning stone floor and smooth walls. It was decorated with small details like a framed book that read *Instructions to Light-Keepers: July, 1881.*

"Thanks." Dawn leaned her head back, as if taking it all in. The ceiling was high, and the staircase that encircled the room went straight up. "It took forever, but somehow we pulled it off." She smiled at us. "Kip went to grab bagels. Would you like the tour?"

"You know I get altitude sickness," Kailyn said. "Don't try and make me go on the roof."

The circular stairs took us up and up and up, twisting beneath our feet. Each room seemed more cozy than the next, which was not an illusion, considering they became smaller and smaller the closer we got to the top. In the final room, Dawn climbed up an old ladder that led past an enormous light. It was beautiful, like a glass honeycomb.

"You're not tricking me into this," I heard Kailyn shriek from the ladder down below. "I'll be down here, suckers."

Dawn burst out laughing. "Kailyn made it farther to the top than usual today," she said when I stepped out onto the gallery that overlooked all of Starlight Cove. "I'm impressed."

"*I'm* impressed." I looked around in awe, the sharp breeze cool on my skin. "This is incredible. I remember my father wanted to see the inside of this place and this view for years. He kept trying to charm the guys in the Coast Guard, but it never worked."

"Well, he didn't miss much back then. It was such a mess when I bought it, and it has been a labor of love bringing it to this state. We're going to open for tours next year."

"Hello, hello." Kip Whittaker climbed up onto the galley, his black hair tousled and a pair of reading glasses pushed back on his head. "May I ask why Kailyn is sitting in our kitchen, shaking with fear?"

Dawn laughed. "I tried to make her come up here. She pulled the ripcord."

"Cruel." Kip rubbed his hands over his tanned arms. "Well, Emma. Should we head down to join her?"

"Too chilly, huh? Darn." Getting to my feet, I followed him down the ladder into the control room, past the bedroom, and into the kitchen. My eyes readjusted to the light, and I settled in at the table next to Kailyn, who was happily eating a cinnamon raisin bagel and hard at work on her phone.

Dawn served us chai tea before heading back upstairs. She planned to finish reading a book, and I wished I could join her instead of spending the next hour feeling as dumb as this was going to make me feel.

Kip sat across from us. "I know this is foreign territory, but I'm glad we're doing this," he said, getting right to business. "The Sweetery is a part of my childhood. I don't want it sold to an outsider, so I'd like to do everything I can to help. Let's take a look at the numbers. The great thing about numbers is that you can't change them. They either work or they don't."

I passed him the monthly reports I'd tried to work with the other night. "The Sweetery has always been profitable," I told him. "My stepmother hired out a manager for years. Since she didn't want to invest anything into the store, everything kind of stayed the same. That strategy, if you can call it that, worked in our favor, really. The tourists know that when they come back to town, we'll still have the same burgundy-and-gold packaging, the same luxury presentation for the hot cocoa, and the same chocolates. That sense of nostalgia is currently our brand. To be honest, I'm conflicted about that."

"Why?" Kip said, taking notes.

"It's nice to see my father's ideas withstand the test of time. That said, I believe in progress. There are so many small changes that could benefit the shop. We need an online presence on our end, rather than relying on random bloggers. I want to offer a few healthy choices, because that matters to some people . . ."

Like a certain Henderson brother.

"I'd also like to make candies appropriate for each season, and the list goes on. If I'm successful in acquiring the store, I'd like to try some of these new things, but at the same time, it seems risky to make too many changes."

Kip nodded. "I hear what you're saying. The good news is that you will have the freedom to make changes slowly, as you see fit. I wouldn't focus on that during the meeting, since banks tend to work with the 'if it ain't broke, don't fix it' approach, but personally, I agree with your take." He entered some numbers into a calculator. "I assume you have the twenty percent down payment."

Embarrassed, I said, "Kailyn thought I might be able to find an alternative?"

She gave a vigorous nod, licking cream cheese off her finger. "There should be some options, since it will be a woman-run small business. Right, Kip?"

"There's a good chance there would be some programs that could help." He frowned at the pages. "Collateral?"

I shook my head. "Not at this time."

The only big-ticket items in my life belonged to my grandmother. The duplex was hers, and so was the car that spent its time growing old in the garage. The only piece of expensive jewelry I owned was my engagement ring from Joe, and I would never part with it. It was only worth about a thousand dollars, anyway. That wouldn't make a difference with a loan like this.

"I have to be up front and tell you that the bank might frown upon that," Kip said, "since you don't have a down payment. However, we can only work with what we have, so let's move forward. Let's talk about the business."

For the next half hour, he grilled me about operating costs, general practices, and my future vision. It surprised me how much information I knew, and he nodded at several of my answers. It made me feel that, perhaps, I would be equipped to speak successfully to a loan officer about all of this.

"I think one of the most important things to focus on," he finally said, "is how long the Sweetery has been in business and the fact that it has always been profitable. That's not always the case for candy shops, even though it might seem like an easy business to get into."

Isn't that the truth?

Candy shops came and went. It was the type of business that seemed to be a guarantee because everyone loved candy. When people were on vacation, they seemed to love it even more. It was an easy gift to bring back home. Besides, northern Michigan had a reputation for making especially delicious chocolate fudge, which left the aroma of sugar floating through the air like clouds. We didn't sell it, because fudge was its own category, but many shops did, and people flocked to it.

In spite of all that, I had watched shop after shop open to high expectations, only to shutter their doors a few years later. The owners seemed baffled and almost ashamed that they couldn't make it work, but really, running a small shop was hard. The new places didn't have experience, so they often spent too much on overhead and could barely hang on, because summer rent was not cheap. If they didn't make a profit quickly, they went under.

Kip considered his notes. "The banks have had experiences with shops like this, so it's really important to reiterate the strength of the Sweetery, even though they'll see it on the balance sheets." He shut his laptop. "This looks great, Emma. I'll put everything into a presentation that speaks bank language, and we'll go from there. The biggest hurdle will be qualifying for the programs that will allow you to bypass the down payment, but again, that's not insurmountable. You might not even need to do that, depending."

"There is one more thing I am worried about," I said. There was an imperfection of the wood on the small table, and I stared down at it, too embarrassed to meet his eyes. It felt wrong to allow him to do a bunch of work without all the facts, so I decided to tell him everything. "Kip, I have terrible credit. Not from credit cards or loans or anything, but because, long story short, I cosigned an auto loan for a friend, and she defaulted."

Kailyn's head snapped up. "What? *Who?*"

I waved my hand. "College friend. You don't know her."

A few years back, I'd reconnected with Nancy, an old friend, through social media. She'd run in the same crowd as Joe and me, but I'd lost touch with her over the years. It had sounded like she was going through a hard time, so I'd reached out to her—sure enough, she'd just gotten a divorce, and her husband wasn't great about child support payments. To top it off, her car had been stolen, and she'd only had liability insurance. She'd had to replace the car or she would have lost her job, but because of her financial situation, she'd needed someone to cosign her loan. Naively, I'd offered to help.

In the end, Nancy couldn't make the payments. She declared bankruptcy, and the bills started coming to me. I had just switched from my job at the nonprofit to the Sweetery and could barely get by, but unless I wanted to declare bankruptcy, too, I was the one stuck paying for her car.

Kip shook his head after hearing the story. "That's a bad break."

I swallowed hard. "Does it ruin everything?"

He tucked his reading glasses into the pocket in his shirt, thinking. "Not necessarily. However, it does create an obstacle. Do you have access to any form of cash for a partial down payment? To be frank, I'd suggest selling your grandmother's duplex, but the sale wouldn't close in time for you to make this deal."

"I can't anyway," I said. "She's not ready to sell."

It would solve a lot of problems, really, freeing up the money to keep her at Morning Lark, but it belonged to her, and she was not ready to let it go. Besides, it also served as a reminder to me that I still had one person left in the world who loved me unconditionally, a thought that made my heart ache every time I considered it.

Kailyn raised her hand. "I'll loan you the money. I'm not going to sit by and watch you lose the store."

"No." My voice was firm. "Sorry, but I've already learned that money and friendship don't mix."

The situation with Nancy had taught me that.

The second I'd volunteered to cosign the loan for her car, she and I had talked almost every day. I had loved rebuilding that connection, since it served as a reminder of the life I'd once shared with Joe. That all ended, though, when things went bad with the loan.

When Nancy declared bankruptcy, she started screaming at me when I told her I didn't have the money to cover the cost of her car. Thank goodness, my grandmother gave me a place to live, and Gillian begrudgingly gave me a six-month advance on my salary. The situation infuriated Gillian, and she tried to get me to get Nancy to give me the car, since I was paying for it anyway, but of course, Nancy refused. From there, Nancy posted a vitriolic message on social media that blamed me for the default. One of our old friends reached out to say the whole thing sounded like a setup from the start and that Nancy had a reputation for being dishonest with money. She'd most likely planned for me to cover the cost the whole time.

Either way, I'd felt like a complete fool, and our friendship had fallen apart. It had been hard to let her go, though, because I'd hated losing that connection to Joe. In spite of everything, he still would have said I'd done the right thing by helping her, but I'd learned that mixing friendship and finances was a bad idea.

"How much of a down payment are we talking about?" I asked.

"Even twenty thousand dollars could make a difference here," Kip said.

Twenty thousand dollars.

Kailyn clapped her hands. "What about that couple you were telling me about? I know you don't want to sell the painting, but there's your twenty thousand dollars."

The spices from the chai tea tickled my nose.

If I used the money as a down payment to secure the loan, I could keep the store and pay the increased monthly fee for the assisted living facility. It would mean letting go of the painting, but that would be a lot less disappointing than losing the opportunity to buy the store.

Still, the thought of letting the painting go hurt. I remembered sitting at the corner table in the crinkling fabric of my party dress, my father reminding me to smile, as Montee worked his magic at the easel. The feeling of hopping up from the table and rushing over to see what he'd painted. The moment I saw myself on the canvas was forever frozen in time. I'd stood in silence, gripping the lace at the bottom of my sleeves.

"That's me," I told my father, amazed. "I'm right there."

It sent me into a fit of giggles to think that somehow Montee had transported me into the sugar plum world he had created, with its pretty lights and silly animal truffles. I'd spun around the store, dancing and laughing for the rest of the day, coming over to look at the painting at least a hundred times.

How could I let it go?

It was impossible to imagine the portrait of me as a child decorating the wall of someone else's home. Everything about it felt wrong. It didn't seem fair that the options had come to that, but I had to make a choice.

"Yes, I could sell the painting." The words were heavy in my heart. "If it turns out the couple is legitimate, I would be willing to take the steps to do that."

Kailyn gave a serious nod. "I know it will be hard to let it go, but we can't ignore the fact that some random couple offered you twenty grand for it right at the time you needed it. That has to mean something. Actually, it's kind of a miracle."

Kip set down his mug of tea. "You two lost me. What painting?"

Kailyn's green eyes sparkled as she relayed the story. Dawn walked in halfway through, so Kailyn started again from the top. By the time she'd finished, Dawn was perched on a chair next to Kip, biting her nails. She and Kip exchanged a troubled glance.

"I don't like it," Dawn said.

"Me neither." Kip sat back in his chair. "They think it's got hidden value."

"Yeah." Dawn gave him a little smile. "They probably think that's what Starlight Cove is all about."

Back when Dawn first moved to town, a national news program did an exposé on her great-grandfather. He was the former ship captain of the *Wanderer*, a ship that sank near the shore back in the thirties. The news program accused him of causing the crash to steal the silver he was transporting. So, while Dawn was restoring the lighthouse, she and her family went on a real-life treasure hunt in an effort to clear her great-grandfather's name.

"Maybe that's where this is coming from," I said. "Maybe they saw you guys on the news or something and decided our town must be full of secrets."

"It *is* full of secrets." Kailyn rubbed her hands up and down her arms. "Like the secret of this painting, because there has to be one. You guys, I have goose bumps. I'm really starting to think that painting might be valuable, and we're too dumb to know it."

"I've considered that," I said. "The painter isn't famous, but I was thinking that maybe the painting could be a big deal in a genre, like small-town Americana or something. Maybe that's dumb. Honestly, I don't know enough about art to figure it out. Sometimes I think there's some big secret about the painting, but I keep coming back to the idea that these are just people who don't know what to do with their money. Or they really love random art."

Kip shook his head. "No. I bet your first guess is closer."

Dawn leaned against the wall, fiddling with her hair. "I wish my parents were in town. They could do a little research and figure it out."

"You should text them a picture," Kip suggested.

That sounded promising. Dawn's parents were not only famed treasure hunters; they owned the local antique shop, Shipwreck Antiques and Treasures. They would probably be able to identify the value of the piece or at the very least, connect us with someone who would know how to find out.

Dawn shook her head. "I would love to, but they're on a submarine, pretty much off the grid for the next month. I would try to send them a message, but I don't exactly have a satellite phone at my fingertips."

Kailyn gave a reverent sigh. "Your family is like the threshold of cool. Do you know who would have a panic attack trapped in a submarine?" She pointed at herself. "This gal. Hey, Emma, did you ever check the security cameras? The couple was looking at something on their phone before they made the offer. I think we need to know what it was."

The three of them looked at me with such interest that I laughed. "You guys, yes, I did. I got a screen grab of the site they were looking at, but it was too blurry to figure it out." Reaching into my purse, I produced the printout and set it on the table.

Kailyn put her hand on her chest. "I have seriously prayed for this moment. The chance to solve a mystery with Dawn and Kip."

The three of them hovered over the picture. The excitement in the room turned to silence. Finally, Dawn shook her head. "I can't see a thing with the lighting in here."

The lighthouse, although spectacular, was definitely dim.

Kailyn held up the page, shining her phone flashlight on it like I had. "Can't we just sprinkle lemon juice on it and light a match or something?"

Dawn burst out laughing. "That's for invisible ink, not people with aging eyesight."

"Have you tried looking at the web-server logs from the store?" Kip asked.

"The web whats?" I considered the bag of bagels Kip had brought and selected one with chocolate chips. "I know my way around the internet as much as the next person, but you're going to lose me if you speak CIA."

"The logs can identify the pages that have been visited on a Wi-Fi system," he explained, as I took a bite of the bagel. "You'd just need to check the date and the time the couple was online and review the sites accessed during that time frame."

"That's only if they were on the public Wi-Fi, though," Dawn said. "Do you even offer it?"

"We do," I told her. "Believe it or not."

Thanks to an initiative from the chamber of commerce, the majority of the stores on Main Street had started offering free Wi-Fi a few years back, in an effort to encourage the tourists to sit and buy an ice cream, coffee, or in our case, hot cocoa. The plan was remarkably progressive, given the fact that our town was usually ten steps behind. I had no idea how many people actually used the internet at the Sweetery, but it was definitely available.

"They would have needed to have their phone set to access the public Wi-Fi instead of their own phone's network," Kip mused. "It's possible, though, because a lot of people do that to save data, especially when they're traveling. I could search your logs and identify the web page they were looking at."

Kailyn put her hand to her heart. "That is so ridiculously *Mission: Impossible* that I could kiss you. Except for the fact that I am taken, so please, hands off."

Everyone laughed.

"So, what do you think, Emma?" Dawn's eyes were eager. "Should we do it?"

My heart started to pound. Could it really be that simple? The fact that all four of us suspected there was more to the couple's offer, that there might be something important about the painting that I was missing, made the decision for me.

"Let's do it." I checked the time on my phone: 9:05. "Speaking of, I have to head into work. When could you stop by?"

"Today's tricky." Kip pulled up his planner on his phone. "I can do tomorrow afternoon."

Kailyn groaned. "That's like a century from now."

"In the meantime . . ." Kip turned his bright-blue eyes on her. "I can dig deeper into the loan options and see what I can figure out. Emma, here's what you have going for you: the Sweetery is a well-known, successful business, and you have proven experience running it. The loan officer has probably eaten more than one piece of chocolate from there. Still, there are rules and regulations when it comes to loaning money, and if the bank can't justify lending to you, they may have no other choice than to turn you down."

My stomach dropped. In spite of his enthusiasm, Kip was basically telling me that I could fall flat on my face.

Taking chances was not one of my strong suits. I'd already experienced so much loss in my life that I was afraid to set my sights too high for fear of being disappointed. I didn't want to humiliate myself in front of Gillian by failing at this, especially when she expected me to. So, if Kip was telling me it was unlikely I'd get approved, it didn't make much sense to move forward.

"Kip, that changes things," I said. "If it's going to be a no regardless, I don't know that I—"

"Emma, stop." Kailyn put her hand on mine. "You have to try."

"There's trying, and then there's trying and looking like a complete idiot." I gave a forced laugh. "I'd rather not waste Kip's time if it's not going to work out."

"You won't know that until you walk into the bank and ask for what you want," Kailyn said. "You have to do it, Emma. Otherwise, you will spend the rest of your life regretting it."

Kip gave me a kind look. "I wouldn't do this if I was sure it would be a no. There's a strong chance you could pull it off. Besides, the candy shop is a part of who you are. Let's go in with our eyes open but give it everything you've got."

The words rang in my ears on the walk to the store. The act of applying for a business loan still felt entirely beyond my skill set, but it was the only way I could buy the store. Besides, it had to mean something that Kip was willing to stand in my corner and that, in spite of the obstacles, he thought it was worth it to try.

I hoped he was right. If I got turned down, Gillian wouldn't hesitate to take the deal from Talbaccis. The thought was too terrible for words. The Sweetery was a part of my story, my history.

I was not about to let it get away.

Chapter Twelve

Like always, the candy shop was busy from the second I opened the doors until I turned the sign to "Closed." There was not a spare moment to work on any of the tasks on Gillian's list. It seemed like a waste of time to bother with them, considering I was trying to buy the store myself, but I couldn't risk making her angry. There was always a chance she could back out of our agreement. So, once I locked the door, I stayed late to tackle some of the things that needed to get done.

To keep my spirits up, I decided to focus on the tasks that would need to be completed regardless of who bought the store. The first thing I picked was drafting emails to our suppliers and billing companies to let them know the company had changed ownership. I had just settled into the desk chair in the kitchen to get started when there was a loud knock at the front door. It was most likely a customer trying to bypass the posted hours, and I was tempted to ignore it, but the delivery people sometimes went to the wrong door, so I decided to check it out.

After stepping back into the shop, I stopped. Cody stood on the front stoop, peering inside. Surprised, then flustered, I quickly crossed the room to unlock the door and let him in.

The fact that he was setting foot in the sugar factory felt like a victory of some sort. Leaning against one of the marble tables, I raised my eyebrows. "What, no muscle shirt?"

He eyed me, then adjusted the collar of his cotton T-shirt. In reality, it *could* have been a muscle shirt, the way it hugged his broad chest and enormous arms.

Something I was doing my best not to notice.

"We have plenty of things for you to choose from." I gestured at the store. It looked like a burgundy-and-gold present, waiting to be unwrapped. "Do you want diabetes tonight? Or a side of obesity?"

Cody crossed his arms. "That stunt with the box of candy was cute."

For some reason, the way he said *cute* made my cheeks warm. I avoided his gaze, letting my eyes fall on the painting instead. The girl sipping the hot chocolate looked amused.

"I'm so glad you liked it." I brushed an imaginary piece of lint off my shirt. The shirt was pink, with a low neckline, and it suddenly felt too revealing. Tugging at the collar, I said, "So, what's up?"

"I wanted to talk to you about the kid."

Of course. That makes sense.

A lot more sense, actually, than the idea of Cody Henderson stopping by to hang out with me.

He took a seat at a table by the front window. "What do you know about his situation?"

I briefed him on the little I knew about Lydia's history. "Their relationship is rocky. He resents her for leaving him with his uncle when she went to get treatment for her depression."

"Yeah, I kinda got that." He tapped his knuckles against the marble. "The part about him being angry with her."

"Why, what happened?" Hopefully nothing too bad, because I didn't want to feel obligated to share the information with Lydia. It also made me sad that it was so obvious Jamal was angry at her, because I knew how deeply she cared for him.

"Nothing happened, really." Cody shrugged. "It was more about what didn't happen. Each time before we start our activity, everyone sits in a circle, and I give a quick talk. Motivational-type stuff." His eyes darted to mine; then he looked out the window. Main Street was still busy, as the families moved away from the beach in search of a bite to eat.

"I'll usually ask a personal question," he continued. "The kids have the opportunity to participate or pass, depending on their comfort level. Today, I asked each kid to talk about the person they admire most in their family and why. Jamal passed. I figured it was 'cause he's new and was finding his footing, but when I tried to get an answer from him while we were working on a part of the project together, he clammed right up. Nothing about his father either. I wanted to see if you knew what was up."

"His father's in jail," I said. "For what, I don't know. Lydia—that's his mom—she's the sweetest person, but it's obvious she's been through it. It sounds like her husband was a jerk, and she struggles with depression because of it."

Cody grunted. "How long are they going to be around?"

Before I could answer, the couple that wanted to buy the painting walked by the store. The angle of the sun must have made it so they couldn't see me and Cody, because they peered into the window and took another look. I tensed, wondering again what they knew about it that I didn't. Then, the wife noticed me and gave a cheerful wave before nudging her husband to move on.

"Emma?" Cody was still waiting for an answer.

"Sorry." I turned back to him. "Lydia's waiting for her car to get repaired. There are some parts on back order, so at least two weeks, but I'm going to try and get her to stay longer. My grandmother doesn't like the place to stay vacant, and the new tenant isn't moving in for a couple of more weeks. Hopefully, that will give them enough time to rest and to figure out what to do next."

"Yeah." Cody seemed lost in thought. Then he frowned. "That kid's hurting, Emma. I'll do what I can to try and break through, but he's carrying a burden."

"I know," I said quietly. "That's why I sent him to you."

Our eyes met. Cody's typical tough expression had a vulnerability I hadn't seen before. I wondered what it was that had called him to this type of work, but that was a bigger conversation for another time.

"I should go," he said, getting to his feet.

"Thank you for your help," I said. "Let me know if there's anything I can do to help."

He stopped at the front door. The sun was bright behind him, making his silhouette look like the statue of a warrior. "There is something you can do."

Eagerly, I nodded. "Name it."

"Talk to a dentist and get some complimentary toothbrushes to hand out," he said. "This place is like a walking cavity."

I felt the silliest impulse to throw a piece of candy at him. "Good night, Cody."

"Night," he said, and banged out of the shop.

I stood in silence for a minute, my hands resting on the marble table. Then I shook my head. "Toothbrushes," I grumbled.

It was a good thing I wasn't interested in Cody Henderson. We were definitely not a match.

I could never fall for a guy who didn't like chocolate.

Chapter Thirteen

Cody's concern regarding Jamal stayed with me. I was tempted to bring dinner over once again so that I could talk to Jamal and see how the program had gone, but it was late and they'd most likely eaten. They had plenty of food in the fridge, too, because I'd ordered more groceries for them from the corner store. Besides, there was a fine line between being helpful and being overbearing. I didn't want to cross that line for fear Lydia might pack up their things and go.

So, I ate alone, baking some chicken in a pan on the stove and adding it to a garden salad. It was boring compared to the flashy breakfast I'd made this morning. It also reminded me of the disastrous dinner with Gillian, where she had criticized the fact that I'd ordered my chicken fried.

"You'd love this salad, Gillian," I mumbled, stabbing at a wilted green. "It's about as plain as plain can get."

The series of family photos I had hung on the wall in the living room caught my eye. Gillian was in most of them, because she had been such an active part of my life prior to her abrupt exit. It bothered me to see her in the pictures, and I'd been tempted many times over the years to take them down, but that would mean losing the photos of my father too. But it was hard to see her be such an integrated part of my family, considering that she'd left me behind.

The feelings it brought up in me made me empathize with Jamal's anger. I had the same type of rage simmering somewhere beneath the surface, but I had always kept it pushed down deep. Because really, the fact that not only one but two mothers had left me was too much to deal with.

My father had only told me vague details about my birth mother. Her name was Camille, and she was the love of his life. He'd met her back when he was an apprentice in Bruges. Her family was well-to-do and important around town, and he worked for the most popular chocolate maker. Needless to say, her family did not approve of their daughter's starry-eyed romance with the help. They did everything possible to keep them apart, but Camille still managed to become pregnant with me.

Her family was outraged. They sent her away, 1950s style, so that no one would discover her dirty little secret. My father was heartbroken. He had no access to her until he finally managed to convince one of her friends to reveal where she was hiding. Camille and my father reunited days after my birth, but I had already been given away to an orphanage, and she did not want to try and get me back.

Heartbroken, my father worked with the embassies and scurried home to America with me before anyone could change their mind. He wrote my mother several times, but she never responded. My father learned she had become engaged to a banker who had no knowledge of "the incident." Since my father's interference had the potential to ruin her carefully cultivated life, he made the decision to set her free.

On the heels of his heartbreak, my father met Gillian. She showed up at the Sweetery to report on the new shop and found herself completely tongue-tied. My father thought she was just nervous, since it was one of her first reporting jobs. That is, until Gillian blurted out that he was the reason she was distracted. The frank comment jolted my father out of his misery, and their romance was off and running.

Gillian was the best thing that could have happened to my father, because she helped him to move on from my mother, but she ultimately had the opposite effect on me. Thanks to Gillian's rejection, I went through a phase when I was eleven where I was determined to connect with my birth mother. I planned to find Camille's last name and get in touch, regardless of how it would affect her. My grandmother talked me out of it. She explained that a secret like that could put my mother in danger, assuming her husband truly knew nothing about me. But later, my grandmother admitted she had feared my mother would reject me, too, which would have been beyond my scope of understanding at that point in my life.

Looking back, I was grateful my grandmother had protected my heart. It had been a complicated situation, and now I could see it with clear eyes. My mother most likely would not have wanted to reconnect, and it would have crushed me at a time I was most vulnerable.

"Thanks, Grandma," I said, getting to my feet. "I owe you one."

Pushing away thoughts of the past, I rinsed off my salad dish and loaded it into the dishwasher. It was another pretty night, and Lydia was already outside enjoying the weather, her back to me. Her hair was down, and the burnt red looked pretty in the gold light of the evening.

I was eager to talk to her because one of my friends owned an office building and needed help cleaning it. The job would be a good way for her to earn some money while she was here, if she wanted it. I didn't want to insult her, but I had a feeling she'd be grateful for the offer.

I found a bottle of sparkling cherry wine from Harrington Wines in my fridge. The bottle was cold in my hands, and its ripe, fruity scent practically bubbled into the champagne flutes. I poured two glasses and headed outside.

The grass was soft under my bare feet as I walked across the yard to the bench.

"Sometimes you have to lie to people," Lydia said in a hushed tone.

I stopped suddenly, realizing she was on the phone. Not wanting to intrude, I started to turn away. That is, until she said the next part.

"Look, Emma gave us a place to stay. She wouldn't do that if she knew the truth."

I paused. It was the same type of thing Lydia had told me at the bed and breakfast.

What's she hiding?

"I did my best, Billy," she said. "*No.* I'll get your money, okay? I just need a little more time."

The words made me shiver.

I crept toward the back door, but suddenly, Lydia called to me.

"Emma! Hi, are you coming out?" She had stood up and was waving at me, a shy smile on her face.

I hesitated. The phone call made me nervous. I didn't know who she'd been talking to or what it had been about, but the idea that she was lying and needed money meant there was much more to her situation than met the eye.

Why would you be nervous, though? She's not asking you for money. And if there's something in her past she's ashamed of, she's under no obligation to share it with you.

Still. Something felt off again. I didn't know what, though, and it wasn't fair to her to make assumptions.

Talk to her. Find out what's going on.

"Is Jamal asleep?" I asked, joining her on the bench.

"Yes, if you can believe it." She sat back down. "He usually doesn't go to bed until late. He passed out with the video game lying across his chest."

"Saving the world is hard work." I held out one of the champagne flutes. "Here. It's cherry wine."

"Oh. Thanks, but I don't drink." Her cheeks flushed. "I'm not an alcoholic or anything. It just makes me feel depressed."

"Then let me get you some pop," I said. "I have Sprite or Rock and Rye. Which one would you prefer?"

"Emma, you don't have to keep giving me things," she insisted.

If this was a person who wanted to deceive me, who planned to try and trick me into giving her money like Nancy had done, she definitely wouldn't say that.

She gave me a searching look. "Your friendship is more than enough. You know that, right?"

If the things Kailyn had said to me the other evening were true—that I was afraid I wasn't worth much and waited for people to leave me—then no, I didn't know that. Maybe that's why I was always trying to give someone something: a box of chocolates, a hostess gift, a free lunch. On some level, maybe I did feel like my friendship wasn't enough. Like I wasn't enough.

Lydia looked worried. "I've upset you."

"No." I squeezed the stem of my glass. "I just have some things on my mind. Hey, don't feel obligated, but I have a friend who needs help cleaning an office building, if you're interested. It'll pay a pretty good hourly rate."

Her face lit up. "Yes. That would be great!"

"Perfect. I'll text you his information."

I was relieved Lydia took the opportunity. Maybe that would help her with whatever financial issues she and this Billy person were discussing on the phone.

"It might lead to more work," I told her. "If you want it."

Was I doing it again? Trying to give too much? We sat in silence for a moment. The birds were settling for the evening, and lightning bugs flitted across the yard. The mosquitoes were also coming out, and I rummaged under the bench for the bug spray.

I spritzed myself, then passed it to Lydia. She pulled the cilantro scent through her hair and spread it on her arms. Then she turned and gave me a tentative look.

"Do you want to talk?" she asked. "I can be a pretty good listener."

Even though my problems were nothing compared to hers, the offer still felt good. She didn't know my stepmother and could be objective in a way Kailyn could not. Before I knew it, I'd told her everything about the stress of trying to buy the store.

"It's brought up a lot of feelings," I said, gazing out at the yard. "Not only am I scrambling to keep my job; I'm trying hard to hang on to something that shouldn't be given away in the first place. It's hard not to be angry with my stepmother because of it all. We were so close before my father died, and then she completely shut me out. It wasn't easy." I took a drink of the cherry wine. "Were you close with your mother?"

"My brother and I were just arguing about that." Lydia pulled out her cell phone. It was such an old model I barely recognized it as a phone. She turned it over and over in her hands like a worry stone.

I watched the phone, thinking. Really, they couldn't have been saying anything too bad, if she was bringing up the conversation.

Should I mention it?

Before I could, Lydia said, "My parents got divorced when I was five. My mother was into some bad stuff, so me and my brother never knew her. She tried to be a part of my life once Jamal was born, but I refused to see her. It was a mistake. I should have let her back in, because in spite of the fact that I was angry with her, I wanted a mother more than anything in the world."

I could relate to that. "You should reach out to her."

"I've tried." Lydia gave a hurt little laugh. "She won't talk to me. I blew it. We're headed to Pennsylvania because my brother is there, and I'm hoping that he can help, but things aren't good between him and me either."

"I'm so sorry," I said.

She glanced back at the house. "That's why I worry so much about Jamal. My mother was rotten at raising me and my brother, and now I'm messing up with my son. The apple doesn't fall far from the tree."

"Keep trying," I insisted. "Be there for him, and do the best you can. It's what I wished my stepmother would have done for me, but she never did." I took a long sip of the drink, letting the alcohol cool my tongue. "You know, I'll never forget the time the girls in my third-grade class decided to throw a Mother's Day brunch." The moment the words were out of my mouth, I was surprised to hear them. This wasn't a story I liked to tell, but now that I'd started, I felt compelled to finish. "I didn't want to bring Gillian, because she didn't seem to want to have anything to do with me, but it's a small town, and she would have heard about it. So, my grandmother told me to invite her, and you know what she said? She said, 'That wouldn't be appropriate. I'm not your mother.'"

Lydia drew back. "That's awful."

"Yeah." I half laughed. "It was humiliating. The girls in my class made me come anyway, so I spent that morning hating my friends for having such great relationships with their mothers. I went back to my grandmother's house hoping that somewhere my birth mother was having a day as terrible as mine."

"Where is your birth mother?" she asked.

I explained her history, and Lydia's face brightened. "Emma! You should find her."

"No." My response was automatic. "That ship has sailed. Besides, I can't mess up her life."

Lydia looked genuinely puzzled. "You don't know that it would. What if she's spent her whole life wondering what happened to you? I imagine it would be really hard to give up your child. Especially when someone else is making that choice for you."

The words filled me with hope, but quickly I pushed them away. "Starlight Cove is not a large town. I'm sure she could have been pointed in the right direction if that's what she wanted." The topic made me uncomfortable, and I got to my feet. "Have a good night. I should get to bed."

Lydia looked embarrassed. "Sorry I kept you. It's late." She hunched her shoulders as we walked back to the house.

"Oh," I said. "The plumbers will be here in the morning to replace the toilets. Sorry—I know it will be an inconvenience."

"Not at all," she said. "I'll let them in. Night," she said and slipped inside.

I stood at the back door for a moment, feeling guilty for ending the night so quickly, but it was impossible for me to discuss the topic without getting upset.

The idea of connecting with my birth mother was one I'd given up ages ago. I didn't want to revisit that subject, to feel that sense of longing. It pained me to think that she was somewhere out there, living a life without me. But when I really let my mind run free, I allowed myself to imagine she ached to be with me too. That was a fantasy, though. Trying to track her down would most likely cause more hurt and heartache, two feelings I was ready to live without.

Chapter Fourteen

Owning the candy shop felt closer than ever when Kip called with a meeting time at Starlight Cove Central Bank.

"Thursday at ten a.m.," he said.

"That's in three days," I cried, delighted.

It was hard to believe that in only a few days, I'd know whether or not I could carry on my father's legacy. The thought was scary and exciting, all at the same time.

"I'm feeling optimistic about this," he said. "The Sweetery is so well known. Focus on that and the proven success it has to offer. I'll have the presentation materials ready for you by tomorrow."

The sense that things could come together stayed with me throughout the day. Still, I put the majority of my time and energy into the tasks Gillian had asked me to do, once again focusing on the things that would be helpful if I managed to buy the store.

At the end of the day, Ashley popped her head into the kitchen, where I was pulling outdated equipment from the back of the cupboards to be recycled. She had a pink-and-purple bicycle helmet in hand.

"Kailyn's here. You're really going to do hot yoga? I'm superimpressed."

"Hot yoga?" I scrambled to my feet, brushing dust off my dress. "I never agreed to that."

"Don't try and weasel out of it." Kailyn bustled in behind Ashley. "You committed last month, and I pulled some serious strings to get you on the schedule, so let's go."

Leave it to Kailyn.

I had a vague memory of committing to the class at the start of swimsuit season, but by now, summer was already in full swing. Didn't that make me exempt? Besides, Kailyn had said her class was on a waiting list. I never dreamed I would actually have to go through with it.

"I could have plans," I grumbled. "A hot date or something."

"You do have a hot date." Kailyn flashed her dimpled grin. "With yoga."

Ashley stood in the door, giggling.

I glared at the two of them. "If I die, you better not bury me in a swimsuit."

"Ooh, great idea." Kailyn rubbed her hands together. "Let's roll."

It had been years since I'd set foot in a gym. Not because I didn't like to exercise, but because I preferred to exercise outdoors. One of my favorite things to do was hike the bluffs. During the winter, it was even more of a workout because the deep snow required snowshoes, which was a workout in itself. That said, it certainly did not prep me for the agony I knew my body was about to go through doing hot yoga.

"I'm not sure about this," I told Kailyn as we walked down the gym hallway toward the designated classroom. There were fit people everywhere, prancing to their cycling class or fresh from the area with the ellipticals. Most of them looked like they didn't need to spend time at the gym, which seemed unfair.

"You'll love it," Kailyn said as we walked in.

The room was sweltering, and I stopped. "It's like a thousand degrees in here."

"Thus the name," Kailyn sang. "Hot yoga. We're over there. Lay out your mat."

Ugh. I couldn't imagine why anyone would voluntarily step into this, considering we'd just finished the heat wave outside. The room smelled too. The odor was hard to place, but it made me think of a sickly sweet smell from a piece of fruit that had fermented in the back of the cupboard.

Was it everyone's sweat trapped in the floor?

Very possible, considering the room was carpeted in this thin, gymnasium-looking stuff that probably broke all sorts of health codes.

Still, I unrolled my purple mat and laid it out on the ground next to Kailyn's. She got into some weird, cross-legged pose and gave me a thumbs-up. Then, she closed her eyes and took in deep breaths.

Now's my chance. I could make a run for it, and she'd never know.

Her eyes flew open. "So, I meant to tell you. Since you have been so brave, stepping out of your comfort zone and applying for the loan and everything, I've decided I need to step it up too. I'm going to tell Dana yes, that I'd love for them to put me up for the nomination."

"Really?" Leaping forward, I gave her a huge hug. "This is a big deal. They will pick you—I just know it."

"Doubt it. But . . ." Kailyn took in an exaggerated Zen breath. "I will simply hope for the best."

"Good evening, everyone," boomed a familiar voice. "Ready to get started?"

Our instructor walked in, and I almost sank through the floor.

"Since when does Cody Henderson teach hot yoga?" I demanded in a furious whisper. "I thought he only liked to lift weights and eat small billy goats in his spare time."

Kailyn giggled. "He does it to keep his muscles loose. Something about weight training making everything tight. The yoga balances it out. Didn't I tell you he was the teacher?"

Nope.

No, she did not.

I sneaked a look at him.

Cody wore a pair of black workout shorts and a muscle tank top and had a white towel draped across his neck. He looked like an advertisement for a men's muscle magazine. I wished I'd worn a few more layers. My black yoga pants and purple tank shirt left little to the imagination.

There was a time, before Kailyn started dating Carter, that she would have freaked out at the very thought of walking into an exercise facility led by a Henderson brother. Now, here she was, acting like it was normal that we were practically sitting in a sauna with Cody Henderson. He strutted to the front of the room and got into some pose that made me think of him standing in the door of the candy shop the night before.

"Everyone ready?" His eyes landed on mine, and he gave a slight grin. "If you're new, push through it. It's supposed to be hot."

I looked past his right ear to a space on the wall and took in a deep breath. This could be it for me. But I was determined to keep up, because I was not about to have Cody tell me that the reason I fell behind was the small plate of chocolates I'd had for lunch.

In the past, I had tried regular yoga, but I'd found it boring. This was not. Cody led the charge, taking us through pose after pose. His deep voice reminded us to take a sip of water, withstand the heat, and enjoy the freedom of the stretch.

I had just convinced myself to not pass out for the third time when Cody guided the class into downward dog. I was focused on breathing into the stretch when two strong hands pressed against my lower back. The lightning heat that shot through my body confirmed that yes indeed, Cody Henderson had his hands on my hips.

"Let your body ease into the stretch," he said. "Breathe through it."

I took in a deep breath, and as I exhaled, he pushed down on my hips. The move was firm but gentle, and my muscles relaxed deeper into the stretch.

"Good," he said, before moving on to Kailyn.

I tried to keep my breathing steady, and only one thought ran through my head: *No wonder this class has a waiting list.*

The workout was forty-five minutes. By the end, I was soaked but flushed with achievement and extremely proud I'd managed to keep up. Turning to Kailyn, I gave her a victorious smile.

"You did it," she said and gave me a fist bump.

We gathered up our mats. On the way out, she called, "Bye, thanks" to Cody. He caught my eye as if he wanted to say something, but an older woman was raving to him about how the yoga relieved her back pain. I was happy to escape.

"What did you think?" Kailyn asked, toweling off her face as we walked out of the room. The cool blast of the gym's air-conditioning hit, and I shivered. "Where's your jacket?" she scolded, draping a fresh towel over my shoulders. "You'll get chilled without it."

Kailyn had made me bring a sweatshirt, but I had been so hot after our workout that I had accidentally left it sitting on a chair by the door.

"It's in the room." I turned and eyed the gray hall, debating whether or not I had it in me to return to the classroom alone. "You know, I'll just get it out of lost and found."

"That's ridiculous." Kailyn grabbed my arm and propelled me back to the room. "Let's just go back and . . . oh, great. Thanks, Cody."

Cody had just stepped out of the room. He had my purple sweatshirt in one hand and a protein shake in the other.

"Hello, ladies." He held up my sweatshirt. "The room suddenly reeked of chocolate, so I assumed this was yours."

I couldn't believe he'd said that. Ever since I'd started working at the Sweetery, I liked to joke with everyone that investing in perfume was a waste of money. That each day that I left the shop to meet friends, run errands, or return to my house, the scent of chocolate, vanilla, and sugar spun in my wake. He tossed the sweatshirt at me. "How did you like the class? The poses can be hard the first few times, but you kept up."

My brain clicked back to that moment when he'd touched my hips. "It was good."

"You'll be back?" Cody took a swig of his shake.

"Under duress." I pointed at Kailyn. "She signed me up for the month, so I'm stuck."

He grunted. "Knowing you, you'll probably bring chocolates for people. Don't. They'll melt."

Knowing you.

Kailyn cleared her throat. "Um, hello, Cody."

He winked at her. "Kailyn." Shifting his eyes back to me, he said, "Nice job." Then he sauntered off to the men's locker room.

Kailyn and I watched him go in silence, and then she turned to me. "*What* is going on there, and why have I not heard about it?" Her whisper was high pitched with delight.

"Nothing." I pulled her toward the exit. "He thinks I'm ridiculous. That's all."

The laugh that spilled from her lips filled the hallway. "That's *not* all. Cody Henderson just flirted with you. And he *meant* it."

"Cody Henderson flirts with everyone," I mumbled.

"No, he does not," she said. "Remember how he dated that one woman with a kid for the longest time? He ended it because she didn't want to take it to the next level, but Carter says he was really in love with her. He hasn't dated since. Lots of women have asked him out, but he's not interested."

"Well, he's not interested in me either."

"Seemed like he was to me."

The sun was bright, and I squinted at her. "Can we drop it?"

"Sure." Kailyn gave one more stretch before climbing into her car. "But I will say this: he was eyeballing you like a piece of protein-rich chicken."

Even though Kailyn was just kidding around, I didn't like the way it made me feel. It had been nearly a decade since Joe's ring was on my

113

finger, but the feeling of belonging with someone else was a hard one to shake. I was supposed to be married at this point, not standing in a parking lot after a hot yoga class, giggling about the instructor.

It's been long enough. It's okay.

It was just . . . the memorial and the prospect of seeing Joe's family once again had brought up feelings I didn't want to face.

Maybe his mother's right.

Maybe I hadn't quite let him go. It was something to consider, but for now, all I wanted to do was get home, take a shower, and snuggle up in some cozy pajamas with a box of chocolates and a movie, preferably one with explosions. Loud explosions designed to push all thoughts of heartbreak and Cody Henderson far from my mind.

Chapter Fifteen

Kip stopped by the shop late the next afternoon with the presentation materials for the loan. His dark hair was tousled, his blue eyes bright, and he gave me a cheerful smile.

"The loan officer's a friend of mine," he said. "I think it's just going to come down to looking at numbers."

"Did you tell him about my credit history?" I asked.

It had to be fine, or the loan officer would not have taken the meeting. Still, it might make the difference in whether or not I would have to sell the painting, a thought that had kept me tossing and turning the night before.

"I told him about your credit history, and he said he'd do his best to work with you to find a solution," Kip said. "Hey, did you want me to check out the web logs while I'm here?"

"Yes, please do," I said, before guzzling from a bottle of water. "Kailyn and I were talking about it last night."

The very thought of Kailyn made my muscles ache. I'd felt refreshed after class the night before, but within three hours, muscles I didn't even know I had started to seize up. Now, I could barely walk. I needed something to take my mind off the pain, and this might do the trick.

Ashley had things under control, so I had time to go to the back and set Kip up on the computer before heading back out to restock the shelves and make sample plates. Today we'd featured the chocolate cherry drops, and they had been a hit. They often got overlooked because they were so traditional, but once people tried them, we could barely keep up with demand.

Kip poked his head out the kitchen door. "Emma. Can you come take a look?"

Peeling off my prep gloves, I headed to the back. "Did you find something?"

"I think I know what they're up to," Kip said, taking a seat at the computer.

"Uh . . . breaking into the Pentagon?" I said. He had pulled up some technical-looking pages that looked cryptic and hard to decipher. "Kip, this looks supercomplicated."

"It's not, if you know what to look for." He tapped the keypad. "Okay, check out this web link. This is the site they had to be looking at. It's right at the time they were here, and the site belongs to an artist. Are you familiar with K. L. Heathwood?"

The name rang a bell, but I couldn't quite place it. "It sounds familiar."

"He's a big-deal artist." Kip closed out the files and got on the internet. "I think my grandmother has plates with one of his prints. Look. He has a very Norman Rockwell, down-home style."

The web page Kip pulled up was definitely the one the couple had been looking at. It had the same color scheme, and at the top, the words that had been too fuzzy to read said *K. L. Heathwood Foundation*. The color scheme, I now realized, was a painting.

"Oh, I've seen this." I leaned against the desk. "It's famous."

The painting featured a happy family seated around a holiday table filled with desserts. The pies were perfectly cooked and ensconced in the midst of plates full of colorful cookies. The lighting was warm, and the sweets looked so real I could practically taste them.

Kip ran his hand through his hair. "K. L. Heathwood was known for mentoring young artists, so I'm thinking that this couple suspects Montee—that's your painter's name, right?" When I nodded, he said, "I bet they think Montee studied with this guy. Their style is very similar."

"Oh, cool," I said. "Maybe that's why they're offering so much?"

Kip frowned. "I don't know enough about art to tell you, but it's a jumping-off point." He got to his feet. "I'd suggest taking the mystery out of it. Contact the professor, and ask her how K. L. Heathwood is connected to your piece. If she's willing to have an honest dialogue, it might end up being a good thing for you and her both."

"It probably would make a difference if I told her I knew there was a connection," I mused, studying the painting. It reminded me of *The Girl with the Butterscotch Hair* in some ways, but like Kip, I did not know enough about art to know if that mattered.

"Thank you so much," I told Kip. "You're the best."

He shook my hand. "Let me know what happens Thursday."

Once he headed out, I turned my attention to the website. Much of K. L. Heathwood's popularity had come about in the last two decades, so the timing was right. Montee could have studied with him, which would give my painting some cachet. I clicked on the informational page to learn more.

K. L. Heathwood has proven to be one of the most popular painters of this century, compared to Norman Rockwell in heart and composition. His rise to fame was cut short by a sudden cancer diagnosis, and his death created a loss in the art world, driving his works to astonishing demand. His final piece, unfinished, was sold by his wife at auction for a startling $1.5 million . . .

I scrolled down the page, glancing at the paintings in the margin. Each one was so personal that I felt like a part of their story. When I got to the bottom, I nearly jumped back in surprise.

There was a picture with a caption that read "Karl LaMontague Heathwood." He sat on a sailboat in a pair of rolled khakis, his feet kicked up in the sun. The wind ruffled his thick, dark hair, and a smile stretched across his large face.

It had been over twenty-five years, but I would have recognized him anywhere.

It was Montee.

~

I called Kailyn immediately. She'd had an afternoon showing out near the peninsula and was headed back into town. There was a whooshing sound in the background, and I pictured her cruising down the highway in her pale-blue convertible.

"Hold up. You're seriously telling me that the painting that's been hanging in the candy shop since we were kids is by *K. L. Heathwood*?"

I stared at his picture, half-afraid to look away for fear the discovery would vanish. "I'm pretty much in a state of shock right now."

"Well, obviously," Kailyn squealed. "Emma, this is too cool! It's like one of those shows where they found that Fabergé egg on that man's counter. Can I please stand next to you when they reveal the painting is worth, like, twenty million dollars? I'll faint of course, as if it were—"

"*Kailyn*," I interrupted.

She went silent.

I gripped the phone. "The website said his final painting sold for one and a half million. *Million*, Kailyn. There's no way this could be worth something like that. Is there?"

"Don't know. Maybe? K. L. Heathwood is one of those artists who everyone likes. I think my grandmother has plates with his paintings on them or something."

"That's word for word what Kip said." We sat in silence for a moment, and I stared at the picture of Montee. "I don't get it. I really don't. I mean, K. L. Heathwood was *here*. How is this possible? Starlight Cove can't keep a secret like that."

"Yeah, but he told everyone his name was Montee," Kailyn said. "The internet wasn't much of a thing back then, so it wasn't like it would occur to people to check up on him, right? Plus, he was sort of a recluse. He made friends with your father, but that was about it."

Absently, I refreshed the website. It was silly, but I wanted to make sure I wasn't seeing things.

Nope. It was still him.

"This is wild." My palms started to sweat as the reality of the situation sank in.

If the painting truly was valuable, I could have the freedom to own the candy shop, keep my grandmother in assisted living for the rest of her life, and even run a small charity on the side, like I'd always dreamed. It would change everything. Yes, it would pain me to sell it, but given the opportunities it could afford, it would be a lot easier to let it go.

Of course, I certainly wouldn't sell it to the couple for twenty thousand.

I sat up straight. "Kailyn." My gaze darted to the door that led into the candy shop. "That couple knew. Should I be worried?"

"Heck, yes," she cried.

The fact that I had an original K. L. Heathwood hanging by a hook in an open public space suddenly made me feel like I was walking down a dark alley all alone. Plus, that couple had tried to dupe me into a sale. To rob me, really. The thought was infuriating but also frightening, considering they could be outside the door at that very moment.

"Are you alone?" she demanded.

"No, Ashley's here. But still . . ."

"I'm ten minutes away." Kailyn's voice was firm. "The banks will be closed. You and the painting should come stay at my house. We'll put it in a safety-deposit box first thing in the morning."

"Thanks," I said in a low tone. "Hurry."

It felt silly to say that, considering the painting had hung undisturbed for the past twenty-five years. I didn't feel safe, though, being responsible for something that could be worth a small fortune. The couple was probably harmless, but if they had told someone about their discovery, that person could have told someone and . . .

Squaring my shoulders, I grabbed the stepladder that leaned against the corner in the back of the kitchen and bumped it out to the candy shop. The richly scented room still bustled with activity. I wondered what would happen if I screamed it out to the crowd: "That painting is by K. L. Heathwood!"

Everyone would think you're nuts.

"Ashley." I left the ladder by the wall and sidled up to her. She had just finished ringing up the final customer and gave me a quizzical look. "Hey, something's come up. Can you finish up today? I have to grab some things and run out."

"Yeah, sure." She swept up a couple of stray candy wrappers and dropped them in the bin. "Hey, have you heard from Gillian? She said she wanted to talk to me about something. It all sounded quite mysterious."

For the first time, the idea of Gillian trying to sell the store did not fill me with rage.

It's all going to be different now.

I smiled at her. "I wouldn't worry about it too much."

Tucking the ladder under my arm, I carried it across the room. It was awkward, and my muscles screamed, but I tried to keep a neutral expression on my face, like late-afternoon maintenance was totally normal. Wiping my hands on my pants, I climbed up on the first step.

The painting was about thirty-by-forty-eight inches, and once I was eye to eye with it, I took a moment to really study it. The colors were so vivid and the composition perfect. My hands practically shook as I took in its incredible beauty.

Bang!

The air-conditioning powered on with a clank, and I nearly fell off the ladder. Scrambling, I steadied myself on the wall. It was time to get off the ladder before I ended up hurt.

I had just lifted the painting off the nails when the security camera caught my eye. Gillian would have questions. In particular, why I'd taken the painting without talking about it with her first.

The safest solution would be to tell her I wanted it removed in case my attempt to buy the store was unsuccessful. It was a weak excuse, but necessary. The painting belonged to me, and I had the paperwork to prove it, but Gillian was sure to flip out when she heard the real story.

I'd just lowered it from the ladder to the floor when Kailyn crept up behind me. Thank goodness she didn't say "boo" or anything, or I would have fallen, and right on top of it too. I scrambled down the rungs, limping the whole way.

Her eyes fell on the painting. "I'm not going to say a word about it here." The exaggerated whisper in her voice made it clear she was just as excited as me.

We rested it in the back seat and covered it with some beach towels and a blanket, keeping our eyes on the street the entire time. Once we were both in the front seat, Kailyn gave me a bear hug.

"What was that for?" I said.

She grinned. "For making my life exciting."

After powering up the engine, we headed for home.

Chapter Sixteen

Kailyn lived in a cozy log cabin that sat at the edge of the woods. It was far enough away from Main Street that she didn't have tourists strolling her block but close enough to everything that, even in the winter, she was only five minutes from the corner grocery store. She'd bought the house with her first major commission from a sale, which had been nearly a decade ago, and I had never been so proud of her in my life.

Now, the tiny house seemed a world away from everything as we pulled up the drive. The asphalt crunched under the wheels of her car, and the forest was alive with the symphony of summer. Bugs, birds, and small animals skittered through the branches, and I could only imagine how the scene would seem frightening in the dark.

"You're sure we're safe out here?" I rubbed my hands over the sudden goose bumps on my arms.

Kailyn gave a firm nod. "We'll set the security system the second we get inside. Plus, Carter's coming over for dinner with his brothers, so we'll definitely have the backup we need."

"Wait." I nearly choked. "What?"

Her green eyes twinkled. "I know. If someone would have told me five years ago that one day I'd have a million-dollar painting *and* the

Henderson brothers in my house at the same time, I never would have believed them."

The thought of sitting at the dinner table with Cody made me all kinds of uncomfortable. Kailyn still didn't know I had strangers living in my duplex, and it was sure to come up. Besides that, no matter how many times I tried to convince myself that I wasn't interested in Cody, his presence was distracting, and I didn't need that tonight.

"Kailyn, no." The panic in my voice was palpable. "When are they coming? You could still reschedule and—"

"They'll be here at seven." She glanced over at me. "Cody's making some sort of superfood salad, so I have, like, five desserts in the fridge so that we don't die of starvation."

I bit my lip. If I made a fuss, Kailyn would know something was up. Especially considering the things she'd said about him flirting with me after yoga.

"Fine." I groaned on my way out of the car. "I'm going to talk to Cody about the fact that I can barely move, thanks to him. Let's get this inside."

We carried the painting to three different rooms before we agreed to hide it in the closet of the guest bedroom.

"This is a great spot," Kailyn said, crossing her arms. "There are no pipes that could burst from overhead or behind the closet wall. If the ceiling collapsed, the angle of the dormer would protect it for at least ten minutes, and I am one hundred percent certain that if the house caught fire, the firemen could get it out of that window without any damage."

I stared at the closet door with a critical eye. "People say they want to win the lottery. Can you even imagine the first night alone in the house with the ticket?"

Kailyn shuddered. "I'd rather not." She thought for a moment. "The K. L. Heathwood Foundation was on California time, right? Let's call them. They could still say Montee's picture's only up on the website because he was commissioned to design it."

I burst out laughing, the sound half-hysterical. The thought was hilarious and terrifying, all at the same time. It would be a huge disappointment, but it would make more sense than any of this. I still could barely wrap my mind around the possibility that the painting was something more than a happy memory from my childhood.

Kailyn and I settled into her living room. It was sweet and cozy, with feather-filled couches, embroidered accent pillows, and several potted trees with blossoms in bloom. I let out a breath, put the phone on speaker, and called the foundation.

The director answered on the third ring. "MacCauley Brandstein."

"Hi." My eyes flickered to Kailyn's. She gave an eager nod. "I'm calling with a rather unusual situation . . ."

Ms. Brandstein listened without interruption. The second I went silent, she said, "Well, this is the best call I've received all week." There was a clattering sound, like she was typing on an old computer. "Yes, your painting is indeed in his work inventory. Let me see here . . ."

Kailyn and I both leapt up at the same time and started dancing around the room. I barely even noticed my aching muscles.

"Yes," Ms. Brandstein said. "It looks like K. L. painted it in northern Michigan and gifted it to the subject. There is no additional information." She paused. "Goodness, we have been trying to narrow this down. We guessed Mackinac as northern Michigan, but of course, he never specified the location. K. L. was very private about where and what he painted, particularly once his work became well known. He did not want the mystery of each piece to be compromised."

"He wouldn't want people to know it was a painting of the Sweetery?" I said, surprised.

"Correct." Her voice slipped into educational mode, as if guiding a museum tour. "Part of his appeal was his ability to capture small-town America. In an effort to make each piece timeless, he would often change key features. For example, his most famous piece is of a full-service gas station run by an elderly couple, where the older man is pumping the gas for a teenager. We have a photograph of the station that inspired the piece, but he changed its color, as well as key features of the subjects. The fact that the setting of your piece is a recognizable location will only add to its value."

I pressed my hand against the couch cushion. "That's part of the reason I'm calling. This discovery was completely unexpected. I have no idea how much my painting is worth or frankly, what to do with it. It's been hanging in the candy shop since he left town."

"Unattended?" MacCauley Brandstein sounded like she might pass out. "My dear, that painting will easily sell for half a million dollars, if not more."

I almost dropped the phone. "Sorry, what?"

Kailyn did another jig across the living room. If I hadn't been so shocked, I would have joined her. The possibility that the painting was valuable had been there from the moment I realized Montee was K. L. Heathwood, but really, that type of money was impossible to even imagine.

There were plenty of wealthy people in town, so I'd been around money most of my life, and I'd seen what it could accomplish. I'd also experienced firsthand the fear and frustration of not having enough. But I also knew that no matter how hard I worked, it would take me a lifetime to make the kind of money that could come from this painting.

I was stunned to be walking into it.

"It's really that valuable?" I echoed. "You're sure? I mean, I thought it would be valuable because of what I read about his last piece at auction, but this isn't a well-known piece or anything, and I . . ."

Kailyn gripped my knee so hard her knuckles turned white. "Shush."

I pressed my lips together.

"My dear." Ms. Brandstein's voice became haughty. "It's an early K. L. Heathwood. Of course it's valuable. Now, several factors do impact that value. The condition of the painting matters. The fact that it's been in a candy shop for twenty-five years does give me cause for alarm."

"This entire situation gives me cause for alarm," I admitted.

I wanted to promise the painting was in perfect condition, that it looked as good today as it did when I was a child, but what did I know? The paint on the wall had been darker than the rest of the wall when I'd removed the picture. Did that mean the sun had been slowly bleaching out the painting? No clue.

"I'm planning to put it in a safety-deposit box first thing tomorrow, but I have no idea what to do next," I said. "Get it appraised, insured, and all of that? Would you have any recommendations on who to contact?"

"It would be my honor to take a look at it personally," Ms. Brandstein said. "The idea that this could be one of his lost pieces gives me chills. Tell you what: Send me a photograph of the painting via email. I'll call an emergency board meeting to seek approval for a visit. Then, I'll come as soon as possible."

"Sounds like a plan," I said.

"Send me the photos, and I'll send you some proposed dates," Ms. Brandstein repeated. "I'll be in touch."

Once I hung up, Kailyn and I stared at each other in silence. Finally, I managed to say, "So . . . there's hundreds of thousands of dollars just sitting in your guest bedroom."

"Yeah. I'm not feeling superconfident about my homeowner's insurance at this moment in time." She got to her feet. "Let's try and get through this night with as little stress as possible."

"How do we do that?" I asked.

She scoffed. "We drink."

~

The Henderson brothers arrived with the expected amount of chaos. Cody carried a huge platter up the stairs with a look of intense concentration on his face, while Carter and Cameron punched him and tried to trip him so that he'd drop it. He shouted at them, and the moment he set the meal safely on Kailyn's counter he took off running after his brothers and had them pinned within thirty seconds.

"Emma." Carter spotted me first, his face half planted in the floor. "You're joining us tonight?"

Cody had been rubbing Carter's face in the rug, but now he stopped and turned. The smile that tugged at the corners of his mouth made my cheeks burn.

"How you feeling today?" he asked, getting to his feet. He straightened Kailyn's lampshade and a few throw pillows that had gotten tossed around and then walked over to me.

"I can barely move," I said. "Thanks for that."

"Come here." He beckoned me over to the rug. "Let me show you a few stretches."

Before I knew what hit me, I was on the ground, and Cody Henderson was helping to stretch my arm across my back. "Breathe," he said. "Breathe through the stretch."

That was easy for him to say, because given the enormous size of his hands and the fact that his aftershave smelled better than even a sea salt caramel, I could hardly catch my breath at all.

This is ridiculous. You really have to stop.

But given the day I'd had, it was kind of fun to fall into the silliness of a crush. It had been ages since I'd been on the floor with a guy at all, let alone a guy like him, so I didn't mind embracing it. Not to mention the fact that the stretches he was doing with me made me feel so much better.

"Thank you," I finally gasped, when he'd practically eliminated every ounce of pain in my legs, thanks to some pull-stretch thing he did. "I truly thought I would never be able to move right again."

"Oh, you'll feel that way again in another hour or two." His voice was cheerful. "The trick is to keep stretching it out."

By now, the rest of the group had headed out to the deck, where they were having drinks and making jokes. We joined them in time to see Cameron running around impersonating a customer who had wanted a nail gun but insisted on saying "ping, ping, ping" each time he picked up a different model. Cameron grabbed his curly hair and tugged on it.

"I couldn't take much more of it. That is *not* the sound a nail gun makes."

Carter crossed his freckled arms. "What sound does it make?"

"Like a *thht, thht, thht*." Cameron took a triumphant drink of water. "I mean, if you're going to do it, do it right."

"Customer is always right," Cody lectured, stalking over to the grill. "They say a nail gun goes *ping*, you better believe it goes *ping*."

Kailyn draped her arm over Carter's shoulders. "Could you make that sound again, Cody? I didn't catch it the first time."

To his credit, he did, and soon we were all doing it. The silliness kept my mind off the fact that there could be a painting worth hundreds of thousands of dollars—that belonged to me—in Kailyn's guest bedroom. The dinner helped distract from that as well.

Cody had marinated a salmon in a lemon-garlic sauce that was one of the most delicious things I had ever put in my mouth. He served it on top of a kale-and-spinach salad topped with blueberries and avocado. I had never been a big salmon fan, but it was so good that I ate every bite and even went in for seconds when everyone else did.

The fact that Cody could cook was pretty impressive. Hardly any of the guys I had dated had been handy in the kitchen, not even Joe. Back when we were engaged, he liked to joke that we should register for a series of toasters when the opportunity presented itself, because cooking a Pop-Tart would be his time to shine.

The evening stretched into night, and once the dishes were done and the desserts Kailyn had served were cleaned up—a chocolate mousse and a berry cobbler, neither of which Cody Henderson deigned to touch—we sat outside, under the stars. That's when Cameron blew my cover.

"How is that woman doing?" he asked. "The one who was sleeping in her car? I heard you were the one who helped find her a place to stay."

"Uh, she's doing great." I glanced over at Kailyn, who was snuggled up with Carter.

"She's still at your house, right?" Cameron asked.

"She's *what*?" Kailyn squawked, sitting straight up.

Great.

Everyone looked at me. Cody actually looked at me with a touch of sympathy, because I had told him the other day that it was supposed to be a secret. The fact that I still hadn't said anything to Kailyn probably made me look like a terrible friend.

I explained about the duplex, and the group stayed silent. Finally, Cody said, "I'm glad to hear you stepped up. We're all a little too conditioned to trust that someone else is going to be the one to solve a problem or help someone. Good for you for actually doing something."

The smoke from the grill still lingered in the air, and I breathed in the comforting summer smell instead of looking over at Kailyn. It was only later, when we were in the kitchen grabbing another round of drinks, that she confronted me.

"Okay, I get it that you decided not to tell me what was happening with that woman." She shut the refrigerator and turned to face me. "You didn't tell me because you knew that I would lecture you, right?"

Relieved she didn't sound too mad, I pressed my hands against the cool granite of her counter and nodded.

"It's just that there are so many resources for people in need," Kailyn said, sounding exasperated. "I don't understand why you have to let her live in your house. It seems dangerous."

"First of all, she's not in my house," I said. "It's a duplex, so there are locks and all of that. Second, why would it be dangerous?"

"Because she's a stranger."

I paused. Yes, Lydia was lying about something, but that didn't mean she was dangerous. Besides, there was something about her that drew me in. I couldn't explain it, but for some reason, I knew I could trust her.

"She has her problems," I said. "But in some ways, she reminds me of me when I was hurting the most. I only got through that because people decided to help me when they could have just walked away."

"Right, but—"

"Kailyn, I get it," I said, touching her arm. "I know you think I'm being reckless, and I also know that a psychologist would have a field day with my need to help people, but when it comes down to it, I think she's a good person. I don't know why, but I do. And I sincerely feel that helping her is the right thing to do."

The bowl of chocolate mousse was on the counter, waiting to be loaded into the dishwasher. Kailyn picked it up and scraped the remnants out of the bowl with her finger. Out the window, the Henderson brothers were loudly debating some sporting event. Soccer, maybe, but it was hard to tell with all the grunting.

"I think . . ." Kailyn stopped.

My eyes narrowed. "What?"

"I think it has to do with the fact that you want to be a mother to everyone. In the way that no one was a mother to you."

The words didn't upset me. Instead, they made a lot of sense. But the night had been so much fun. I didn't know why we had to get into all this. It was the reason I hadn't told her about Lydia to begin with.

"I just want you to be careful," she insisted.

"I know," I said. "I will."

Kailyn rinsed off her hands. "Good."

I headed off to the bathroom. The conversation had worn me out, and I was half tempted to call it a night and go to bed. That would be rude, of course, since the Henderson brothers were still there. It had been surprisingly fun hanging out with them, and they had done a great job of taking my mind off the painting. I came out of the bathroom, torn between going to the guest bedroom to sneak another look at the piece or going back outside, when I nearly ran into Cody.

"Oh. Hey." He stopped suddenly, looking confused. "How are your muscles?"

We stood in the hallway, his enormous body blocking the exit to the deck. There was no way to walk past each other without touching in some way. I moved forward, and he realized that I was stuck and quickly moved backward.

"Sorry," he said. "I'm in your way."

I squeezed past him, cheeks burning. He looked uncomfortable too. I headed back outside and sat next to Kailyn.

Carter had pulled out his guitar and started to sing some folk songs. We all joined in, and Kailyn put her head on my shoulder. Cody walked back out to the porch, and I suddenly felt wide awake. I tried not to look at him, only half succeeding, until the Hendersons finally packed it up and called it a night.

～

Waking up in Kailyn's guest bedroom was like waking up in a field of daisies. The room was painted pale yellow, and the breezy white window treatments, the handmade quilt in the shape of a flower, and the white wicker furniture with fresh daisies in small vases made the crack of dawn a cheerful experience. Given the events of the previous day, though, I really didn't need much to put me in a good mood.

Propping up on my elbow, I looked over at the painting. In my wine-induced haze, I had taken it out of the closet before going to bed.

Now, it lounged against the white wicker of the dresser, and I studied it from the bed. It looked different seeing it without the competition of the shelves and shelves of boxed candies. Here, it seemed even more life-like. It was truly a masterpiece. Something about it had always caught my eye, and if I had to narrow it down, I would say it was the raw emotion that shined through the light.

The painting evoked a feeling of loneliness. The chill of the snow on the street and the clear warmth of the shop gave the sense of being on the outside looking in. I didn't know anything about art, but on some level, perhaps it was a statement on small-town life.

I'd heard those who weren't from Starlight Cove comment that, no matter how long they lived in town, they still felt they were on the outside looking in, so maybe that was it. Or maybe the painting was about privilege and poverty. The idea of the little girl, decked out in her party dress and sipping at her hot cocoa, with no clue that there was a world beyond her sweet confectionary cocoon. Or maybe it was simply a slice of life, a moment that captured the precious, pampered naivete of childhood.

Whatever the intent, the painting offered such a strong sense of emotion that I was not all that surprised to learn that it had come from such a well-known artist. The thing that did surprise me was the fact that it had hung in the shop for years without anyone identifying it. But the idea of a diamond hiding in plain sight made me happy somehow. It served as a reminder to take the time and look around because there was so much beauty out there that otherwise could be missed.

Speaking of things that were beautiful, I followed the scent of hazelnut coffee to the kitchen. Kailyn was eating a boiled egg and a piece of cinnamon raisin toast, flipping through the latest MLS listings on her phone.

"Good morning," she sang, setting it down. "How's my little art mogul doing today?"

"She's beyond excited." I grabbed a mug of coffee, the fragile porcelain delicate in my hand. Sitting at the table with her, I took a sip. "So,

I wanted to say that I'm sorry again about not telling you earlier about Lydia and her son. You're such a good friend to me, and I wasn't trying to deceive you. I just . . ."

Kailyn waved her hand. "I get it. You were afraid I was going to lecture you. Which I did, so it's fair. Still . . ." Her green eyes met mine. "Please be careful, Emma. Especially now. Once this gets out, there's a good chance people might try to prey upon your good heart."

"Be careful with what?" I said, confused. "The painting?"

"It's a windfall."

I sighed. "What do you think I'm going to do? Start handing out money to strangers on the street?"

"With your address on it, so they'd have a place to stay?" Kailyn said, with a straight face.

I glared at her, and she grinned. "Kidding. Look, you actually don't have to worry at all, because you have a best friend who is not about to let anything happen to you. Except the good stuff, of course. Speaking of . . ." She batted her eyelashes. "Did you enjoy your time with Cody Henderson?"

My cheeks went hot. The memory of that awkward moment in the hallway made me feel restless, bringing up emotions I'd been trying to avoid. Embarrassed, I focused on adding creamer to my coffee from the little cow she had sitting on the table instead of answering the question.

"Hmm." She raised an eyebrow. "That's what I thought. Well, let me know when you're ready to talk about it, because I am rooting for the two of you." Hopping to her feet, she grabbed her car keys off the counter. "Pour that into one of my to-go mugs. Banks open in twenty. Plus, I think we owe it to Dawn and Kip to call them and tell them about it on the way. Let's get that painting out of here."

This time, we were a million times more careful as we set the painting in the back seat and covered it with blankets. Then, we headed straight for the bank.

Chapter Seventeen

The moment the Sweetery closed, I headed to Morning Lark to see my grandmother. I could not wait to tell her what had happened and to find out if my father had ever hinted at anything unusual in regards to Montee or the painting. To my dismay, I found her alone in her room, crying. She had the television on, turned to some remodeling show, and the volume was on high. Still, there was no mistaking the telltale shaking of her shoulders. I drew back, not wanting to embarrass her.

"Oh, Emma." She spotted me anyway and slid her glasses back on. They fogged up, which made her take them back off to wipe. "I'm so glad you're here."

I knelt by the couch and took her hand. "Why are you crying?"

"This darn remodel show." She gestured at the television. "The family was so happy to get a new place. It really touched my heart."

I started laughing. "Grandma." Pulling her into a tight hug, I nestled my head into her neck. "I thought something was actually wrong."

"Well, it is." She took her glasses back off and turned to me. "I haven't done a thing with my life, Emma. Here I am trapped in this place waiting to die, and I look back and think, What have I done for anyone?"

The question threw me. My grandmother had always been one of the nicest, most giving people I had ever met. It hurt me to think that, not only was she upset at the prospect of dying one day, but she also felt she hadn't contributed anything during the time she'd had here.

"Grandma, I don't think what you're saying is true. You're amazing. I've seen you do so much for other people."

"Not enough." She wiped her nose. "Did you know I wanted to change the world when I was younger? One of my friends had started traveling the country, helping to build houses for people, and I decided that was the way I could do it. I was just about to sign up, to help give people a place to call home, when I went and got married instead."

The expression on her face was so put out that I smiled.

"I think you made a good decision there."

By all accounts, my grandmother had loved my grandfather from the moment she'd laid eyes on him. They'd met at a drive-in movie, where they were both on dates with other people. They'd kept sneaking glances at one another, and at the very end of the night, the waitress in charge of the popcorn and sodas had slipped my grandmother a note from my grandfather.

I can't tear my eyes away from you. Could I please have your number?
And that was that.

"Grandma, you were in love." I reached into the candy jar my grandmother kept by the couch and ate a root beer barrel. It was from the Sweetery, but I hadn't had one in years. It took me right back to my childhood. "Besides, saving the world doesn't have to be about building people houses. You had my father and raised him to be one of the greatest people alive. But if it makes you feel any better, you gave me a place to live back when I was little and today. So, you pretty much did build me a house. Twice."

My grandmother smiled. "Well, you might be right." Her eyes wandered back to the television, where another episode of the show had started. I picked up the remote control and gently turned it off.

"You're a good person," I told her. "That's what matters." I clicked on the lamp next to the couch to give the room some more light and settled back against the cushions. "I have big news. It's about that painting that's always hung in the shop."

My grandmother's face changed from sorrow to amazement as I told her the story. I left out the details about how much it might be worth, because I didn't want to shock her. Instead, I alluded to the fact that it was valuable, and she gave an eager nod.

"K. L. Heathwood is very well known." She waved at the cupboards in excitement. "I have plates with his paintings on them." She put her hand against her forehead. "I have to admit, though, that I've never liked that painting in the shop. Your father went through too much because of that friendship."

Wait. What?

"You've never liked the painting?" I said, surprised.

My grandmother glanced at the television, as if expecting it to still be on. Then she lowered her voice. "It's not just me. Gillian doesn't like it one bit either. There was . . . there was talk, Emma. People started to notice that your father began spending all his spare time with this artist, instead of his wife. It started rumors that things were not good in their marriage."

"What do you mean? Dad and Gillian had a whirlwind, fairy-tale romance," I said. "Didn't they?"

"For a brief period." My grandmother suddenly looked tired. "You probably don't know this, Emma, because you were quite little, but your father had quite the reputation around town. He loved women of every shape and size, but of course, he loved your mother most of all. That made it difficult for him to give Gillian his full heart, and eventually, that caused some problems."

"This is the first I'm hearing of any of this," I said, grabbing a pillow and pulling it close.

"Good." My grandmother nodded. "It's not something that needs to be said. However, you asked, and I'm saying it. Gillian did not appreciate the fact that your father seemed much more entertained by the artist than by her."

I racked my brain, trying to think back to those times in the shop with my father and Montee. The two had always seemed to have a blast, laughing and drinking. But now that my grandmother mentioned it, there were times I'd stayed there with them much too late into the night and had fallen asleep on the couch my father kept in the kitchen. It was strange to think that Gillian wasn't a part of any of those memories.

"Well." My grandmother folded her hands. She sat in silence for a moment, then said, "Gillian was not happy. One night, when your father missed her birthday because he was carousing with the artist, I had to talk her out of a divorce."

The words floored me.

They were talking about a divorce?

This was all news to me. I studied my grandmother, wondering if she was simply getting confused. It was nearly six o'clock, and she had to be hungry, so I got to my feet. I had been hoping to have a little time to discuss the options with the painting, but given the turn in the conversation, it was probably best to let it go for now.

"Dinner smells good," I said. "You ready?"

Her face brightened. "Yes, I'm hungry."

The kitchen staff served a roast swimming in mushroom sauce, alongside buttered green beans and a corn bread muffin. My grandmother was thrilled with the roast, because it was soft and easy to chew. We talked with her friends, listened to stories, and laughed at jokes. It ended up being a fun night, and the things she'd said about my father and Gillian were far from my mind.

The comments returned on my bike ride home. Since there was still daylight, I decided to take a detour to visit the house where I grew up.

It wasn't something I did quite often. I didn't like that the house had continued on, with different furniture, decorations, and people than the life my father and I had shared together, but I liked to see it. Being there made me feel close to my father, like I'd stepped back in time.

My old house was down a tree-lined street at the very end of a cul-de-sac. It had been far enough off the beaten path for my father to enjoy his quiet time but close enough that it had never been a big deal to walk to work in the snow. Well, except the time the iron gate in the alley had frozen shut, a story that had made me giggle like crazy every time my father had reenacted it.

The house was small, a Cape Cod painted dark green with white shutters, details that had not changed over the years. Of course, my favorite part as a kid was the covered front porch held up by the two pillars, because I used to swing off of them to leap into the bushes. Each time, I'd earned a playful reprimand from my father, although I think he'd been secretly impressed.

I pedaled through the gate in the alley and onto the cozy street. The summer evening was starting to fade, and the shadows were long beneath the trees. I saw Mrs. Price, one of our old neighbors, sitting on her front porch. She and her husband had spent plenty of time socializing with my father and Gillian and had known them well.

I coasted into her driveway, dropping my bike on the pavement. "Hi," I called. "Care for a visit?"

Mrs. Price waved. "How are you, my dear?" Her brisk voice rang out across the lawn.

I walked up the porch steps and kissed her cheeks.

Mrs. Price had worn a too-bright pink lipstick ever since I'd known her, carefully drawn on, and its powdery smell brought me back thirty years. Her lawn furniture was the same, too, carefully maintained dark-green wicker with flowered cushions that were so comfortable they practically molded to my body as I sat down. I'd spent many hours of my life on this porch, listening to her stories and learning the history of the town, and I let out a breath I didn't know I'd been holding.

She squinted at me. "Are you doing okay?"

"Yes." Then, because I wanted to be honest, I said, "Actually, I'm feeling a little emotional tonight. My plan was to stop by and see the house, but seeing you is even better."

"Let me get you a juice," she said. "Then we'll chat."

Moments later, I had a chilled combination of freshly squeezed pomegranate, blueberry, and lemon juice in my hands, topped off with a sprig of mint. Mrs. Price was famous for the juices she whipped together, and I kept trying to talk her into opening a street cart to make some money off her talents, but she wasn't interested. It was just something she enjoyed doing to pass the time.

"Well . . ." She gave me a sly look and settled back in her chair. "I guess since you haven't yet commented, you don't know."

"Know what?" I sipped at the juice. Tart, sweet, and almost spicy. "This is delicious."

"Thanks." She raised her sparse eyebrows in the direction of my old house. "Your home is under construction."

"Wait." I set my drink down on the table. "What?" Leaping up, I peered over the edge of the porch, squinting in that direction. My father's house wasn't visible behind the heavy oaks that lined the street, but I could hear the steady whir of large machinery. Turning back to her, I said, "I can hear it."

"The noise has been somewhat of a bother. Yet, we endure." She plucked the mint sprig out of her drink and waved it around, as if to emphasize her descriptions. "They're building up, knocking out the back to add a sunporch and an open room, and hiring a landscape artist." She gave me a catlike grin. "I'm not nosy, just neighborly, so I've been over there several times, of course."

After pulling out her cell phone, she showed me a quick video of my old house under construction. The side yard was all torn up, and a small digger rested near the side. There was a large dumpster out front as well as a porta potty, which meant the work would continue for quite some time.

"Gosh." I played the video once again, feeling lost. "I don't know why that bothers me so much, but it does."

"It's your childhood home, my dear. We like to operate under the illusion that we can always go back."

True enough. When Joe had first come to visit the town where I grew up, my old house was the first thing I took him to see. I'd worried the gesture would confuse him, since I'd spent the majority of my life at my grandmother's, but he'd figured it out right away. He'd looped his arm around me and held me close.

"I can imagine the two of you here," he'd said, kissing my head. "Your father might have been bold, but he liked his privacy. I can see that by where he chose to live, tucked away at the end of the street. Seeing this helps me to know him." Which was exactly why I'd brought Joe there.

He knew me so well.

Mrs. Price smiled at me. "How's the Sweetery?"

"Delicious, as always." I pulled a small box of chocolates out of my backpack and handed it to her. It was our dark chocolate assorted blend, with the liquid fruit centers. "Have you tried these?"

"I wasn't hinting." She opened the box and breathed it in. "Okay, maybe I was."

Mrs. Price and I caught up on the news about the neighbors, as well as the things she'd been doing for fun. It was nice to chat with someone I had known for such a long time, especially since there had been so much change in my life. Then, since Mrs. Price was such a shameless gossip, I decided to test the waters with the comments my grandmother had made about my father and Gillian.

"Hey, do you remember that artist who was here years ago?" I asked. "He went by Montee."

"Goodness, yes." Mrs. Price smoothed her gray hair. "I had the biggest crush on him. This was back when I volunteered my time at the library. He spent each morning in the back corner, reading the news while he drank a cup of coffee from a thermos. I started bringing him a breakfast sandwich each morning to nurture his talent. Rufus found that *infinitely* amusing," she said, referencing her husband. Mrs. Price spoke of him often since he died, and I knew she missed him something terrible. "That is, Rufus found it amusing until the morning we only had one egg left."

"Who got it?" I asked, playing along.

"Montee, of course. Rufus got a melted cheese." She chuckled, looking out at the yard. "What on earth made you think about all that?"

"I was just thinking of all the time he spent in the candy shop." It was tempting to tell her what had happened with the painting, but if I did, the story would be all over town by morning. I'd give her the update when it was already public knowledge. "He and my father hung out a lot, since he was painting there. Gillian probably didn't like that much."

Mrs. Price studied me for a moment. "No, I don't believe she did."

My shoulders went tense. "Did she tell you that?"

"Emma, is there something you'd like to ask me?"

I paused. Something in her tone held a hint of warning, as if I might not like what she had to say. The fact that she didn't just blurt it out showed remarkable restraint on her part, and I was grateful. There was so much on my mind already that I didn't need to worry about this too.

"Not tonight," I decided, getting to my feet. "I should get home. Would you like me to wash my glass?"

Mrs. Price reached for it. "Emma, I'd ask you to clean my whole house, but knowing you, you'd actually do it." She also stood. "I'm always here if you need me. Are you still planning to bike by your old house?"

"I'm not sure I can." I shoved my hands into my pockets. "The idea of it being under construction doesn't feel right."

"Life's a changing tapestry," Mrs. Price said, then kissed my cheek. "Embrace it."

The words pushed me to head down the block. Sure enough, the corner of the house was torn off, and the owner hammered away at a wooden frame. The sound echoed through the evening. I pulled my bike into the shadow of the trees and watched.

The owner noticed me and waved. I gave him a rueful smile and lifted my hand in greeting, then climbed back on my bike. I hadn't lived in that house for years, so technically, I had no business getting upset at the changes being made. Still, it felt like another thing distancing me from that time in the painting when, for one brief moment, life was only about drinking hot chocolate in the twilight.

Chapter Eighteen

"Gillian? Hey, it's Emma."

I called my stepmother on my walk to work the next morning. The air was brisk from the lake, and the sky was clear. It was already shaping up to be a beautiful day.

Through the gaps in the buildings on Main Street, I caught a glimpse of the lighthouse. The meeting I'd had there with Kip felt like ages ago, but really, it had just been a few days. It was hard to believe that the meeting with the bank was only moments away.

There was a moment when I'd considered canceling the meeting altogether, because the painting had the potential to solve so many problems. Then, reality set in. I still needed money now to buy the store, and there wasn't enough time to wait on the money the painting could bring.

Plus . . . I wasn't 100 percent certain I could let it go. Yes, it could be worth a fortune, but the sentimentality still remained. There were moments when I imagined hanging on to it, as impractical as it seemed.

"Emma?" On the other end of the phone, Gillian sounded irritated. "I'm about to film a segment. What do you need?"

The things my grandmother had said about talking Gillian out of a divorce ran through my mind. It made me think about Gillian in a different light. I'd always believed the relationship she'd shared with my father had been perfect, so it had confused me that she never really spoke about it or him. When Joe died, I had gained a new perspective and decided Gillian avoided talking about my father because losing him had been too painful, but now I didn't know what to think.

"Emma?" she repeated.

"Yes," I said, coming to a stop in front of the bank. "I just wanted to let you know I'm about to go into my meeting about the loan. Can we get together for dinner tonight to discuss the outcome?"

Kip said I'd likely have my answer right away and if not, then within a few hours. If the loan was approved, I wanted to be able to firm things up with Gillian immediately.

"That would be fine," Gillian said. "I'd like to go over some things as well, in the event that it doesn't work out. Let's do six. Text me the place."

With that vote of confidence, she hung up.

Irritated, I set up a reservation at the new Mexican restaurant in town. I would most likely need the assistance of a very strong strawberry margarita to deal with Gillian, regardless of the outcome.

If the loan didn't come through, I'd have no choice but to tell her about the painting. It would allow me to offer her a premium on the store, if she could wait for me to sell it. Of course, that situation would not be ideal.

Telling Gillian about the painting could make things complicated. Once she heard the identity of the artist and the value of his work, she would make a million assumptions about the type of money coming my way, which might not even be accurate. The painting would need to be authenticated, cleaned, and placed at the appropriate auction house before I would see a cent, and in spite of the projections Ms. Brandstein had made over the phone, it could be damaged and not worth as much. So, there was still a chance Gillian would say no if I asked her to wait on the sale of the painting. The reality hit me with a thud. I adjusted my computer bag, which held my laptop and the flash drive Kip had created with the necessary materials for my application, and took in a deep breath. Then, I headed up the stone steps leading to the bank.

This meeting was more important than ever. Gillian didn't think I could pull it off, and to be honest, I wasn't sure I could either. It was so tempting to run in the other direction.

Don't do that. Prove her wrong.

I had to. At this point, there was too much on the line to walk away.

Chapter Nineteen

I felt like I was going to pass out when I walked into the bank. The loan officer called me to the back, made small talk, then slid on his glasses and reviewed the materials Kip had put together. Then, he fired a whole list of questions at me about the current profits and operations, followed by questions about my future plans. The whole process was very similar to what Kip and I had discussed, and I actually felt prepared.

The only tense moment was when we discussed the down payment. There was still a strong risk that I wouldn't qualify for a no-interest loan. But once he heard the story of the painting and that I was willing to put it up for collateral, his demeanor changed. "That is quite an impressive find. I'm sure my boss will include a clause requiring a certificate of authenticity, but given the strength of the presentation, the profit margins, and the potential collateral value, this looks great to me." It took only twenty minutes for his boss to review the materials, and sure enough, I had a preapproval letter sitting in my inbox by the time I walked out the door.

My breath came in short gasps, and I leaned against the front of the bank, convinced I had to be the luckiest person alive. The candy shop, after all these years, was going to be mine! The news meant everything to me, and it would have meant the world to my father. The pastel buildings and brightly colored trees blurred, and I half laughed, wiping at my eyes. It was not time to get emotional—it was time to celebrate.

❧

Heart full, I dipped a chip into the best salsa for miles, relishing its fresh flavor. It was a masterpiece of fresh tomatoes, red peppers, garlic, and cilantro. The string of colored lights draped over my table felt made for celebration, and as mariachi music skittered from the speakers, I placed an order with the waitress for two gigantic frozen margaritas.

The calorie content of the drink alone was probably more than Gillian allowed herself in a day, but if she didn't drink it, I would. Especially since the meeting with the bank had been nothing short of perfect.

Gillian arrived right on time, sporting her casual but intelligent look, which had to mean she'd spent the afternoon interviewing someone. Her hair was pulled up into a bun, and her carefully made-up eyes were magnified behind a pair of tortoiseshell glasses. She set her purse on the table but not without giving the surface a suspicious look, as though checking for stray sauce.

"This is quaint. I'm not certain my stomach can handle it," Gillian said, glancing around. "Or my ears." She gave a pointed look at the speakers, one of which happened to be right overhead.

"Don't tell me you're getting old," I teased, as she slid into the booth across from me. "I never thought that would happen to you."

"It won't." She took a sip of water. "Thanks to my deep respect for the art of plastic surgery."

I smiled. Sometimes Gillian could be a lot of fun. It must have been what my father had once loved about her. He was all about business, but when it came to life, he was the first to bring the wine and chocolates.

"You should be fine." I spotted our margaritas on their trip across the room. "If all else fails, I ordered you a drink."

Gillian laughed as the waitress set two fishbowl-size margaritas on the table. Once the waitress had left, Gillian said, "This place is interesting. It feels progressive, somehow."

The restaurant was run by Mexican immigrants. They primarily spoke Spanish, and the food was mostly authentic, with a few things tailored toward popular taste. I could see Gillian's wheels turning, debating whether or not it warranted coverage for the news.

"It would be a good story," I agreed. "I've heard the food's delicious. You should definitely cover it."

"Hmm." She tapped her manicured fingers against her lips. "Perhaps I will."

The waitress returned and gave us a friendly smile. "Ready?" Her accent was pronounced.

"I'll have the chicken-and-cheese enchilada, please." The gooey cheese and thick tomato sauce looked phenomenal in the picture. I was determined to celebrate with something delicious, and if Gillian made any comments, I was still committed to eating every bite.

Gillian clicked her tongue as she skimmed the menu. "Do you have a salad?"

The waitress tapped at a picture on the menu. "Taco salad."

Beef, cheese, and tortilla chips topped a bed of romaine lettuce.

"Chicken fajitas, please." Gillian sighed, handing over the menu. "When in Rome, I guess."

"When in Mexico," the waitress corrected, and we all laughed.

"So, how did it go?" Gillian's tone was casual. "I assume this is a celebration dinner."

I clinked my drink to hers. "Yep. I have a preapproval letter from the bank." It was hard to keep the pride out of my voice as I added, "I can pay ten thousand over the offer from Talbaccis, as agreed. I'd only require a week to have the books audited, and assuming they're satisfactory, which I know they will be, I can sign off in two weeks. Here's the letter from the bank."

The document from the loan officer was cued up on my phone. Gillian reviewed it, then lifted her eyebrows. Then she nodded. "Big news."

My stomach tensed. Part of me trusted she would shake on the deal. The other part of me still half expected her to find an excuse to walk away.

Taking off her glasses, she set them on the table. "Emma, I have to admit, I'm impressed. When I made the decision to sell to Talbaccis, I didn't think you were capable of this. You've proven me wrong. Your father would have wanted this." She put her glasses back on and smiled.

My heart skipped. "Does that mean you'll accept the offer?"

Gillian considered the note from the bank once again. "Barring any complications . . ." She let out a hearty sigh. "Yes. I should be able to sign off once the funds clear." The colored lights above the table seemed to glow even brighter. "I do have to ask, though. How did you get approved?"

"Kip Whittaker helped me put together a presentation." I reached for another chip. "I'm thrilled. I've wanted to be a part of my father's shop ever since I was a little kid."

Gillian lifted her drink. "Then, congratulations. I'm proud of you."

Proud of me?

It was the first time Gillian had ever said anything like that in my entire life.

"Thank you," I managed to whisper.

The waitress headed back over with our food. Gillian's fajitas hissed, steam rising from the stoneware, and the waitress set an elaborate display of sour cream, guacamole, and chicken alongside it. Then, she presented my enchiladas. The plate was hot to the touch, and the cheese was burnt and bubbling along the edges.

The second the waitress left, I tried a small bite.

Perfection.

"What a relief," Gillian said, digging into her food. "I can't tell you how happy I am to move on." She checked her phone and texted for a moment, then set it down. "It will be good to have one less thing on my plate. I swear, there have been so many random things to deal with over the years that I don't even know where to begin." She stabbed a piece of chicken. "Would you believe that crazy couple you told me about contacted me?"

"Crazy couple?" I echoed, confused.

"The ones interested in the painting."

I almost choked. "What did they say?"

"They wanted to know why we'd removed the painting from the store and if we would sell if they increased the offer." Gillian's gaze was frank. "I did not know how to answer the first question, since no one asked me to remove it. Why did you take it out of the store?"

Does she suspect something?

In spite of her easy approach, she seemed to be looking for the story. I considered confessing everything until I remembered what it could cost me. Gillian could cause all sorts of trouble and even try to claim it as her own. Since the painting served as collateral for the loan, I couldn't afford any complications.

"I took it out of the store because it looked like the deal with Talbaccis was going to go through," I said. "The painting means a lot to me. I didn't want to risk it being sold as part of the store."

The suspicion that had flashed in Gillian's eyes was replaced with understanding. "Ah."

I gave a vigorous nod and took a bite of my enchilada. "What else did they say?"

Gillian took her time folding guacamole, vegetables, and chicken into a flour tortilla. Cutting into it with her fork, she said, "They offered me thirty thousand dollars for it."

My mouth dropped open. "What did you say?" I said, swallowing hard.

"I said I couldn't make that decision for you." The shock on my face must have been apparent, because she said, "Emma, the painting is yours. I don't want a thing to do with it. I should have taken that horrible thing down years ago."

My grandmother's comments about my father's relationship with Gillian came rushing back once again. I turned my fork over and over, wondering if I should address the topic. Probably not. It wasn't my business, and I had no right to bring it up.

Besides, this let me off the hook. Gillian had flat-out said the painting belonged to me. She might change her mind later, once she found out the identity of the artist, but this changed things.

The mariachi band in the corner strummed the guitar.

"Well . . ." I shrugged and lifted my drink. "To the exciting things on the horizon."

Gillian lifted her drink and, to my absolute disbelief, downed it. Then she flagged down the waitress and signaled for two more.

"When in Mexico," she sang, shrugging off my shocked expression.

The band strolled over, singing "Guantanamera." Gillian and I clapped along with the music, talking and laughing. For the first time in years, it finally felt like we'd actually landed on common ground.

Chapter Twenty

The strawberry margaritas left me with a dull headache that replaced the revelry from the night before, but when I woke up, the sun bright outside the window, the future seemed full of possibility.

The night with Gillian had been so fun and so strange. For the first time in my life, she'd gotten drunk in front of me. She was a happy drunk, like my father, all arms around the shoulder and unexpected compliments, like how much she had always admired the gray/blue color of my eyes. The compliments hadn't always been directed at me. She'd talked a lot about my father as well.

Once we'd stopped drinking and decided to share coffee and a dish of fried ice cream—which I still could not believe—Gillian had started to talk about how much she had loved him. His laugh, the way he'd made her feel, and most of all, the way she'd felt every time he walked into the room.

"My heart died when we lost him, Emma," she'd said, clutching my hand. "I'd already lost him anyway. I knew that much."

I'd tried to press her for more information, but some customers who recognized her from the news had come over and tried to get us up to dance. To her credit, she'd done it, and we'd gone home right afterward.

Gillian's comments made me wonder again if there was truth in my grandmother's words. I'd never noticed any trouble in my father's marriage to Gillian, but maybe there'd been something going on that I hadn't seen. Either way, I'd been surprised to learn that she'd questioned his love and that the issue had never been resolved.

When I'd gone to bed the night before, I'd been resolute to talk about it with her further. To let her know that, based on everything I had seen, my father had loved her until the end. In the light of day, however, it didn't seem like the best idea, because we still weren't close. It was better to forget the things she'd said, the hurt she'd shown, and move on.

Stretching, I got up and out of bed. I wanted to put together a breakfast and check in on Lydia and Jamal. It had been a few days.

The way I'd left my conversation with her the other night, cutting the visit short because I hadn't wanted to talk about my birth mother, had been a mistake. It was obvious Lydia struggled with confidence, and my abrupt exit had to have hurt her. It was just that the suggestions she'd made about getting in touch with my mother had brought up emotions I didn't like to face.

I drank a green juice and a cup of coffee as I put together a basket of muffins, boiled eggs, and fresh oranges for Lydia and Jamal. Then I knocked on their door. One of the house numbers looked loose, so we'd need the workers to fix that, too, before the new tenant moved in. It was strange to think that in a matter of a few weeks, Lydia and Jamal would not be my neighbors and even stranger to think I would miss them.

Lydia opened the door and gave me a surprised smile. "Oh! Good morning." Her eyes fell on the basket, and she shook her head. "Oh my gosh. Thank you. We were just about to leave for the hardware shop."

"That's actually why I stopped by." I had my portable coffee mug in my free hand and took a sip. "I wanted to see how you guys were doing, but I also need to talk to Cody about a few things. I thought I could walk over with Jamal." Then, in case the idea of sending her son with someone who was still a stranger made Lydia uncomfortable, I added, "Or we could all walk over together."

"It would be fine if you took him." Lydia looked delighted at the idea. "I was hoping to stop by the library this morning."

Even though Lydia was not a resident, I had asked the librarian if she and Jamal could use our facilities while she was in town and put her items on my library card. There were so many books and movies that she and Jamal could enjoy for free, as well as internet access. Lydia had been so pleased at the privilege, and she'd been there nearly every day.

"What do you say, Jamal?" She opened the door all the way. "Do you mind if Emma comes with you?"

Jamal was sitting on the couch, his face buried in the comic book that someone had left in the candy shop. I'd dropped it off for him a week ago, and it already looked well loved. It was a huge improvement over burying his face in that video game.

"Jamal?" his mother repeated.

He grunted.

"Great," I said brightly. "Let's do it."

The sun was hot, and the birds chirped as we walked to Henderson's Hardware. There was a light breeze from the lake, and the air smelled fresh and damp, in that unique way only a coastal town did. It was nice to spend time outside, especially since, for the first time in ages, I felt like I didn't have a care in the world.

"What do you think of Starlight Cove?" I asked Jamal as we crossed the residential street and moved toward Main Street.

Since he had to put one foot in front of the other, he couldn't hide his face behind a book or a video game. I wanted to use the opportunity to get him to open up. I was still a little worried about the things I'd heard Lydia say on the phone the other night, and if anyone was going to give me the scoop, I figured it would be Jamal.

He glanced at me with his wide eyes, then shoved his hands into his pockets. We crossed the street in silence, and I assumed he wasn't going to answer at all.

Then, out of nowhere, he said, "I like it."

I nearly stumbled over my flats. "You like it?"

He gave me a look like, *What, can't you hear?*

"I'm so glad," I said quickly. "I've lived here my whole life. It's small, but I like it, because everybody knows each other and . . ."

Not things a ten-year-old would care about.

"That comic book looked cool," I said, switching gears. "What's it about?"

Jamal's face lit up. He told me the story from beginning to end, even acting out some parts. By the time we reached the hardware store, he was jumping up and down, shouting, "Pow! Pow! Pow!"

I laughed, delighted to see him so fired up about something. So much for having a heart-to-heart, but at least he was happy. I'd have to tell Lydia to get him some more comic books from the library. That would give her a new way to connect with him.

The bells on the door jingled as we walked in. Cameron was busy ringing up a customer at the front register, his ringlet curls practically covering his eyes. Looking up, he smiled and pointed toward the back. "Hey, little man. They're outside. You're building a castle today."

Jamal's face lit up. "All right!"

Just then, Cody banged through the screened door and barreled up the aisle. He stopped for a brief moment, spotting me.

"What is that? Dirt?" He squinted at my face, then reached up and brushed his thumb against the side of my cheek. Peering at it, he said, "Nope. Chocolate. Should have known."

The move brought me right back to that moment in yoga class when he'd pressed his hands against my hips.

155

Get it together, Emma.

Cody turned his attention to Jamal. "You ready to get tough on a hammer and some nails?" He shot out his hand for a fist bump.

They shared some sort of complicated handshake and then laughed like old friends. I had to admit, it was pretty impressive to see the relationship Cody had managed to build with Jamal in a matter of days. It was something I probably couldn't achieve in a lifetime.

"Get out there," Cody told him. "Some of the guys are already reviewing the plans. We need all hands on deck."

Jamal scampered out the back door. It warmed my heart to hear a couple of boys shout a greeting. There was no reason for Jamal to feel on the outside because everyone seemed happy to let him in.

"He loves the program." Cody rested his hand on a shelf. "You made a good call on getting him here."

"Thanks." The last time I'd really had a moment with Cody was in the hallway at Kailyn's house, and the memory made me feel bold. "You're the one who's done such a great job making him feel welcome."

Our eyes met, and I looked away. There was a long pause; then Cody said, "Why did you walk him over today?" He nodded at my mug. "Need a shot of protein powder for your coffee?"

"It's a mocha," I said in a lofty tone. "Even though the copious amount of sugar in it might mask the chalky taste of your fake food, I think I'll pass."

He shrugged, his enormous shoulders heaving with the effort. "Well, when you have to take a nap by ten o'clock this morning, think of me."

The idea of Cody Henderson anywhere near a bed was not something I needed to be thinking about at all.

I cleared my throat, then said, "I stopped by because I wanted to check in with you about something. Do you have some free time to advise me on setting up a nonprofit?"

The idea was one I'd had after Joe died. Back then, the plan had been to create a retreat where battered women across the state could take control of their lives and learn how to start a side business selling candy and baked goods. Now, I also wanted to open the opportunity to low-income and marginalized women, as well as single mothers. The emphasis would be on developing business skills so that they could create a side business that was right for them.

"Since you started this program for the kids, you know what to do, and I don't have the first clue," I said. "I'd be happy to take you to lunch or dinner or something to talk about it."

He actually looked surprised. In fact, the look on his face made me realize I was making a bold move. Still, I didn't want him to get the wrong impression.

"Strictly business," I said quickly. "And I'll buy you a salad. With lots of protein. Like tuna, chicken, and I don't know . . . soybeans or something equally suspicious?"

"I'm happy to help." He nodded at the back door. "This experience has been one of the best of my life. There's something about looking outside yourself that makes the world seem like such a better place, you know? Let's go tonight. Six o'clock. I'll pick you up."

"It's not a date," I clarified.

He raised an eyebrow. "Never said it was."

"It isn't, though," I said. "For real."

Emma, what are you doing?

So many women in town, tourists and locals alike, made a daily habit of flirting with Cody Henderson. I wasn't trying to be rude; I just didn't want him to think I was doing the same.

Aren't you, though?

I never asked anyone for help. But I was willing to ask Cody?

It was only because I needed information on how to start a nonprofit. He was the only person my age in town who had that experience. Learning from him would save me a ton of time. Yes, there was the small detail that I was attracted to him, but really, who wasn't? He was whip smart, all man, and he had a big heart. There was nothing wrong with noticing that.

"Six sounds good," I said. "See you then."

I gave him a brief smile and headed out without stopping to make small talk. Cameron always said the most random things that made me laugh, but I felt too far out of my comfort zone to have a normal conversation with him, thanks to Cody.

It had been a long time since a guy made me feel that way. It almost made me want to pick up the phone and talk about it with Joe's mother, which was completely ridiculous. I'd been on plenty of dates with guys over the years. It was just that I had never found anyone I was interested in.

It's not a date.

Then why did I feel like I'd made some big emotional leap asking Cody to have dinner with me?

Thrown by the whole situation, I headed out to Main Street and down to the lake. I stood in silence, watching the waves crash to shore. Finally, I scooped up a handful of icy water and splashed it on my face, before heading back into town.

Chapter Twenty-One

The cold water had snapped me back to reality, but once I keyed into the candy shop, I felt giddy all over again, for a different reason. I stood in reverent silence, staring at the familiar space.

It's going to be mine.

The rich wooden interior gleamed in the early-morning light. I breathed in the scent of chocolate, gazed at the marble tables, and admired the perfection of the burgundy-and-gold wrapped boxes. The candy shop was a dreamworld, a fairyland, and the place that was my one true home. Finally, *finally*, it would belong to me.

I hugged myself tightly, practically dancing with excitement. This achievement felt like the completion of something, like I'd pushed through a secret door into a magical place. I could turn the Sweetery into whatever I wanted it to be. I would decide what candy to offer, the window displays at Christmas, and even the hours that we opened and closed. I could build on what was working, change what I saw fit, and call the candy shop my own.

My father must have also loved that sense of ownership when he'd first opened the doors. It had been his dream since he was a little boy to open a shop, and he'd trained his whole life to perfect the art of candy making. I could only imagine his joy when he had first achieved his dream, and I felt closer to him than I ever had.

In honor of the moment, I decided to make myself one of our famous hot chocolates. The doors wouldn't open for another thirty minutes, and I settled in at a table in the window, reveling in the joy of dipping the hard chocolate into the steamed milk and watching it dissolve. I had just brought the mug to my lips when I saw Lydia barreling up the stone steps. Her cheeks were flushed and her shoulders hunched, but she looked excited. Spotting me, she gave a frantic wave.

"Hi," I said, throwing open the door. "I'm so sorry. I should have thought to call. Jamal's there; he's great—"

"I found her." Lydia burst into the store. Her hands were clasped and her eyes shining.

"Found who?" I said, confused.

Lydia rushed over to the table where I'd been. "Please, sit down." It was a bold move for her, and I hid a smile, wondering what had her so revved up.

"Okay." I hesitated. "Would you like a hot cocoa?"

"Emma, come on." She looked frustrated. Then, once I sat, she gave me a hopeful smile. "First, I want to apologize for being so completely and utterly nosy. I couldn't help it, though. I wanted to give something back after all that you've lost and everything you've done for me and Jamal. Emma . . ." She looked flushed and nervous, as if expecting me to start shouting at her at any minute. "I think I've found your mother."

My body went cold. I couldn't speak for the longest time. Instead, I stared at the plate of shortbread biscuits next to the cocoa. The recipe, my father had said, was one that had been shared with him by my mother.

It was something I hadn't thought of in twenty-five years.

"Oh, no." Lydia touched my arm. "I didn't mean to upset you." It was only when she returned to the table with a box of tissues from the bathroom that I realized I was crying. "There's still a chance it's not her, but based on the information you gave me, I think it is. Her name is Camille, she lives in Bruges, and she looks so much like you."

"You saw a picture?" My head snapped up so quickly my ears started to ring. "Let me see it."

"It's on the computer. I've been researching her at the public library. I can pull it up if you have a computer here, if you'd like."

Feeling numb, I nodded.

We headed back to the kitchen, and Lydia got to work. She was fast on the keyboard and quickly produced a picture from a business magazine. A group of well-dressed couples attended what looked like a holiday party. In the very front stood a man in a tuxedo who had one hand placed on the shoulder of a woman wearing a strapless gown. She eyed the camera with a half smile on her face.

Wow. That's her.

Not only did the woman look just like me, but the caption below the picture had her first name, Camille. More than that, I felt it was her. Taking in slow, measured breaths, I studied her face.

We had the same eyes and the same turned-up tip of our noses, but I did not have her physique. My mother was rail thin with a heart-shaped face, while I was stocky like my father. Even with those differences, there was no question we were related. Her beauty was haunting, and my heart ached just looking at her.

"Do you think that's her?" Lydia asked shyly. "She's married to a banker, which matched up with your description. He seems to be prominent in society, based on the information I found."

"It's her," I whispered. "How did you find this?"

Lydia ran her hand across her forehead. "Before my life fell apart, I had a relatively high position in loan collections. I was very good at tracking people down." She gave me a rueful look. "Sometimes, I can't help but think that anything bad that has happened to me is my karma for working in that field."

The comment made me smile. That was the charm of Lydia. There was something funny and sweet about her, in spite of all the question marks.

"Thank you for finding this," I said quietly as I returned to staring at the picture. My eyes fell on the time in the lower right-hand corner of the computer. It was almost time to open the doors of the shop. Reluctantly, I pulled my attention from the photograph and stood up. "I have to get back out there." Lydia made a move to close the screen, and I leapt forward. "Wait." Quickly, I took a picture of my mother with my phone and also emailed it to myself.

We walked back into the store, and because my legs still felt weak, I sat back down at the table in the front.

"You're not mad?" Lydia asked, and I shook my head. "Good. I was afraid you'd be mad, but based on the things you've said, it seemed worth the risk. I also think that contacting her is worth the risk."

"How would I do that?" Then, in a rush, I said, "No. She might not want to talk to me. She probably won't want to talk to me. That's what my grandmother was afraid of, because there was a reason my mother gave me away. Her family didn't want me to ruin their perfect life plan for their daughter. It looks like she's living that plan, so should I really step in and destroy it all?" My words came quick and frantic, and I found it hard to catch my breath. "I can't. I can't risk destroying her life. Especially if she never wanted to hear from me in the first place."

Lydia touched my hand. "Emma, what would you want to say to her? If you only had one chance?"

It was a great question. One I'd thought of many, many times. Especially during those games in college when people would say things like, *If you could have dinner with one person, who would it be and why?* I never gave the true answer, because I didn't want anyone to feel sorry for me, but it was her.

It had always been her.

"I would ask if she ever wondered what happened to me." I stared down at my hot cocoa. "If she thought of me on my birthday. If she ever almost picked up the phone." I looked out at Main Street, watching the leaves on a tree shift with the wind. "I'd ask if she would have stayed with my father if her family would have allowed it. More than that, I'd ask why she didn't fight harder for the life she could have had. If she regretted that. I'd ask her . . ." I felt my voice catch and took a steadying breath. "I'd ask if she knew—if she could feel—that I've loved her my entire life, and I would tell her that I would give anything to spend just one more second in her arms."

Lydia was silent, and I turned to look at her. She had her hand to her mouth, and her eyes were bright with tears. Nodding, she said, "You have to take the risk, Emma. It's worth it. You have to. I can find her phone number, email, whatever you need."

Lydia's conviction was so great that I almost said *let's do it right now*. Instead, I closed out the picture on my phone and reached for a napkin to wipe my nose.

"It's a lot to process. I'll need some time."

"Understandable." She peered at me. "I have to head over to the Laundromat. They called me to help clean, thanks to the job you got me at the office building. If you need anything, please call, and I'll do what I can."

There was a dull ache in my head and my heart. I stood in silence at the window, watching Lydia go. The traffic had started to pick up on Main Street, and any moment, the tourists would walk up the steps to the shop.

There had been so many times when I was little that I had dreamed that my mother would walk through those very doors. That she would seek out my father, which would lead her to the candy shop, which would lead her to me. Now, I stood in the very same place as I had for so many years, hoping for something to change, and it had.

The power had shifted. I didn't have to wait for her. Finally, it was up to me.

If I wanted to, I knew where to find my mother.

Chapter Twenty-Two

I spent the day in a haze, alternating between two emotions: pure joy at the prospect of owning the candy shop and complete confusion about my mother.

One would think the fact that the painting was in a safety-deposit box because of its potential value would have taken up more space in my brain, but surprisingly, it didn't. Until the director of the K. L. Heathwood Foundation received approval from the board to come to town and educate me on the next steps, the scope of my imagination was limited. Instead, my focus remained on the issues close at hand.

When Cody walked up the steps for our dinner meeting, some of the tension drained out of me. It would be good to get out in the world with him, because it would pull me out of my own head. I smiled and unlocked the shop's door.

"Hey," I said. "Thanks again for doing this."

Cody looked casual and relaxed in a pair of gray cargo shorts and a close-fitting black T-shirt. Practically gym-wear, but not quite. He also smelled all man, like musk and the earth after a rainstorm.

Stop. It's not a date.

The reminder helped bring me back to earth.

Quickly, I set up the final few boxes on the new summer window display I'd been working on and turned back to him, brushing off my hands. "Ready?"

"Yeah." He gave a suspicious glance around the shop. "What's that smell?"

I put my nose in the air and sniffed. "Don't know. Sugar?"

"Is it taffy?" He shoved his hands in his pockets, looking irritated. "It smells like taffy or something."

How hilarious. I'd pulled taffy over four hours ago when Ashley was still here. The fact that Cody Henderson had picked up on it meant that I might have found his kryptonite.

"You're a pushover for taffy, aren't you?" I said. "Even though dark chocolate has several documented and proven health benefits, if you were stranded on a desert island, you would wish with all your heart for a few stray pieces of taffy to wash to shore."

That attractive smirk tugged at the corner of his mouth. "Look, if you send me a box, it's going in the garbage."

"No doubt," I said. "Filled with empty wrappers." After grabbing my silk wrap, I headed to the front door. "Shall we?"

Cody held the door open, and we headed out. I made a move to lock up, but before I could, he stuck his head back inside the shop and took in one last deep breath. Then, he gave me a big grin.

"Let's get out of here."

I insisted on treating Cody to dinner at Sugar Cane. In spite of its name, it was actually one of the healthiest restaurants in town and offered a wide selection of fresh fish, innovative salads, and vegetarian options. It also had an open-air seating area right on the water, which I loved.

I'd called to make the reservation the second Cody had agreed to meet with me, and the owner had slipped us in, even though they had to have been booked solid on a Friday night.

The breeze was already chilly, and I pulled the wrap close around my shoulders. I'd worn slacks to work that morning, so I was perfectly snug, and happy to be sitting outside. We ordered, and then I pulled out a small notebook.

"Is it cool if I take notes while we talk?" I asked.

Cody draped one strong arm over the back of his chair. "Sure. I also emailed you a whole series of links to the resources you'll need."

"Even better." I slid the notebook back into my purse. Then, I let out a breath, letting his calm demeanor, the steady motion of the waves against the shore, and the evening light calm my nerves. "First off, I want to tell you the work you're doing with those kids is incredible. The change I've seen in Jamal since he got here is so great. It's because he's making friends, growing in confidence, and happy to be a part of something. I've heard it from other parents around town too. Your program is a valuable asset. I know you have a lot of knowledge, and I appreciate you talking with me about my plans."

"Thanks. Hearing things like that lets me know I'm moving in the right direction."

If someone had given me such high praise, I would have deflected. I would have blamed the program's success on chance or the kids or heck, even the weather. Cody owned it in a way that I admired.

"So, I'm curious." I took a sip of water. "What prompted you to start it all?"

Just then, the waitress arrived with a complimentary appetizer, a beet-and-tomato salad sprinkled with ricotta cheese. It was common for Gillian to get this type of treatment, as the restaurant owners and shopkeepers liked to help each other out, and I knew they were sending it to Cody. Still, I gave a secret smile, since there were actually two shopkeepers at the table.

I wonder what he'd say if he knew.

"That looks great." Cody dished up the portions, and we dived in. "Tastes great too." He chewed for a minute, then said, "I wanted to start the nonprofit because of what happened with my parents. You know all about it. You were there."

Cody's parents had been killed in a small plane crash when we were in high school. The news had rocked our small town, because they had been survived by three sons, but also because Cody was supposed to have been on the plane too. He had been sick that day, so he had ended up not traveling with them, and that had saved his life.

There were times after that when I had looked to Cody to see how he was handling the situation. There was something mournful about his eyes that pulled at my heart. In high school, I actually went so far as to pull out pictures from our elementary school yearbooks to see if he'd had that type of sorrow in his eyes before his parents had died and was surprised to find that he had. He had already been an old soul, and that situation made him grow up even more quickly.

"It was a wake-up call," he said. "I was falling into some bad stuff, and it made me take a look at my life in a way that most people don't." He gave me an apologetic look. "I don't mean to say that I'm more introspective than anybody or anything. It's just that most people aren't forced to take the time to evaluate their life at that age."

I ran my hand over the mint-and-white striped vinyl tablecloth. "I can relate. It was like that when Joe died."

His death had been so violent and unexpected that it had changed the way I looked at everything. Decisions I'd made, the things I'd believed to be important, and the choices I wanted to make moving forward so that I could create a life worth living again.

"Yeah. That must have been so tough." Cody looked out at the water. "Back then, it felt like a gift to still be here, you know?"

I nodded. "I do."

"So, I thought, what do I do with that? Taking care of myself was a big part of things. Taking care of my brothers was another. The outreach program came about from guilt, really. Because no matter how hard I tried, I never felt good enough to deserve the second chance I got."

The confession touched my heart. "Cody," I said gently. "That's a lot of pressure to put on yourself. There are plenty of people walking around, not feeling particularly inclined to prove their right to be here. You shouldn't have to either."

"Maybe not. Still, I couldn't shake the feeling that I needed to do something bigger with my life."

I ate some more salad, impressed at how sweet and tender the tomatoes were. "You know, I had a philosophy professor who liked to say, 'You don't have to change the world. You just have to live in it.' I think he might be right."

Cody scoffed. "That's rich, coming from you." I must have looked confused, because he said, "Look, I've seen you around town. The things you do for people. You're not just living in the world. You're always trying to change it." He scraped up the last bites of the appetizer. "You'd be the first to run into a burning building to save a mouse."

"I'd probably rescue the chocolates first."

He laughed, a sudden and surprising burst of sound. It made me happy, somehow, to know that I'd made him laugh. The food arrived then, and both his perch and my stuffed grouper smelled like heaven. The sky was a deep blue, and it reflected in the lake, creating a spectacular backdrop for dinner. The night was exactly what I'd needed, given the emotion of the past few days.

We ate in companionable silence. Then he said, "Tell me about your project."

The idea of sharing it scared me. I hadn't really talked about it with anyone, not even Kailyn, and I hoped it didn't sound completely ill conceived.

"It's a nonprofit to help women develop business skills, with the goal of teaching them how to start a small side business like selling candy, baked goods, or whatever is right for them to earn extra income."

Grateful to get the words out, I sat back in my chair and held my breath. Cody looked at me for such a long time that my heart sunk.

He thinks it's a terrible idea.

"You hate it," I mumbled.

"No, I'm thinking." He took a big drink of water. "Where would it be? Who would educate the women?"

Cody seemed genuinely interested, which was heartening.

"Kailyn's always stumbling across this property deal or that," I said. "I'm hoping to find a ranch right outside town and build a bed-and-breakfast-style house or maybe a dormitory, for better safety and privacy. I'd commission different people, because my skill set is pretty much limited to making chocolates."

"Would it be year round or during the summer?" he asked.

"I think a week each spring and fall." It didn't sound like much, saying it out loud, but I knew the work behind organizing each session would take up a ton of time.

He nodded, a pensive look on his face. "You might also want to find a way to use the building during the off times, instead of letting it sit vacant. Lodging, groups that want to rent it for their own retreats, things like that."

I hadn't thought that far, but it was a great idea, and I told him that. From there, he explained the ins and outs of becoming a legitimate nonprofit organization, and we started brainstorming additional ideas. By the time we'd finished talking, it was late, and we were one of the last remaining tables.

"I should get the check," I said, looking around for the waitress. There were a few busboys rolling silverware in napkins at an empty table in the corner, but I didn't want to bother them. "I'm sure she'll be out in a minute. She'll probably want to start to close things up."

"We're good." Cody got to his feet. "Let's get out of here."

I gave him a blank look. "What do you mean?"

"The check's paid," he said. "I called earlier and took care of it."

"You did *what*?" Heat rushed to my face. "Cody, I wanted to take you out to dinner, not the other way around. Get the waitress. I want to pay for it."

"Not a chance." His voice was firm. "Let's go. I'll walk you home." We walked in silence for a few moments, and then he chuckled. "I just realized we didn't order dessert. Sorry about that."

The statement caught me so off guard that I burst out laughing. "Cody, I never in a million years thought we would order dessert."

"You're a chocolate addict, though. I thought it would be necessary to survive."

I smiled. "Not always, but there's nothing a piece of chocolate can't cure. I don't care if it's an illness, grief, or heartache—taking the time to eat a piece of candy every day is an opportunity to enjoy life to the fullest."

Cody rolled his eyes, and I nudged him. "Seriously. Chocolate can be an emotional experience. That first bite of the smoky carob flavor right before it dissolves." The thought of its sugary sweetness filled me with longing, and I did regret the fact that we didn't think to order anything. "My father used to like to say that a good piece of chocolate can promise everything from comfort to nostalgia to pure joy."

"So, it's about the emotion, not the sugar," Cody teased.

I held up my hands. "Look, I have seen customers stand at the counter and eat an entire piece of chocolate with their eyes closed and a look of pure rapture on their face. Chocolate might not actually be able to solve problems, but it certainly can make them seem unimportant for however long you can manage to savor the bite. I've had more chocolate than most people in this life, and I'm here to tell you, it's one of the great wonders of the world."

Cody stopped walking for a moment and studied me. We were under a tree, and one of the lamplights cast a golden hue over us. There was a split second where it felt like he might lean forward and kiss me, and embarrassed, I started walking at a clipped pace.

"I'm telling you," I said brightly over my shoulder as he caught up to me. "There are some health benefits to dark chocolate. I'll send you the links."

He gave me a sideways look. "I'd love to learn all about it."

We walked on in silence, confusion troubling my heart. I'd had such a great time with him. Every word of the conversation had been easy, like I was talking with a good friend. Still, I felt awkward about the moment back there and also about not paying the check. It made it feel too much like a date, and it wasn't.

Which is unfortunate.

The sentiment surprised me, but it shouldn't have. Now that I'd spent time with Cody, I liked him. A lot. He was such a good person, incredibly smart, and made me feel like he was really listening. Plus, we had the same sense of humor, which I appreciated. It wasn't often that someone could really make me laugh, and he did.

It would never work, though. We're too different.

That could be a good thing, though. We challenged one another. At least, I wanted to believe I challenged him, too, but that didn't mean he would be interested in me.

I felt let down when we reached my front door. The odds of having another dinner like that anytime soon were minimal, and I was sad it was over.

"Thanks again for all of your help." I pulled out my keys. "I'll start working on everything and keep you posted on the progress, if that's okay."

It was dark by now, and moths danced in the outdoor porch light, casting eerie shadows across the door.

Cody opened the screen and held it for me as I keyed in. It put our bodies in much closer proximity than they had been all night, and I flushed. Turning to him, I said, "Have a good—"

In the most casual way possible, Cody cupped my chin midsentence and tilted my face up toward his. Then, he held my gaze for a brief moment and leaned in to kiss me.

Every single thought left my brain. The only thing I could do was grip his forearms and kiss him back.

My legs were weak when he pulled away. The only sound was our breath and the crickets in the woods. We looked at each other in silence. Finally, Cody grinned.

"It might have been a date," he said.

I nodded.

"Maybe we should do it again."

"Good plan."

Then, before I could do or say something to ruin this absolutely perfect night, I rushed inside and shut the door. I slid down to a sitting position and put my head in my hands.

It had been a long time since a kiss had made me feel like that. The thought scared me. For the first time in years, it felt possible to find something real, something that mattered. And for the first time in years, the idea didn't make me want to run in the other direction. It made me want to run toward that beautiful sense of possibility and see what it could become.

Chapter Twenty-Three

By morning, the sentiment changed to panic. Steam rose from the flat iron as I pulled it through my hair and tried to forget the way Cody's lips had felt on mine. The idea of crossing that line had seemed like a good one when he was standing in my doorway, but in the light of day, I knew I'd made a big mistake.

What was I thinking, getting involved with him?

I wasn't ready for something serious. The night before, when Cody's lips were on mine, something had passed between us, this feeling that the kiss had so much more behind it than a fun night at dinner. In that moment, I knew that spending time with Cody wouldn't be about grabbing a bite to eat with the cute guy down the street. It would be intense and would require stepping into real feelings in a way that I might not be ready to handle.

Cody wasn't the type of guy to do the minimum. He'd told me as much at dinner. Being in a relationship with him—because let's face it, that's what it would be—would be an opportunity to connect with someone who could capture my heart. That connection, however, meant opening myself up again to the potential of hurt, heartbreak, and loss.

I'd had more than my fill of all those things. It would be so much easier to find a plain, nice guy who I could go grab burgers with once in a while. Instead, I had to walk into this.

You should have thought of that before kissing him.

True, but I'd been so swept up that I hadn't stopped to think. Now, it was too late.

I set down the flat iron and was about to put on makeup when my phone lit up. My heart skipped, and in spite of all the admonitions I'd just put myself through, I half hoped it was Cody calling. Instead, it was a number I didn't recognize.

"Emma? This is MacCauley Brandstein," said the voice on the other end. "The board has given their approval for me to visit Starlight Cove!" She sounded delighted. "Every bit of research matches up, and based on the picture you sent, I am confident this is the lost painting. I can be in Starlight Cove on Tuesday, if you'd like to meet then?"

In the mirror, my eyes went wide with delight. "Tuesday . . ." Joe's memorial was later in the week, on Friday. That was the only thing I had on the schedule that couldn't be changed. "Yes, of course. When would you like to meet?"

"My flight would arrive midday. Shall we say one p.m.? I assume you'll want to meet at the bank where you have the painting stored. I wouldn't recommend moving it at this point unless absolutely necessary. There's too big of a risk of damage or theft."

I gave a vigorous nod. "Perfect. I can't wait for you to see it. I've loved this painting for my entire life. It really is something special."

"I have no doubt," said Ms. Brandstein, with a smile in her voice. "Send me the necessary information, and I'll look forward to seeing you then."

I hung up the phone and let out a breath. Ready or not, some big life changes were coming my way.

~

I stopped by Lydia's on the way to work, cradling a pork roast in my hands. Since she had put all that work into finding my mother, I had wanted to do something to thank her. The roast smelled like the holidays, had just come out of the oven, and was still warm. I'd also added vegetables in the pan alongside it, including carrots, asparagus, and portobello mushrooms. It was a good meal, and I half hoped Lydia would invite me to join them for dinner later, because I wanted to talk with her more about how to contact my mother, and also because she was starting to feel like a friend.

"Who is it?" Lydia's voice was tinged with suspicion, like always.

"Me," I called. "I brought dinner. It's heavy, so open up."

The locks jiggled, and the door opened. The sound of gunfire rang out, and I jumped a mile, nearly dropping the roast. Lydia caught it, gently taking it from my hands.

"Jamal, turn off that game," she scolded and gave me an apologetic look. In a low voice, she said, "We had a rough night last night. He started asking all these questions about our future plans, and I didn't know how to answer. It wasn't good."

"I'm sorry." I sneaked a peek at him. He didn't appear to be listening, but it was hard to tell. "Did something happen to prompt it? Cody said he seemed to have a blast in the program yesterday morning."

Lydia sighed. "I don't know. I can't get anything out of him." She headed for the kitchen. "Come in, please."

I followed her into the kitchen and stopped short.

Lydia must have cleaned it from top to bottom again, because the place seemed to shine. The wood floors looked bright and free from dust, the kitchen counters were clear and white, and even the windows seemed to let in more sun than I'd ever seen.

"What on earth did you do in here?" I demanded. "It looks better every time I stop by."

I took in a deep breath, which reminded me of Cody breathing in the smell of the taffy the day before. I would have to send him a box of it, just to see what he'd do. But the duplex didn't smell like taffy. It smelled strange and sour, like something I couldn't quite place.

"Vinegar." Lydia set the roast on the counter, put her face close to it, and breathed in. "The smell leaves something to be desired, but it's cheap and gets the job done."

It was something to keep in mind. I practically wanted to FaceTime Kailyn, to show her how good the duplex looked on Lydia's watch and to prove that having her here was a good move. *Not* that I expected Lydia to keep cleaning. In fact, I felt a little guilty about it. This was the type of cleaning job that would have been expensive if I had hired out the help to do it.

"It looks incredible." I walked through the apartment, still baffled at the change. The spots on the walls were gone, and even the floorboards were white. Then, because Lydia was watching and I didn't want her to feel like I was trying to invade her space, I returned to the kitchen. "It's never looked better."

"It keeps me busy." She nodded, surveying the space with a critical eye. "I'm one of the strange ones. I like to clean. It's one of the few things in life that make absolute sense, like math."

I laughed. "You've lost me on both the math and cleaning part."

"One plus one will always be two, and a counter wiped down with water and vinegar will always shine," Lydia said with a definitive nod. "I really appreciate you setting me up with that job at the office building. It went well. They're having me back, and it's led to so many others."

"That's great," I said. "Keep me posted. I can see if I can ask around and find some more things for you."

Gunfire started up again. This time, I didn't jump. Instead, I walked into the living room and sat down next to Jamal on the couch.

"Cody said he had fun with you at the program yesterday," I said. "How was it building the castle?"

Jamal made a face and went after his video game with a vengeance.

"Don't you like it?" I asked. "I thought you had fun the first day?"

He grunted but didn't answer.

"There's another session next week," I said, propping my feet up on the coffee table. Just as quickly, I took them down, not wanting to set a bad example. "Cody said everyone will get to make their very own bow and arrow."

That caught his attention. He glanced up for a second, and based on a sound from the game, it threw him off.

"Dammit," he shouted, leaping to his feet.

"Jamal!" Lydia sounded horrified. "Don't use that type of language. You know the consequence." She took the video game and placed it on top of the refrigerator.

Jamal had a flat-out fit. He started kicking everything in sight, wreaking havoc on the couch and coffee table, and for a second, he turned and eyeballed me. Then he ran down the hallway and slammed the door.

Lydia stood in the kitchen, hand to her throat, her face stricken. "I'm so sorry. I don't know why he's acting like this."

"It's understandable," I said, embarrassed at her embarrassment. "He's away from his friends, his home, and he doesn't know what's going on. He's just upset, Lydia. It's not your fault."

"It *is* her fault." Jamal came storming back into the room. The rage in his eyes was so intense that, for a moment, I was afraid. "She's a fraud and a grifter. You're so stupid for trusting her. She's a liar!"

Lydia rushed forward. "Go to your room right now, and do not come out."

"It's not my room. None of this is mine. It's not yours, either, so quit acting like it!" Jamal stormed out of the house and slammed the front door.

"Jamal," Lydia called, chasing after him. "Jamal!"

I stood in silence in the foyer, his words ringing in my ears.

She's a liar and a grifter.

What did that even mean? The comment scared me, because it was such a strange and specific thing to say. Plus, it was much too close to the type of warnings Kailyn had been giving me from the beginning.

Stop. He's a kid. He probably doesn't even know what it means.

Heck, I barely knew what it meant.

Still, my hands were shaking, and I didn't know whether to chase after them or stay here. I looked around the house. I'd never really snooped to see what they were up to, because it felt wrong, even though I had a spare key. Now, I couldn't help but think that maybe I needed to get a better idea of whether or not I was making a huge mistake trusting a complete stranger.

I poked my head outside the door. Lydia was halfway down the block, chasing after Jamal, who was running. It was my chance to see what I could figure out.

My heart started to pound, and I walked back toward Lydia's room.

The space was immaculate. The boxes and crates that had held their clothes were neatly stacked in the closet, her clothes hung on hangers and neatly placed in the drawers. There were no personal artifacts anywhere that could give me any additional information.

Jamal's room was a different story, of course. It smelled like sweat and dirty shoes. His bed was unmade, and clothes were tossed on the floor. The comic book was bent and half hidden beneath a pillow that had the case hanging off, but I had a feeling Lydia would sweep in and clean things up the moment she got the chance.

I decided to rescue the comic book, and when I pulled it out from the pillow, a well-worn picture fell out. It was of Lydia and Jamal standing with an older woman at the Grand Canyon. When I went to tuck it back in the book, my eye fell on an inscription on the back written in Lydia's neat penmanship: *Mom and Jamal, Grand Canyon, 2017.*

Mom?

I looked at the picture again, completely confused.

Lydia said she hadn't seen her mother in years.

Why would she lie about something like that?

Because it would be an easy way to connect with you.

Cold seeped through me. That couldn't be true. That was the one thing, the one topic that was so painful to me . . . I couldn't imagine she had faked a story of her own just to gain my trust.

There had to be another explanation as to why there was a photo of her and her mother from just a few years back when she'd told me she hadn't seen her mother since she was a kid. Could it be a mother figure, someone she'd adopted in her mother's place?

The front door banged, and I jumped, dropping the picture. Quickly, I put it back where I'd found it and tried to figure out how to make a quick exit.

"Emma?" Lydia called.

One hallway ran from the two bedrooms, with the only bathroom in the house right between them, and it could be seen from the living room. I could give no explanation for being in her son's room, because it wasn't like I didn't know where the bathroom was.

She's a fraud.

Jamal's words rang in my ears. If it wasn't for what I'd just found, I'd chalk up the words as the angry accusations of a young boy mad at his mother for uprooting his life. But now, there were too many warning signs to ignore.

Lydia had flat-out told me at the bed and breakfast that I would not want to help her if I knew the truth about her past. I'd stopped her from continuing when she'd teared up, but given the things I'd overheard on the phone with her brother and now this, it might be time to start asking questions.

Such as, what if she's been manipulating me from the start?

I couldn't think of a reason for her to do that, though. She had never asked me for money. She didn't seem to be after anything at all. In fact, she seemed like a good person, but maybe I was wrong, and it would be dangerous for her to catch me snooping.

Heart pounding, I considered hiding in the closet. She'd think I'd left, and I could sneak out when she wasn't paying attention. But of course, I couldn't do that. I had to face her, in spite of the sick feeling in my gut.

"I'm here," I called, stepping out into the hallway.

Lydia's back was turned, and she was peering out the living room window. I took a few quick steps forward and rested my hand on the doorjamb of the bathroom, as though I'd been there the whole time.

"He's not with you?" I asked.

She shook her head. "He bumped into some boys from the outreach program. They were on their way to play basketball at the park and needed one more. I don't want him out there alone, but there was no way he was coming back with me, so I guess I'd rather he's out there with them."

The defeat in her voice was mirrored in the slump of her shoulders. Lydia always struck me as a person who handled a bad situation with humor and grace, but in moments like this, I could see the stress that weighed on her every day. It worried me that the problems with Jamal could put her back into a depressed state.

Maybe she never actually was depressed either.

The thought made me angry with myself. I had no business judging her, especially when I was doing it because of a picture I knew nothing about and because of the angry words of her ten-year-old son. She had never been anything less than polite and caring to me, and she had even tracked down my mother. She deserved the benefit of the doubt.

"I think it's great news that Jamal has found some friends to hang out with," I said slowly. "The park here is very safe, so you don't have to worry about that." I took a few tentative steps into the living room and sat on the edge of the couch. "Plus, if he's making friends with the guys in the group, he'll be more apt to want to go back. I really think it's a good place for him to spend time, because that's where he's going to meet good people."

"You're sure the park is safe?" The pinched look between her eyes seemed to soften. "I never would have left him alone at a park at home, but if you could have seen the look he gave me, Emma, when I tried to stay." She sighed. "There were already lots of kids, though, and parents that were there for the toddlers on the swings." She turned back to the window. "I guess it's like stepping back in time here. To a day and age where things were different. When you could trust people."

The words were ironic, given what I'd just found.

"Did what he said about me scare you?" Lydia turned to face me. "My brother said that to me the other day. I had him on speaker, and he blew up because I still owe him money from back when he had to take care of Jamal. I fully intend to pay him back; I just don't have the resources to do it yet. But please don't doubt me because of that. It's from another time."

My cheeks heated with embarrassment. "What do you—"

"I know you weren't in the bathroom." She waved her hand. "Look, I don't blame you for not trusting me. The things Jamal said . . ." The low light of the room cast shadows beneath her eyes, and she gave me a troubled look. "I would wonder too."

"Well, it's not just that."

Lydia's forehead wrinkled. "What do you mean?"

I hesitated, worried at how she might react to getting caught in a lie. "Lydia, I found a picture of you with your mother."

Her face went pale. "My mother?"

"The picture of you, Jamal, and *Mom* at the Grand Canyon," I said. "It was taken in 2017."

Lydia looked tired. "Emma, that was my ex-husband's mother."

Relief flooded through me, but before I could comment, she said, "We'd always been close. It nearly killed her to find out the truth about her son, and we stayed in touch. She reached out when it looked like he was going to get early parole, begging to see me and Jamal. It was one of the things that . . ." She ducked her head. "His mother was the main reason I never left him. Seeing her triggered those memories. That visit started me down a bad path, in spite of the fact that I still love her."

Relief flooded through me.

"Thank you for telling me that." I walked over and tried to take her hand, but she flinched and moved away. "It's my mistake," I said. "I should have trusted you."

Her expression was so hurt I felt terrible. "Why would you trust me?" she said. "You don't know me. And *how* could you trust me, after what Jamal said? No matter what I do or say, he finds a way to throw my mistakes back in my face. Maybe I deserve it, but it kills me. I wish there was something I could do, but it's like he knows exactly the right thing to say to break my heart. He's been so angry at me for leaving, for taking him from his friends, from his life. I . . ." Her shoulders tensed. "I'm a terrible mother, Emma."

I shook my head. "You're a great mother."

"I don't know how I've survived, to be honest." Her voice was quiet. "The things that have happened in my life were so far beyond my control. Still, I can't help but blame myself." Her eyes went raw with pain. "I still do."

Silence hung between us. I wanted to ask her to tell me more, but I didn't want to risk making her think I was still trying to figure out if Jamal's words were true.

"Do you want to have some coffee?" I asked. "I still have a half hour before I have to be at work. I'd be happy to talk about all of this."

Lydia hesitated. Finally, she gave a tired nod. I'd included some ground coffee from Chill Out the day I'd brought over groceries, and bustling around, I made us a strong-smelling pot of it.

"Here." I walked a mug over to her. "Drink this."

We settled in at the kitchen table, the early-morning sun bright outside the window. She looked outside as if hoping for a view of the park, but of course, it was too far away.

"I promise he'll be fine," I said. "The only thing you should worry about at all is the fact that he's probably not wearing sunscreen."

Lydia gave a weak smile. "That will give me a good excuse to go back and check on him." She turned the coffee cup in her hands. "I told you. He'll never forgive me for leaving him behind. He shouldn't either. What kind of mother does that?"

"My stepmother," I said. "My birth mother."

Lydia pressed her lips together. "I bet you're furious with them both."

I didn't know how to respond to that. In some ways, it was true, but in others, I'd accepted the situation. My grandmother had given me a good childhood, and I'd never trade the time I got to spend with her.

"It's complicated," I said.

She looked down at the table. "You know, Emma, I've kept all of this buried for so long, and . . . I don't know. Back then, I just snapped. I sold my house, bought a camper, and took off to the mountains. There were days I thought would be my last, days I wanted to be my last, but it was the thought of Jamal that kept me here. That kept me alive." She shuddered. "My brother finally tracked me down and called the authorities. I was put away for treatment for my depression, thank God, and I was there for almost a year. Once I came out, Jamal wasn't exactly ready to leap into my arms. Good for him. I screwed up. He knows it, and he's not going to forget. It scares me to think of the type of damage I did."

I didn't know what to say. The fact that she'd struggled with serious mental health issues meant that she needed more than just a pep talk. Plus, I didn't know enough about depression to make any type of grand proclamation. From what I understood, though, I knew it was beyond her control.

"Your son loves you, Lydia. I can see how much he loves you, and like I've told you before, I can see how much you love him. In the end, that's what matters."

Lydia's body went so still that I couldn't tell she was crying until she spoke. "That doesn't fix things. He's too young to understand why I left. He only knows that I did, and he hates me for it. I failed him, and he's probably scared it will happen again."

I wondered if she was scared it would happen again.

"Life is long," I said. "You're his mother, and it's your job to teach him that no one is perfect. It's the best you can do. You can't turn back the clock, but you also can't spend the rest of his life feeding him chocolates and ice cream and saying sorry."

Embarrassment crossed her face. "I don't even know what a grifter is." She took a drink of her coffee, shaking her head. "Is it someone who lays bricks?"

I chuckled. "No clue. But it sounds pretty bad, which was his intent, I'm sure."

"Is that why you searched our rooms?" she asked.

There was no point in beating around the bush. The relationship that Lydia and I shared had shaped up to be pretty direct, in spite of all the heartache.

"Yes."

"I understand." She took another drink of coffee. "I probably would have done the same thing." We sat in silence for a minute.

Then I said, "Jamal will come around. I know you want to be firm and raise him right and all of that, but if you want my advice . . ."

"Please."

"Give him a break," I suggested. "Tell him you love him. Let him play his video games. Let him go to the park and be a kid. Hug him. Because no matter how angry he is, you're the one who has the maturity to make it better."

The hope on her face nearly broke my heart. "You really think so?"

"I know so. I've been as angry as he is now, and let me tell you, it would have been so simple for my stepmother to make things better. The only thing I wanted was to know she loved me."

The words sounded childish coming from my lips, especially at this point in my life. Still, the hurt had never gone away, and the sentiment was true. It would have been so easy for Gillian to try and make me understand why she chose to leave, but instead, she acted like nothing had changed, even though my world had been turned upside down.

"I have to get to work," I said. "Let me know when he comes back home."

The talk I'd had with Lydia made me feel a lot better, so I hoped it did the same for her. Still, the moment I was alone with my own thoughts, walking to the store, I wondered if I could actually trust the things she'd told me, or if I was being naive.

Chapter Twenty-Four

The candy shop was absolutely slammed. It was a Saturday, the weather was perfect, and there was a steady stream of people eager to try our candies. Halfway through the morning, the couple walked back into the shop.

This time, the man wore a short-sleeved button-up shirt with the same expensive watch but no glasses, which made his face look less defined. His wife was dressed up in a brown-and-white starched sundress that fell past her knees and a pair of high-end flats. I had been about to run someone's debit card, and instead I stood as still as a statue, trying to fight the fury that shot through me at the sight of them.

"Ashley." I reached out and tugged at the sleeve of her shirt. She had just finished boxing a selection of dark chocolates from the glass case and gave me a confused look. "I have to go deal with something," I told her in a low tone.

"Sure." Her eyes got big, probably because I never got angry at work. "I'll handle the register."

I stomped out from behind the counter, my breath coming in angry little bursts. Putting my hands on my hips, I stared them down. "What are you doing here?"

Margot looked confused. "My dear, we couldn't help but notice you removed the painting." Today, she was the one wearing glasses, and they made her eyes look wide and calculating. "We're hoping it's a sign that you've decided to sell it to us. We contacted the store owner and increased our offer to thirty thousand and had been certain we'd hear from you, but you haven't called, so we wanted to check in."

I took a moment to really look at the two of them.

The man stood next to his wife, with a slight look of impatience, as if he couldn't believe their money had not already achieved its goal. Margot looked falsely cheerful, the laugh lines around her eyes strained with the effort. Because of the way they stared at me, with such intense pressure designed to have me bow to their wishes, I made the decision to put them in their place.

"What did you hope to accomplish?" I asked. "By trying to take that painting from me?"

"What? We're offering thirty thousand dollars," her husband said, as if in disbelief. "That's hardly taking it from you."

The disappointment I felt in the charade topped any sense of professionalism. Plus, I was no longer worried about getting fired for telling off a customer. But there was that little matter of treating others the way I wanted to be treated, so I decided to use the conversation as a teaching moment rather than unleash all the things I actually wanted to say.

"*The Girl with the Butterscotch Hair* was painted by K. L. Heathwood," I said. "One of the most popular mainstream artists of this century. I'm sorry I didn't tell you that when you first asked, but the truth of the matter is, I didn't know it then."

Their shocked expressions were comical. It was almost a surprise to me, not to mention an insult, to confirm that the couple knew full well who had painted the piece. They really, truly thought I was just a dumb small-town girl, too oblivious to see through their nonsense. The thought infuriated me.

"It's wonderful that you brought it to my attention," I said. "I don't have a lot of money, and to me, this discovery is a windfall. The thing that has made me profoundly sad—and let's be honest, incredibly angry—is the fact that the two of you chose to be so dishonest about it. You planned to rip me off and sell the painting to the highest bidder. I have to ask, How do you sleep at night?"

"Now, hold on." The man held up his hands. "We suspected, but—"

"Then why wouldn't you tell me?" I demanded. "You knew how much it could be worth. Plus, I am *in* the painting. It's a painting of *me*, as a little girl." The rage was building again, and I gave a quick glance around the store to remind myself that it would not help anyone to make a scene. "I am truly in disbelief that you would be so incredibly dishonest that you would actually try to take a work of art from *the subject* for your own personal gain. I gotta tell you, the world needs more good people. I would suggest that, moving forward, you try and give a little more and take a little less."

Margot's eyes narrowed. "Excuse me—you should be thanking us, not judging us. I completed my dissertation on K. L. Heathwood. I know every detail about his work and his history, including each of the lost paintings, which is not common knowledge. The fact that I identified this for you deserves thanks, not criticism, because you never would have known."

I was about to comment when she cut me off.

"Don't argue," the professor said. "Simply tell me: Do *you* know that there is half of an orb of light at the top of each of his paintings? I'm sure you don't. It's his silent signature. Sometimes it's noticeable, sometimes it's not, but it's always there."

I thought back to the painting. Now that she mentioned it, the lighting at the top of the painting was curved into a gentle half circle. It had certainly never caught my eye, but now I couldn't wait to pull out the painting and take another look at it.

The man looked at a fixed point just past my shoulder, because he was probably too embarrassed to look me in the eye. "So, I think we deserve a thank-you, not a lecture."

Unbelievable.

I put on my best Mona Lisa smile. "You know what, this was fascinating, and you're right. Thank you. You did me a big favor, and I appreciate it. Now, do me another favor. Get out of my store."

For a split second, I half expected the room to erupt in applause. Of course, no one was paying attention. The couple simply stormed out, banging the door behind them. I looked up at the wall where the painting had hung for so many years and imagined the little girl smiling down at me. Then I turned to head back to the register and almost bumped right into someone.

It was Gillian.

Chapter Twenty-Five

Gillian's face was like stone. Like always, she was immaculately dressed in her newscaster clothing with her makeup perfectly done. She iced me with a look. "I will see you in the kitchen immediately."

Shit.

Gillian sailed past the candy counter and through the door. I stood in silence, a sense of dread replacing the momentary feeling of victory. Ashley had just made a hot cocoa for a customer, and even the languid scent of warm milk did nothing to calm my nerves.

I wondered how much Gillian had overheard. Maybe nothing at all. The kitchen conversation might turn out to be a lecture on treating each customer with respect or because I'd said, "Get out of my store," and she didn't want me to say that, because I didn't own the place yet. There was still a chance she didn't know. Still, I could barely stop my knees from shaking.

"Ashley," I said, heading behind the counter. My voice sounded strangled. "Gillian needs to talk to me. You okay out here?"

She gave a grim nod, scooping up chocolates and ringing purchases at the same time. "I got it."

"Thank you," I told her. The girl had not stopped moving since she'd arrived. I'd have to slip her a couple extra bucks from my pocket, because without her, we'd be in trouble. "If I come out of this meeting alive, I promise I'll make it up to you."

"Ha. Good luck," she said, laughing. We'd both bonded over the fact that Gillian could be scary. This time, though, I had a feeling that my talk with Gillian would not be a joking matter.

Squaring my shoulders, I pushed open the door. The fluorescent lights made the kitchen feel like an interrogation room, and I started to sweat.

Gillian sat at her desk, hands folded. "A bit hypocritical, no? You just spent five minutes berating them for not telling you the truth about the painting. When were you planning to tell me?"

So she'd heard.

"Gillian, I . . ." I rubbed my sweating palms up and down the side of my dress. "I planned to tell you."

"Oh, I'm sure." She gave a slight smile. "When you closed on the store, right?"

It was amazing. Some people told lies 24-7. I never lied. Yet, the one time I chose to be slightly deceptive and only for the purpose of self-preservation, I managed to get caught.

I took a few steps forward, not sure where to stand or what to say. "I thought about telling you the whole story, but I was scared."

She raised her eyebrows. "Of what, exactly?"

The anger that simmered beneath her words frightened me. More than the outrage on the couple's face or the idea that Lydia could be those terrible things her son had said about her. It scared me, because I had no idea what Gillian planned to do next, and she held so much of what I wanted in the palm of her hand.

"I was afraid you would try to take it from me," I admitted, and she drew back as if I'd slapped her. "I'm sorry," I said quickly. "I know it wasn't fair of me to think that way, but that painting means a lot to me and—"

"Take it from you?" She got to her feet, her eyes bright and angry. "I told you when we went to dinner that I don't want a thing to do with it! You don't know what that damn painting cost me."

"What did it cost you?"

"My marriage." She sank back into the desk chair. "Emma, your father and I did not have a great love story for the ages. Did you know that?"

That familiar cold feeling started somewhere in my stomach as I considered the things my grandmother had told me. "What do you mean?" I said, tentatively taking a seat.

"Your father was not faithful to me. Oh, he would never admit it, but I knew." The pain in her voice chilled me. "He claimed to be hanging out with that painter, but I knew the truth. It was a cover, so he could be away from me and with other women. I don't know how many there were. I don't want to know, but boy, did people love to talk."

This side of Gillian surprised me. She'd always presented me with the same perfect facade people saw on the news. Now, I could actually see the bitterness beneath it all—the hurt, scorned woman. It made sense, actually, based on what she'd said about my father that night at the Mexican restaurant, about how desperately she had loved him. Rumors that my father had been unfaithful would have crushed her.

"It was all a shock to me. I thought we'd had something rare." She ran the back of her hand over her forehead, and I was surprised to see her hand was shaking. "Once I figured it out, I attempted to confront him, because I was not about to live a lie. He laughed in my face and said the only thing he had time to fall in love with was that painting, which was completely untrue. The fact that he could joke about it so easily hurt the most."

"Gillian, I don't know what to say," I told her. "I remember you and my father together. He adored you. Maybe he *was* laughing because it wasn't true."

Gillian scoffed and twisted her rings. They were her wedding and engagement rings. She'd never taken them off after he died. She'd only switched them to another finger. I'd always assumed it was because of the huge diamonds, but now I realized it was because she'd never stopped loving my father.

"I mean it," I said. "This doesn't sound right to me."

"Oh, it is. It was the talk of the town for a while." She flipped her hair. "All I know is that I had never been more humiliated in my life. He never admitted it, but I could never trust him again."

"Why would you believe gossip, though?" I said. "Instead of your husband?"

"The gossip was truth, Emma, started by a former friend of mine who did not deserve to be called a friend, because she was there when I found a love letter written to your father. It was from another woman."

My mouth dropped open.

"You're kidding."

"I wish I was." Her lips were pressed so tightly together they were nearly white. "'These past few months captured feelings that no one else could have. I trust you will keep our secret to the grave and back . . .' I was literally sick after reading it; the betrayal cut so deep."

I put my hand to my mouth. "Who was she?"

Gillian shrugged. "I never found out. It was signed with a *C*. Probably a tourist, because even though everyone was eager to whisper about it, no one knew."

"You didn't ask?" I said. "When you confronted him about the letter?"

"I never told him I saw it." Her eyes went dull. "He'd already laughed in my face once, and I was not about to let it happen again. It was easier to pretend nothing had happened. That was the end, though, for me. Did you know that we'd agreed to get a divorce right before he died?"

My heart sank. "No."

My grandmother had said she'd talked Gillian out of a divorce. That decision must not have lasted long.

Gillian shrugged. "It was not a good time in my life. There were so many times over the years that I wanted to take that damn painting off the wall, and I did take it down a couple of times, but then someone would complain, and I'd have to put it right back up. So, I don't want to take it from you, Emma. To be frank, I'm delighted to see it go."

"I'm so sorry, Gillian."

"It's fine." She got to her feet and brushed off her hands. "Of course this has to come back to haunt me, now that I'm trying to move on. It will be a big story. I'd like to get an exclusive, please, because everyone's going to be talking about it."

"Of course," I said quietly. "The director of the foundation will be here on Tuesday to look at the painting. You can interview her."

Gillian gave a sharp nod. "Please set it up. I'll plan to talk to her then. Thanks."

She swept out of the back door without a second glance.

I sat in silence, trying to imagine what it must have felt like to find that letter. The idea that my father had betrayed her like that was a complete shock. They had seemed so happy. The fact that Gillian had loved him so deeply only to have that happen must have broken her heart.

Part of me wanted to run after her, to tell her that there must have been more to the situation, something that she wasn't seeing, but what did I know? Maybe my father liked the idea of being in love more than the reality. There was nothing I could say that could change what had happened. The whole thing made me want to sink into the chair and have a good cry.

But it was Saturday, the shop was still slammed, and by now, Ashley had to be desperate for some help. Getting to my feet, I headed back to work.

Chapter Twenty-Six

Kailyn came over to have a drink with me in the backyard, most likely because she wanted to hear what had happened with Cody, but the only thing I could talk about was the situation with Gillian. I told her everything, from the moment I'd confronted the couple to the rumors about my father, and she listened in disbelief.

"I don't even know what to say. I'm shocked, actually, to think she doesn't want anything to do with the painting, but if that's the history behind it, I guess it makes sense." She scratched a bug bite on her wrist. "It's a surprise, really, to think that she and your father almost split up."

"Even if my father had lived, Gillian might not have been a part of my life," I mused. "Maybe she and I weren't meant to be."

I wasn't in the mood to have a drink, so I was binge eating gumdrops instead. They had been a weakness of mine ever since I was little. Our shop didn't carry them, but the candy store down the street did. Popping a red one into my mouth, I bit down, feeling the granulated sugar dissolve before getting a blast of strawberry flavoring.

"I can't believe you're eating those." Kailyn eyed the gumdrops with suspicion. "I feel like that's one of those foods that will sit in your colon for seven years. Like if you swallow gum."

Rolling my eyes, I said, "Did you hear that from Cody?"

Her eyes brightened. "How was dinner?"

Drat. The fact that I'd brought up his name at all opened the door to the topic. I brushed away a mosquito.

"Fine," I said. "Fun."

I must have blushed, because she squealed. "Did you kiss? Did he kiss you?"

"Would you be quiet?" I whispered, embarrassed. "I do have neighbors."

"That's a yes." She leapt to her feet and did a ridiculous, Kailyn-style victory dance. "That is one hundred percent a yes."

"You have to stop," I insisted.

The smell of charcoal and roasting meat wafted over the fence, which meant my neighbors were outside. It was a small town. I could only imagine word getting back to Cody that Kailyn and I were sitting in my backyard squealing about him like two adolescents.

Of course, that's exactly how I felt when I thought about the kiss we had shared, and I had to fight to keep the smile off my face.

"That is the best news I've ever heard." Kailyn beamed at me. "We could have a double wedding!"

The words were sobering, and I reached for another gumdrop. Green, this time. It was impossible to tell if the flavor was apple, lime, or what, and I could only imagine what Cody would say.

"Look, I'm just happy to get back out there." I kicked off my sandals and buried my toes in the grass. "Let's start there."

The dinner with Cody had been great. Yes, we'd kissed, and that was even better. But the whole thing still freaked me out, because I still didn't know how capable I was of being open to love again. And if I wasn't, what was the point?

Kailyn could probably see me shutting off, because she held up her hands. "No worries. You don't have to talk about it if you don't want to."

"So, what's going on with the chamber?" I asked.

"The vote's later this week." Her face clouded. "I'm really starting to regret the fact that I decided to go along with all of it. I practically have a panic attack every time I think about it. I might have made a bad move with this."

"No." I gave a vehement shake of my head. "It's absolutely the right move, and I'm proud of you."

"We'll see." She grabbed her glass and hopped to her feet. "I'm going to run inside for a refill. Want anything?"

"Some water would be great." I held out the bag of gumdrops. "Take these. I think you might be right about the whole seven-years-in-the colon thing."

Crickets chirped in the stillness of the evening, and I considered checking my phone to see if Cody had called or texted, but I ignored the impulse.

"Emma." I turned toward the house. Lydia gave a tentative wave from the back porch. "Jamal and I are just finishing up dinner. The roast is delicious. Thank you."

I hopped up and jogged across the yard. "How is he?"

"Good." She kept her voice low. "He had a lot of fun at the park, but he said he's not going back to the hardware shop thing again. I don't know what happened."

"Really?" Cody hadn't said one word about things being hard for Jamal this time around. "I'll talk to Cody," I said. "Find out what's going on."

The idea of talking to him again made my heart pound. Quickly, I pushed the feeling away. I had no business thinking about that at the moment.

"Thank you," Lydia said. "I'd appreciate that."

Kailyn came back out. Lydia ducked back inside quickly, as if not wanting to be seen. Once Kailyn and I were seated on the bench together, she frowned. "That's the woman? How long is she planning to stay?"

"Lydia," I said. "Her name is Lydia. I invited her to stay for six weeks."

Kailyn's eyebrows shot up. "Six weeks?"

"Look, she's great. The place would be vacant otherwise, and really, she's become a good friend."

"I'm a good friend," Kailyn shot back. "You barely know her."

"Please don't give me a hard time about this." The thought of launching into a detailed description of my connection with Lydia sounded exhausting. There was the whole story about finding my mother, and after everything that had happened today, I couldn't even get into that. "I know you're worried, which is the only reason you're asking, but we've had this conversation. I'm a pretty good judge of character."

Kailyn snorted. "No, you're not. I only wanted to be your best friend because I knew you owned a candy shop."

It was an old joke, one we'd laughed about for years. The first day of kindergarten, Kailyn plunked down right next to me at snack time and informed me she planned to be my friend because I owned a candy shop. I corrected her, saying that my father owned the shop, not me, but she said she'd be my best friend anyway. It was a good move, because I had sneaked a pocketful of candy to school and shared half with her.

"I haven't left your side since," she said cheerfully.

"Thank goodness." I put my head on her shoulder.

My phone rang. Pulling it out of the pocket on my dress, I nearly dropped it.

"It's Cody," I whispered.

Kailyn squealed, stomping her feet against the ground and sloshing her rosé. "Put it on speaker," she whispered, as if he could hear. "Please."

"No way." Getting to my feet, I scampered over to the cherry tree and stood underneath it. The blossoms were bold and fragrant, the perfect complement to the summer night. "Hello?"

"I've come up with a thousand different things to say to you today." Cody's voice was low over the receiver. "Because I didn't want to end up saying something stupid, like your kiss was as sweet as sugar or anything."

I laughed, touching the smooth bark of the tree. "So, you failed at that."

"I did." He cleared his throat. "But for real, sorry you're just hearing from me now. The store was slammed today."

"We were too."

"It was fun last night." He paused. "Would you like me to make dinner for you next week?"

My palms went damp.

It was official. This could move forward.

I still had a chance to back out. To make an excuse and walk away. But I didn't want to.

"Depends," I finally said. "How healthy are we talking?"

"It's a yes-or-no question."

The determined tone in his voice made my heart soar.

"Yes," I said. "I'd like that."

"Good."

There was a long pause, and I could tell he was ready to get off the phone now that his mission was accomplished. Still, I had to find out what had happened with Jamal.

"Hey, one thing," I said. "Lydia said Jamal kind of flipped out today about the program, said he wasn't going to come back. Did something happen?" Briefly, I updated him about the fight he'd had with Lydia and running off to the park.

"No." Cody sounded surprised. "He had a great time. We built that castle, and everyone got to be king at one point or another, which he owned."

"Huh." I swatted away a mosquito. "Yeah, he—"

"Wait," Cody said suddenly. "Something did happen, but it didn't seem like a big deal. I ordered shirts for everyone with their last name on them. The printer messed his up, didn't give him the right last name. I added the order on last minute, so maybe it's my mistake. That could have made him feel on the outside, since all the other guys put theirs right on."

"How do you spell Billings wrong?" I teased, reaching for a cherry blossom.

The only reason I even knew their last name was because I was there when Lydia signed in at the bed and breakfast.

He paused. "How *do* you spell it?"

"B-i-l-l-i-n-g-s. How did *you* spell it?"

"Exactly like that, smarty-pants. Hmm. Maybe the shirt was just an excuse, because we got it right." He was quiet for a second. "Tell you what. I'll stop by tomorrow, if it's cool with his mom. I can take him to the park. Or actually . . ." He thought for a second. "They've got that dog over at Search and Rescue, Captain Ahab. All the kids like him. I could take him over there, let them run around on the beach together or something."

The idea of Cody cooking me dinner had been attractive, but this melted my heart.

"You're a good one, Cody Henderson," I told him.

"Nah," he said, but he sounded pleased. "Text me and let me know if his mom says it's okay. I'll be free anytime in the afternoon. My derelict brothers can do some work tomorrow. It won't kill them."

I laughed. "Have a good night."

Kailyn was waiting for me on the bench, as eager as a puppy. "So . . . what did he say?"

"It's a nice night," I said, looking up at the sky.

"Come on," she pleaded. "Give me something."

"The sky's so clear."

"You're really not going to say anything?"

"Look, there's the moon," I said, pointing.

Kailyn slapped the bench in mock frustration. Then she reached over and took my hand. "I'm happy for you, you know."

I squeezed her hand. "I know."

Chapter Twenty-Seven

Later that night, I texted Lydia to get permission for the excursion to Search and Rescue. She called right as I was climbing into bed.

"That would really make him happy." Her voice sounded stuffy, like she'd been crying. "He's back to sitting around shooting me mean looks. I keep trying to break through, but I'm not getting anywhere."

"Cody's great with him." I pulled my pillow close to my chest. "He might be able to get through to him tomorrow. Let me know a time. I have the day off, and I'll stop by your house when he's going to be there."

"I don't blame you." There was a hint of a smile in her voice. "Cody seems worth stopping by to see."

"I hadn't noticed," I said, embarrassed.

She laughed. "Yeah. Me neither."

~

The following afternoon, Lydia and I sat at the table drinking hot tea and waiting for Cody. It had been years since I'd had plain black tea. It was delicious with cream and sugar, and I was quick to accept a second cup. Lydia gripped the kettle tight while pouring it, as if scared to spill a drop. It seemed like there were many things that she did where she was afraid to make a mistake, and I could only imagine it was from living under the shadow of her abusive husband.

"Have you given any more thought to contacting your mother?" she asked, sitting back down.

"No." With cream, the tea looked like freshly made caramels. It hit me that a series of candies designed to go with tea might be good, and I made a mental note to try some ideas out in the kitchen.

Lydia waited for me to say more.

"I know you went to a lot of trouble to do that for me," I said. "It couldn't have been easy to find her. It's information I've wanted to have my entire life. The thing is, I don't know what to do with it. There are so many factors, and really, this is it. I want to wait until I'm at a place where it won't destroy me if I reach out and she pushes me away."

"Gosh." Lydia looked down at her hands. "You seem so strong. I never would have guessed you'd be scared."

"I'm strong about some things. Not this."

"Take your time, then." She added sugar to her tea and tapped the spoon against the side of the cup. "At least you know how to find her."

There was a rap at the door, and I jumped. Then, I smoothed my hair and went to answer.

If possible, Cody looked even better than he had at dinner in a pair of faded jeans and a soft white T-shirt that snuggled up against his muscles in a way that I couldn't help but envy.

"Oh, Cody." I attempted to sound surprised. "What are you doing here?"

He rolled his eyes at my performance. "Jamal around?"

We'd all agreed that it would be better if it seemed like Cody's visit was completely coincidental, rather than something Lydia had set up.

"Yes. Come on in."

He walked in, and for a split second, we smiled at each other. Then, embarrassed, I turned back toward the kitchen. Lydia was walking out, and she gave him a shy smile too.

"Hi, Cody. Thank you so much for letting my son be a part of your program."

"Sure thing. Hey, do you mind signing a few permission slips? I thought I'd swing them by." Then he looked around. "Jamal here? Oh, hey, buddy."

Cody strolled into the living room. Jamal barely looked up from his video game. I had to give the kid credit. At least he was consistent.

To my surprise, Cody didn't push or tell him to put down the game. Instead, he picked up the remote control and clicked on the television. There was some sort of soccer game playing, and Cody leaned forward, watching it like it was the most fascinating thing he'd ever seen.

"Nice pass," he said after a few seconds. "Get it down the field. Down the field!"

Jamal glanced up and watched for a second, then went back to his game.

"Get it in," Cody shouted, making me jump. "Yeah. Almost!" He applauded loudly, and this time, Jamal set down his console. He started watching the game too.

"You play soccer?" Cody glanced at him.

"Nah. I might want to, though."

Lydia and I looked at one another in amazement. Then, since Cody seemed to have it under control, we ducked back into the kitchen.

"He's a kid whisperer," Lydia said. "No one has ever gotten through to Jamal like that. It's moments like this . . ." Her voice trailed off.

"What?" I prompted.

She ducked her head. "I get so upset about the situation with his father. He should have been the one to have those moments, but he was never that kind of man. It makes me sick to think about him."

The words were said with such sorrow that I couldn't help but wonder what he'd done.

"I'm sorry." I waited to see if she'd say more. "What was he like?"

"A monster." Straightening her shoulders, she peeked back out in the living room. "They're watching the game." She sat at the table and folded her hands. "Jamal finally looks happy. So did you when Cody walked in."

"Lydia." I shushed her, terrified he would hear.

"He's a good man, Emma." She nodded. "That's what a good man looks like."

I took another look in the living room. The two sat in silence on the couch, watching the game. Every couple of seconds, they'd grunt or offer a word of support to the players on the television, as if we were all on the same team.

"Yeah." I sat back down at the table. "I think you might be right."

Chapter Twenty-Eight

My eyes flew open at 4:45 Tuesday morning.

Today's the day.

I'd done such a great job of putting the painting out of my mind, because until I had the chance to show it to MacCauley Brandstein, I didn't dare think about what it could all mean. But today was the day she was coming to town, and it felt like Christmas. It would be incredible to share the painting with her, because she was an expert on K. L. Heathwood and his art, but I could also tell from her voice that she was extremely passionate about it too.

After reaching for my phone, I pulled up the foundation site. The painting with the series of desserts greeted me, and I clicked on the "About Us" page to read her bio once again. She'd studied art in New York, fallen in love with K. L. Heathwood's work, and traveled to California to meet him. She'd spent three years working as his assistant, cataloguing his work and managing the press prior to his death. Showing her the painting was going to be educational and, of course, life changing.

I tried to go back to sleep but only managed to toss and turn. Finally, I gave up. It was almost 5:30 in the morning, which was manageable. I could go into the shop and get to work on the series of tea candies I'd been thinking about. That sounded like a great way to keep my mind off the meeting with MacCauley Brandstein, because otherwise, I knew I'd be counting the minutes like years until she arrived.

∾

MacCauley Brandstein looked exactly like her picture in the bio. Shoulder-length black hair streaked with gray. Her eyes were hooded and fiercely intelligent. She wore a relaxed-style sundress with earrings made of thin wire that encircled two jade stones, and she shook my hand for at least a minute when we met outside the bank.

"This is quite an honor for me." Her earrings jiggled as she spoke. "I have spent so many years updating the archives and researching the lost paintings that it feels like a moon landing when one of them finally crops up. This will be quite the splash in the art world. I hope you're prepared for that."

My stomach tightened. The idea was frightening to me, because I knew nothing about art. I did know about candy, though, and since it was featured in the painting, I figured if anyone asked, I could just talk about that.

Speaking of . . .

"The local news would like to do an interview with you," I said. "Later this afternoon?"

Gillian had insisted on having her news crew present for Ms. Brandstein's evaluation of the painting, but I had drawn the line. I wanted to wait until I'd had plenty of time alone with Ms. Brandstein so that I could really absorb everything she had to say. It was my moment, and I didn't want to be distracted or have it splashed all over the news. In truth, I wanted to keep the entire situation private, but I knew word would get out, and people would want the details. Everyone around here had a story at some point. This time it just happened to be mine.

"That would be fine. I imagine quite a few news outlets will be interested in hearing this." Ms. Brandstein straightened her dress. "Shall we go take a look?"

Starlight Cove Central was the oldest bank in town and as a result, the most intimidating. It had perfectly polished white marble floors, enormous chandeliers that hung overhead, and black iron cages where the tellers sat. To access my safety-deposit box, I was whisked down a hallway where I had to sign in.

The teller used my key and hers to open the box and then helped me lift the large metal tray that held the painting. It was placed on a pushcart, and then we were transported to a large private room with pictures of Starlight Cove hung on the wall.

Ms. Brandstein did not hover over the box, as I'd anticipated. Instead, she studied one of the portraits on the wall. "Your town is quite pretty."

In the picture, Lake Michigan stretched along the horizon, its haunting deep blue a striking contrast against the pale-blue sky. It was a windy day, and the whitecaps on the water roiled, leaving puffs of white like clouds in their wake.

"It's not a surprise to me that K. L. chose to work here." She gave a sharp nod, as if marking the idea worthy to catalogue. Turning back to me, she said, "I should like to see it in the winter. Originally, he came here to study the way that light fell on snow. How interesting that he chose to capture the lights around and within the shop, but even in the picture you sent me, I could see what he had accomplished. He was skilled at creating a sense of warmth, an invitation to step inside the world of the painting. It's what I most love about his work."

I pressed my hands against the edge of the frame, my heart full. "That's exactly how I've felt, but I didn't know how to put it into words. Yes. The scene is inviting. Every time I look at it, I want to step back inside that life, that moment, and have a hot chocolate. I always want to have a hot chocolate, though, of course. That's what our store specializes in. You should have one, maybe before the news report, to have the full experience."

Ms. Brandstein lifted an eyebrow. "Certainly an attractive offer." Stepping away from the window, she walked over to the table. "Shall we?"

The look on her face the moment I unveiled the painting was momentary rapture, followed by an expression I couldn't place. Concentration, maybe? I stood in silence, trying to see it from her eyes.

The light from the ceiling reflected off it, showing the bold brush-strokes in a way it had not from the wall of the shop. The colors were exquisite. Lush blues, reds, and of course, the multilayered brown of the chocolates. For the first time, I noticed the fact that my nails were painted a light pink in the painting, something I hadn't done since I was a little girl.

My heart gave a little twinge. It was going to be hard to let it go.

Ms. Brandstein turned to me.

I met her eyes and gave a brave smile. "What do you think? Is it as good as his later works?"

It would be interesting to hear how they compared. In my opinion, nothing could be better than this, but I'm sure she had her favorites. I waited, the silence stretching between us. Finally, she blinked, looked at the painting again, and brushed her hand against one of her earrings.

"This is disappointing," she said.

Disappointing?

For a split second, I felt insulted.

"What do you mean?" I asked, pulling my arms to my chest.

Art was subjective, but I'd never heard anything but praise for the painting. I hadn't considered the fact that the art world could refer to it as subpar because it was done early on.

Trying not to sound as offended as I felt, I said, "I think it's great. I mean, I don't have the experience—"

"It's a fake."

My heart must have stopped for a moment, because for a split second, her words seemed to echo in the complete silence of the room.

Ms. Brandstein fumbled in her bag and pulled out a Polaroid picture snapped on her cell phone and handed it to me. It was of the painting, but the photograph was old. I squinted at it, confused.

"This is the original photograph taken of the completed work." She sank down in the chair, as if too tired to continue to stand. "K. L. was meticulous about documentation. He had a folder marked for *The Girl with the Butterscotch Hair* that included vague information. His notes said the painting was completed in northern Michigan and gifted to the subject. However, if you look closely in the photograph, you will see a small detail is missing, but that's not what tipped me off initially. I could tell it was a fake from the brushstrokes alone."

"Now, hold on. I sent you a picture of the painting. Nothing has changed from what I sent you. Look, it has the orb."

With a determined gesture, I pointed out the part of the painting the professor had spoken about in the shop. Still, Ms. Brandstein shook her head.

"This isn't it," she said. "The tail of the cat is missing."

"The what?" I demanded.

Was this some sort of a setup? Was she here to try and trick me out of the painting? Based on my run-in with Margot and her husband, it wouldn't surprise me. I sat down and pulled it closer to me, as if she would be able to dart out the door with it undetected.

"If you look closely, there is a tail of a cat sticking out from beneath that table," she said, pointing at it. "Your photograph was dark, and to be quite honest, it was a detail I missed. I never would have thought to look for it if the brushstrokes had not been such a giveaway."

I peered at the photograph on her phone once again. Sure enough, there was a black tail jutting out from underneath the table in the corner. Putting my hand to my mouth, I sat back in the chair.

"I haven't thought about that cat in years," I said, stunned.

My father used to break all sorts of rules by letting this stray cat come into the shop. We called it Smokestack because it was as black as coal and had eyes like orange embers. It spent the majority of the winter slinking in and out of the shop and slept there at night. I had cried bitterly during the spring when it was warm enough that Smokestack had left the shop and never come back.

The memory was so unexpected that in the heightened emotion of the situation, I teared up.

"My dear, I can understand if you're upset . . ."

"It's not the painting." My sleeve went damp as I brushed it across my eyes. "It's the fact that we forget the things that once mattered the most." Letting out a shaky breath, I tried to make sense of all this. There had to be an explanation. "Look, I see the differences. But you said yourself that he gifted the painting to the subject. That's me. I can show you a photograph of me when I was younger, and you'll see that I'm her . . ."

For the first time, Ms. Brandstein looked sympathetic. "My dear, that would be impossible to prove. Perhaps the subject in the painting is you; perhaps it is not. I cannot be the judge of that. The fact of the matter is, the original painting got lost somewhere along the way. Perhaps it was sold; perhaps it was stolen. Either way, this is not the painting in this photograph, and it is not his work."

"He could have done two versions," I suggested. "It's possible he didn't like this one and decided to do it again. Or . . ." I sucked in a sharp breath. "What if he didn't like the cat? A lot of people don't like cats. Maybe he decided to paint over it or something. If we had it analyzed . . ."

"I'm so sorry." Her earrings rattled as she shook her head. "You, of course, may follow up to your level of comfort. However, I can guarantee the photograph would not have made it into K. L. Heathwood's records if anything had been changed. He was very particular about the records he kept of his work."

"He changed as an artist, though, over the years." The conversation felt like it was going round and round, but I refused to accept MacCauley Brandstein's opinion as the final verdict. "You said yourself that he started to disguise the people and places he was painting. That's not what he did here."

Ms. Brandstein paused. "Strong argument. However, this was in his records, and so, that's that. K. L. struggled with mental illness, my dear. Certain quirks would not have allowed him to deviate from his record keeping. He needed to have his records just so, or he could not create."

"What do you mean?" I said, confused.

"His records helped keep him on task." She shrugged. "I cannot explain it. I can simply communicate the information. I suspect that he shared his identity with your father. He was already becoming quite popular around this time, which is why he needed an escape. Perhaps your father needed money at some point, sold the original, and replaced it with a copy."

The words were like a slap in the face. Mainly because it was very possible. That meant the original could be out there, hanging on someone else's wall. The very thought hurt me. It was a moment from my childhood, and it belonged to me. At least, that's what I'd always believed.

When I remained silent, Ms. Brandstein said, "You are welcome, as I said, to have the painting examined by another source. However, it's no longer a pursuit I can justify to our board. I truly am sorry, my dear. I was quite excited. It's a strong forgery, but ultimately, I cannot endorse it as his work."

I didn't know what to say. The idea that I had, in a sense, stumbled across a treasure had felt too good to be true. Still, so many of the pieces of the puzzle had fit that it had never occurred to me the painting could be a fake.

My father wasn't one for pretense. He would have told me flat out if it was a copy, wouldn't he? Something had to have happened to it.

Had someone figured out the truth behind the painting and stolen it? Even Gillian hadn't known its true origins. The only people who had access to the Sweetery beyond business hours were her and the management company she'd employed. Maybe they had figured it out, had a copy made, and replaced it?

The idea seemed far fetched, though. I loved that painting and how it stopped people in their tracks, but I'd never thought it was valuable. It seemed unlikely that someone would decide a random painting in a candy shop was worth some elaborate heist.

On the other hand . . . this had all started because that one couple had identified it.

Tourists passed through town on a daily basis. What if an art expert like the professor had guessed the origins and had found a way to steal it? Gillian had only installed the security system a few years ago, and it couldn't have been that difficult to jimmy the door. Most of the shopkeepers in Starlight Cove operated under the illusion that we lived in a bubble where crime couldn't touch us, which made us the perfect target.

"I'm going to return to the airport." Ms. Brandstein looked at her watch, the displeasure on her face highlighted by her pinched expression. "I'll see about switching my flight."

Our eyes met. For a second, I saw it: disdain and anger. The verdict was still out, but she half believed I had tried to trick her into condoning a forgery.

My cheeks burned with shame. "Ms. Brandstein." I reached out and touched her arm. "I promise you, I had no idea . . ."

"Oh, I'm quite sure of it." Her voice was so polite it froze my blood. "Mistakes happen. Best of luck."

The ramrod posture of her shoulders felt like a rebuke as she walked out the door, not bothering to wait for me to follow.

I swallowed hard, trying to figure out what to do next. If the painting was a forgery, that meant the real one was still out there. It felt like a violation somehow to think that it was hanging on a wall somewhere, and I would never get to see it.

Quietly, I packed up the painting.

Should I bring it home?

Regardless of the situation, this was the painting that was special to me. I needed to keep it here, safe, until I figured out the truth. *If* I figured out the truth, something that didn't look promising at the moment.

I stepped out of the room and into the main section of the bank. There, I stopped short. I was supposed to provide the loan officer a certificate of authenticity by the end of the business day. Without it, the loan offer I'd received to purchase the candy shop was null and void.

Chapter Twenty-Nine

The loan officer was apologetic but confirmed that the bank would not be able to move forward without collateral. Since I had nothing else to offer, the preapproval letter was null and void.

I contacted Kip from the entryway of the bank.

He was surprised and disappointed, I could tell, but he approached the news with typical pragmatism. It didn't have to be the end of the world. There had to be an explanation about the painting, and there were other banks. It was possible that one of them would give me a chance. It would just take time.

The problem was, I didn't have time. Gillian expected to close within two weeks. It would take a major leap of faith for her to agree to wait for me to pursue other options, but maybe that was a possibility.

My hands shook as I walked into the candy shop. I had texted Gillian with the news about the painting, since her entire crew was there, waiting to film. Then, I'd asked if we could talk in private, because I needed to tell her I'd used the painting as collateral for the loan.

When I walked in, Gillian took off her glasses and looked up from her computer. The blue light made the features on her face appear sharper than usual.

"Have a seat." She gestured at the chair in front of her desk.

"Thanks for meeting with me." I sat in the chair and cleared my throat. "There's a problem with the loan."

She nodded, as if she'd expected that. "What happened?"

"The painting was my collateral."

"Ah." She stared at me for what felt like an eternity. Then she clicked her tongue. "The thing that's so disappointing to me, Emma, is that for a moment, I thought I'd have the opportunity to do the right thing." She switched off the computer and stared off into the distance. "It was hard on me to inherit the Sweetery," she finally said. "Did you know that?"

I wanted to point out that it was hard on me to lose the Sweetery, but that was a given.

"It was hard, because I didn't think that would be what your father would have wanted. In my heart, I always felt he would have wanted the Sweetery to go to you."

The words rang in my ears. It was a thought I'd had many times over the years. Yes, my father loved Gillian, but I was his daughter. He had watched over and protected me from the moment I was born. There was no doubt he would have wanted to make sure that Gillian was taken care of financially, but he would have wanted me to be taken care of as well.

"There were so many times I struggled with the idea," Gillian continued. "I wondered if it would have been the right thing to hand over the keys to you." She rested her hand against her forehead. "Then, when I had to bail you out of that situation with that girl and the car and your creditors, I realized that you weren't ready for the responsibility. Maybe that wasn't the right choice. It has not been a simple decision."

Her words were confusing. It sounded like Gillian was considering hanging on to the store or even—I swallowed hard—thinking about passing it on to me.

"Is that the only reason?" I asked. "Because I can assure you, I never would have taken it for granted."

"It wasn't the only reason. You were a minor, for one. You were little when he died, so that meant I'd have to be responsible for it anyway, for years." Gillian ticked the reasons off on her fingers. "There was the fact that when you were at an age where you could legally take over, you weren't there emotionally. In the end, though, it was the money that made me keep the store for myself.

"To put it quite simply, your father promised me a certain lifestyle, and the candy shop made it possible. If candy making was truly in your blood, like it was with your father, you would have found another way to carry on that legacy, like opening up your own store or at the very least, setting one up online, but you were never motivated enough to do that."

Never motivated enough to do that?

The words hurt.

"Gillian, I wanted to set up a store for the Sweetery online, but you wouldn't let me. It's hard to appear motivated with zero support. Besides, you own the rights to all of my father's recipes," I informed her. "There's not much I could do without those."

"Oh, please." Gillian brushed dust off the desk. "There are a hundred different ways to make a piece of chocolate, Emma. You do it all the time, making up this concoction or that, but I understand the need to make the excuse. You've always been full of excuses, and to be perfectly frank, I saw that as a good reason to let you make your own way. In the end, that's why I never handed you the shop."

"Why are you telling me this?" I demanded.

The idea of kicking me when I was down jumped to mind. I was tempted to get up and walk out, but I needed to know what was next. If Gillian could wait just a few more weeks so that I could find another way to secure financing, it would still be possible for me to follow through.

"Because." She let out a sigh. "I want you to know that I did my best to teach you how to make your own way. Like I said that night at dinner, I've often hoped you would come to me and make an offer on the shop. You never did. Even now, the way you've handled this particular situation with obtaining a business loan has been a fiasco.

"So, with all of that in mind, I feel I've waited long enough. Talbaccis is still interested in purchasing the shop. I have a contact at the bank who shared the news early this morning that the loan would not go through. I signed the papers agreeing to sell to Talbaccis two hours ago. I do hope you understand."

The world around me went silent. A sharp, metallic ring in my ear was the only thing I could hear, followed by the slow beat of my heart. Moments passed, minutes or perhaps seconds. Then reality set in.

"You signed the papers?" I repeated.

"Yes." She gave a brisk nod. "Quite frankly, I got tired of waiting."

"I can't believe you did that." The words came slowly, like cold caramel. "Gillian, you can't *do* that."

"Emma, I can, and I did." She snapped open her purse and pulled out her cell phone. "It's a shame that I could not have followed through with my intent to sell to you. I have to do what's best for my future. Their offer was not going to last forever, and I couldn't afford to lose it." Getting to her feet, she paused. In a much softer tone, she said, "I am sorry, Emma. It would have meant quite a bit to me to see the candy shop go to you, but I couldn't wait. I really hope you understand."

Understand? I would never understand. Not in a lifetime.

With that, Gillian left. I couldn't figure out what remained in her wake. Determination, anger, sorrow?

There were so many memories in this kitchen. So many beautiful, sweet moments that had shaped my life. Now, all of that was about to go away. The Sweetery was going to be a thing of the past, and there was nothing I could do to change that.

Chapter Thirty

The moment I opened my eyes I had the feeling of being caught in a bad dream. The sun was bright outside the curtains, and I pulled the pillow over my head. There were so many things about everything that had happened that made me feel sick inside that I barely knew where to start.

Yes, Gillian's decision made sense. She'd been more than fair by giving me the chance to buy the shop. I understood that accepting the other deal was the best choice for her, but that didn't make it any easier on me.

Losing the candy shop and the painting in one day was like losing everything I'd ever loved, all over again. For a moment, the future had seemed so clear and so right, and now it was nothing but a big blank space.

Rolling over, I closed my eyes and went back to sleep.

~

I was awakened by the sound of a key jiggling in the lock of the front door, followed by frantic footsteps. Then Kailyn burst in through my bedroom door in a waft of apple-scented perfume.

"Why aren't you picking up your phone?" she demanded. "I've been worried sick."

I had stayed in bed for two days straight, ignoring phone calls, texts, knocks on the door, and even the rumbling in my stomach. By now, I was so disoriented that I could barely process what she'd said. The stare I gave her must have been blank as could be, because she actually looked frightened.

"Okay, hold on." Moments later, she was back, pressing a glass up against my mouth. "Drink this."

Cool water slipped through my dry lips. It tasted incredible, but after the first sip, I drew back. The sour feeling in my stomach couldn't take it, but Kailyn forced it back to my mouth and made me drink. I finished the entire glass and, head pounding, lay back against the pillows.

"I stopped by the store when you didn't answer my calls or texts." Kailyn put her hand on my forehead, as if checking my temperature. "Gillian said you never showed up to work. She told me what happened."

"With the painting or the store?" My voice was like a croak, and I cleared my throat.

"Both." Kailyn frowned. "Hold on. I'll be right back."

She returned with another full glass of water and a plate of sliced apples. I tried one, then pushed it aside. The idea of food did not appeal.

"You have to eat," Kailyn insisted. Then her green eyes studied me with concern. "Emma, tell me what I can do to help you."

The answers that came to mind were glib, but really, they came down to one simple thing.

"You can't." I smoothed the sheets with my hand. "There is absolutely nothing you can do. The store's gone. I have to figure out what's next. Find a job. Tell my grandmother she should prepare to move." Kailyn had opened the window and switched on the ceiling fan, and

I stared up at it, watching the blades whir past the light with a slow, hypnotic effect. "Lydia found my mother. Did I tell you that?"

Kailyn's mouth dropped open, and she grabbed for my hand.

"Did you contact her?" she whispered.

"No."

The word was barely out when Kailyn let out an enormous sigh of relief. "It's just not the time," she said, noting my incredulous look. "You have enough going on. How on earth did Lydia find her?"

In a dull tone, I explained Lydia's history.

"The world never fails to surprise me." Kailyn drummed her fingers against her lips. "I contacted Henry at the police department about the painting. He's going to call you."

I turned to her in surprise. "Why did you do that?"

"Because something stinks," she said. "It doesn't make any sense that your father would hang up a forgery and not tell you or Gillian the history. If he'd sold the real one, he had nothing to lose by telling Gillian the identity of the artist, right? Besides, several people have had access to the candy shop over the years, and I think it's worth looking into."

I set down the glass of water. "Something did dawn on me while I was here resting."

For a split second, it looked like Kailyn considered making a joke but thought better of it. "Tell me."

"What if Gillian took it?" I bit into an apple and the inside of my cheeks tingled at its tart sweetness. "I mean, my father must have shared Montee's true identity with her—she was his wife. That means she would have known what it was worth, and she had access to his files. She knew the painting had been left for me. What would have stopped her from selling the original and putting up a fake? Maybe that's why she told me she didn't care what I did with it—she knew it wasn't real."

Kailyn wrinkled her forehead. "I think she'd have a lot more money, don't you? I mean, I did a little research, and that painting is worth more than a couple of hundred thousand dollars, Emma. It's worth a lot."

The comment made me pull the blankets close. During my time in bed, I'd mindlessly scrolled through my phone several times and had also learned more about K. L. Heathwood's work. The painting would have been worth a fortune, if it had been real.

"Maybe the money is hidden somewhere." I chewed another bite of apple. "Or maybe the painting is hidden somewhere, and she hasn't sold it yet. If she buys a fancy beach house in Florida, who could say she didn't get that money from the sale of the store? It's possible."

"It is possible." Kailyn frowned. "In fact, I wouldn't put it past her."

It was terrible to think that my own stepmother would steal from me, but it made the most sense. If the painting had been taken and not sold by my father, the most likely suspect would be someone close to it.

"The thing that really made me think about it was the fact that I noticed the painting that one day, the day I met Lydia, when her car was going up and down the block . . ." I lay back against the pillow. "That was the same day that the couple noticed it. The professor's husband was in. It seems kind of funny that something that had faded into the background suddenly caught my eye. What if she'd just replaced it and that's why I noticed?"

Kailyn's eyes brightened. "I bet there's a way to tell how recently something was painted. I'm sure of it. Jolene studied art history, and she helps the women's chapter of the Starlight Cove Society with historical artifacts sometimes. She might know how to tell."

Jolene Winters had gone to school with us and was a talented artist in her own right. She had turned her mother's old photo shop into an art gallery. I'd heard it was doing very well, even though I hadn't been there in a while. Either way, I knew she'd be happy to help.

Even though I'd been planning on spending plenty more time in bed, the idea of getting to the bottom of the forgery was much more appealing.

After throwing back the sheets, I got to my feet and yanked on the dress I'd dropped on the floor two days ago. "Let's go find out."

~

It took only a half hour to contact Jolene, get permission to drop by, and take the painting out of the safety-deposit box. It was the middle of the day, and I had forgotten my sunglasses. Considering my eyes were so raw from crying that they actually hurt, Kailyn slid off hers and passed them to me.

"That's what friends are for," she said, when I tried to protest.

The gravel in the drive of the art gallery crunched under the tires of the convertible as we pulled in. The building had seen better days. It needed a new paint job, the porch looked ready to cave in, and the roof sagged under overgrown wisteria. Still, the enormous paintings propped next to the front door and the wind chimes blowing in the breeze made the space seem like an oasis.

"Your work is beautiful," I said, giving Jolene a quick hug. She was so petite that it was like hugging a little blonde doll. "Thank you so much for looking at this for us."

"Well, you had me so intrigued on the phone. I made a space for the painting on the table."

We hadn't told her much over the phone. I appreciated her casual approach, as though people brought her old paintings to assess every day. I laid it down and hung back, feeling almost as nervous as I did the day MacCauley Brandstein appraised it.

Jolene stood over the painting, pulling her white-blonde hair off her shoulders in a waft of sweet orange oil. "Hmm." She picked up a magnifying glass and gave the painting a closer look. "Yeah. No, this is old. For sure."

Kailyn looked surprised. "It is? I really thought you were going to tell us this was painted, like, two weeks ago."

222

"No." She pointed at a corner with a mixing brush from her painting supplies. "See how faded it is here? That's from years of sun damage. This was up in the shop, right?" Her bright-blue eyes met mine. "Who's the artist?"

"I don't really know." Her little white dog was nudging my feet, so I scooped him up and buried my face in his fur. "I'd love to know who painted this. I thought I knew its history, but as it turns out, I don't know much of anything about it that's true."

Jolene tapped the mixing brush to her chin. "Hmm."

My phone rang. The number was blocked.

"Be right back." I set down the dog and slipped onto the porch as Jolene and Kailyn started playing catch-up. "Hello?"

"Emma?" The voice on the other end was gruff and male. "This is Henry with the Starlight Cove Police Department."

My cheeks flushed. Brushing a horsefly away, I said, "I appreciate the call."

"Kailyn Barnes said you wanted to speak to me about a stolen painting?"

I didn't know where to start. Our police chief did not have a reputation for being warm and fuzzy. The last thing I wanted to do was have him dismiss me, which meant making sure I could give him all the facts. But I still didn't feel like I had my head on straight.

"Um, yes. Could I come down to the station?"

That would buy me some time to get my thoughts together.

"Filing a report at the station would be normal protocol." Henry sounded impatient. "Kailyn, however, was quite insistent that I contact you directly."

Because Henry sounded ready to hang up on me, I decided to run him through the full story. There was a long pause on the other end of the line. Then he made some sort of a sound that could have been a chuckle.

"Let me get this straight. You want me to track down a painting by K. L. Heathwood that may or may not have been in your father's possession twenty-five years ago and that could have been taken from the walls of the Sweetery at any point?"

"I'm sorry," I said, embarrassed. The request sounded completely ridiculous. "We shouldn't have asked. I know you're busy."

He gave a hearty sigh. "The best place to start, I think, is to take a look at the note that was provided by the artist and given to your father. We've got a guy who's interested in that sort of thing. He can check it out when we get a minute, and then we can go from there."

The note. MacCauley Brandstein had said there was no way to prove that I was the subject in the painting, and therefore it could have been gifted to anyone. Her words had embarrassed me at the time, but if I could authenticate the note, I'd be one step closer to proving I was in the painting and that my family had once owned the original. Proving that piece of information would be a small step in the right direction.

"Thank you, Henry." I felt a glimmer of hope. "I appreciate it." The wind rattled the trees, and the smell of pine was strong in the air.

"I'll send one of our guys by to pick it up," Henry said. "Can you have it at the candy shop this afternoon?"

"It's at my house." I rattled off the address.

"Good deal." Henry grunted. "I knew your father, kid." His voice took on a kinder tone. "He was a good man, a hard worker. We'll try to help you out the best we can, but with something with this type of history, I can't make any guarantees. Still, we'll do our best."

I hung up and looked out at the woods, thinking. There had to have been a theft somewhere along the way. If the copy of the painting wasn't a recent development, something had happened to the original years ago. Like Henry said, it might be impossible to figure out where it went, but at this point, I didn't have anything else to lose.

The scent of freshly brewed chamomile tea hit me when I walked back in. Jolene offered me a cup, but I shook my head. Kailyn stood in the corner, talking numbers to someone on the phone, probably negotiating a sale.

"Hey, do you care if I take the frame off?" Jolene ran her hands over the wood, her tanned arms flexing with the motion. "Frames have a way of hiding things."

It wasn't like taking off the frame would lower its value.

"Sure," I said. "Go for it."

I leaned against the sharp edges of the table while Jolene separated the wood from the canvas and set the frame aside. Her shoes were off, and a silver anklet shimmered as she made her way around the table, studying the painting from every angle. Suddenly, she said, "Huh."

"What?" I asked.

"Nothing, it's just . . ." Jolene looked from the frame to the canvas. "I'm surprised. He wouldn't have painted this, so what's the frame doing here?"

My heart skipped. "I'm lost. Who?"

"Charles Randolph." She held up a section of the frame, flipped it, and pointed at the corners. They were not held together by nails but by an intricate series of carved, interlocking wooden latches. It was a work of art in itself. "People have been known to buy his artwork just for the frame," she said. "But this painting is not his style at all, so I'm wondering . . ."

"Could he have still painted it, though?" I asked quickly.

"I mean . . ." She clucked her tongue. "No. It's nothing like anything Charles does. He's modern, all the way. The frame is his, though. For sure."

"How could I find him?" My heart pounded at the potential lead. "Maybe he could help me find the painter."

"He's been at the Belden Gallery in town for years," she said. "He's prickly. It depends on his mood whether you'll get any answers." Her dog was half asleep in a dog bed on the floor and grunted as if in agreement.

That didn't sound promising. It would be just my luck lately for this Charles guy to decide he didn't like me and not tell me anything. Either way, it was a lead, and I was grateful.

Kailyn noticed we were packing up and headed back over, still working on her deal. She covered the receiver and mouthed, "Thank you so much" at Jolene, who nodded and walked us to the door.

I was just about to step outside when Jolene touched my arm. "Why do I get the sense that this was about more than the age of the painting?"

"Because it is," I admitted.

"I hope you'll come back at some point and tell me what's going on."

"I'd love to." I looked down at the painting and shook my head. "But for now, Jolene, I don't even know."

Chapter Thirty-One

I called the Belden Gallery the second we were in the car. They informed me that Charles was on vacation and would return on Monday. I left a message, asking to have him call me back as soon as possible. Then I sank back into the seat.

"You okay?" Kailyn asked.

"Frustrated, I think," I said. "Too much time has passed. I don't think we're ever going to figure this out."

"We just have to be patient," Kailyn said. "The fact that this Charles guy made the frame is a strong lead."

I could only hope.

Kailyn dropped me off at home with a container of chicken curry salad, grapes, and some crackers from the deli at the corner grocery.

"Eat every bite," she said. "I'll have Henry stop by to make sure you did."

"I don't doubt it." I shut the car door and tapped it, my mind still on Jolene's discovery. "Thank you. Seriously. I don't know that I'd be out of bed yet if it wasn't for you."

"Speaking of Cody Henderson," she said cheerfully, "have you talked with him?"

"Funny." I ran my hand through my hair. It really needed to be washed. "No, not yet. He called and left a message, but like everyone, I haven't called him back."

The truth of the matter was, I didn't know that I was ready to talk with Cody. He was so great, and he had his life together. The fact that I'd spent our dinner talking his ear off about a nonprofit that now would never happen made me feel like a complete failure. It was a miracle I hadn't told him about buying the store, or I'd never be able to look him in the face again.

Kailyn must have sensed my hesitation. "Don't blow him off, Emma. I get it if you're scared, and I get it that it's bad timing, but he really is one of the good ones. If you need some time, tell him."

"I will." The words felt like a fib, because really, I couldn't imagine being bold enough to bring it up.

Lydia's side of the house looked quiet as I keyed into my apartment. Since Cody was on my mind, I was curious how Jamal's day had gone with him a few days back. He and Cody could have just sat there and watched soccer all day, for all I knew. The lack of information helped me realize that I had been hopelessly out of touch, but on the other hand, I didn't have the energy to pick up my life right where I'd left it. Things were still too much of a mess.

I sat down at the kitchen table, then jumped to see a blur of black run across my backyard. "What on earth?" I rushed to the kitchen window and stared in surprise.

There was a black lab leaping up into the air to catch a Frisbee thrown by none other than Cody himself. Jamal raced after the dog, tackling it and laughing hysterically as it licked his face. It had been a while, but I recognized the dog as Captain Ahab, the chocolate lab from Search and Rescue. The dog was known for making instant friends with every little boy in town.

"Heads up!" Cody's shout rang through the windowpane, and he tossed the Frisbee again. The dog took off and snapped it up in his white teeth. Cody turned then, looking toward the house. Quickly, I ducked away from the window but not before confusion clouded his face. I sank to the floor, heart pounding.

It unnerved me to think that he had built such a strong relationship with Jamal simply because I'd asked him to. The fact that he was in my backyard, playing Frisbee with a dog and a boy made him even more irresistible than ever. But I hadn't showered in two days, my eyes were still dry from crying, and I felt like a shell of the person he'd seen on the date the other night.

Even though it felt devious, I pretty much army-crawled to the kitchen table, reached up and grabbed my food, and sneaked it off to my bedroom. I'd explain it to him another time, if he was still willing to listen. For now, though, I needed to figure myself out.

Unfortunately, Cody was not about to let me do that alone. He knocked on the door and when I didn't answer, sent a text.

Sometimes it's better to let people in.

I held the phone for a brief moment before texting back.

I'm not good at that. But see you in a minute.

Cody and I sat on the couch together, my feet in his lap. He rubbed his hand gently over my socks as I told him the whole story. Then he shook his head.

"That's incredible," he said. "That's a lot for you to deal with."

"The fact that Gillian and I have our issues hasn't helped matters."

He gave a slow nod. "She doesn't exactly seem like the motherly type."

"That's the understatement of the century." Maybe because of my mood or simply because he was so easy to talk to, I told him our history. "Eventually, I had to accept the fact that I wasn't meant to be a daughter."

"What do you mean?" Cody gave me a searching look.

I fidgeted. "I don't know. I guess there's something about me that drove away both of the women who had the option to be my mother."

"Don't put yourself down. Words are powerful."

I slid my feet off him and sat up. "I'm just saying that the whole thing is messed up. I've always wanted kids, badly, but when the time comes, how am I going to know how to be a good mother? I don't have the first clue."

"Sure you do. You're always trying to take care of everybody else." Cody folded his hands behind his head, his arm muscles flexing with the effort. "The fact of the matter is, you got shafted. It's a shame you're blaming yourself because of the shortcomings of the two women who could have raised you. It has nothing to do with you."

His words made me uncomfortable. Mainly, the fact that they were so kind.

"It has to have had something to do with me," I said. "If I had been the type of daughter Gillian wanted, she would have put the time and effort into raising me, into getting to know me, into . . ." I wanted to say *loving me*, but the words choked in my throat. "I don't want to complain. My grandmother was phenomenal. The days I shared with her in this house were some of the best of my life, and I wouldn't trade them for the world. I just wonder about it sometimes. Why some people have everything and others have to struggle. I'm thinking about Lydia right now, not me, by the way. Because I didn't have to struggle."

"Yeah, you did." He took my hand, running his thumb over my skin. "Your experience was different than hers, but it wasn't easy. You have every right to have emotions about what happened, and they don't have to be positive.

"You know, I miss my parents every day. Sure, other people have it worse, but you know what? It sucks. It sucks that my grandparents had to raise me and my brothers those last few years, it sucks that my parents weren't there to help us out, and it sucks that I miss them every day." In his eyes, I could see that the pain was still raw. "Yeah, I could sit here and think about all the people in the world who never had parents, like how you never had a mom and how you lost your dad when you were young and compare myself and say wow, I had it good. But you know what? I didn't. It wasn't fair. That's the way it was for me, and your story is the way it was for you. Comparing it to anyone else isn't going to change it."

The words caused a sting at the back of my eyes that I didn't want to feel. Cody was wrong. There were a lot of people who had it worse than I did.

When I started to argue, he held up his hand. "Emma, sometimes it's okay not to be happy," he said quietly. "It can destroy you, trying to fight the dark. Spit it out. Get it out. You'll feel better in the morning."

I shook my head. "I'm not bitter. Sorry if I gave you that impression. It's all a part of the past."

"No, it's not. Gillian's still giving you a hard time, and you're still thinking it's because of something you did. Let it go. It's not your fault."

Well, Cody Henderson just seemed determined to be the expert on feelings, and that was fine. Maybe he still harbored anger from what had happened with his parents, but I did not want to waste any more time reliving bad memories. Life was too short.

"It's getting late," I said, getting to my feet.

He squeezed my hand. "I should head home."

Too many emotions coursed through me. It felt like a big mistake to talk to him about everything that was going on, because I didn't need to share that type of thing with people. Families were complicated. That didn't mean I had to waste a ton of time on self-reflection.

The people who do that are the ones who are afraid to just live their life, I wanted to tell Cody. *That's not me.*

There were plenty of people who had it worse.

∼

I was still trying to convince myself of that fact the next day, on the drive to Joe's memorial.

The fir trees passed by my window in a blur as I headed downstate, keeping one eye on the clock and my foot on the gas. I'd left late, because for a moment, I'd almost skipped. Then, reality had set in. Honoring my late fiancé was the right thing to do, and I had to be there.

The church parking lot was full when I pulled in. The spire was tall and bright in the early-morning sun, and the sight brought me right back to Joe's funeral.

It was hard to believe it had been ten years since his death.

We were supposed to celebrate anniversaries, Joe, but not like this.

In the church, the fragrance of flowers was heavy in the air. The ones I'd sent, a cheerful bouquet of roses, lilies, and baby's breath, rested on a table full of framed photographs. The pictures of me and Joe were oldies but goodies, and I hadn't seen them in years.

There we were at his college graduation, kissing while he held up his diploma. I'd always loved the one in the Rockies with the cutesy matching sun shirts we'd bought on a rare trip to a mall. Finally, there was a series of our engagement photos, taken on the dock at his family's house.

Gosh, we look young.

Young and so incredibly naive. Even though we were planning for our lives in the real world, we had no sense of the road waiting for us ahead.

"Emma. I'm so glad you came." His mother wore a lilac lace gown. She looked older than I remembered, but there was no trace of sadness in her eyes.

I hugged her and then his father. He looked so much like Joe, with his earnest expression and the dark eyes that turned down at the corners.

"It's a nice showing," he said, and I nodded.

The church was full. There seemed to be a lot of people my age, and suddenly I felt nervous. It had been so long.

Joe's mother seemed to notice my unease. "Would you like to sit with the family, Emma?"

Was it still right to do that? His brother and sister were already in the pew. I'd sat with them at the funeral, but so much time had passed.

My cheeks burned as I walked up the aisle, feeling incredibly out of place. It wasn't a feeling I'd expected to have, but it was there, coupled with a vague impatience that I was back in the same spot, once again mourning this loss.

Spit it out; get it out. You'll feel better in the morning.

Cody's words rang in my ears. Letting out a breath, I slid into the pew.

The program Joe's parents had put together was well done. It was printed on a heavy ivory-colored card stock, with an adorable picture of Joe's smiling face on the front cover. Each page was full of thoughts and quotes and memories.

It was the type of remembrance people made once there was time to do it, and I imagined Joe's parents working for months to get it just so. I held it tight as the service moved through the acoustic versions of songs he had loved, a heartfelt sermon from the priest, and a general sense of celebration, not sadness. Joe's brother even made a funny speech about how Joe just had to try everything first, even death, and people laughed out loud at the jokes and anecdotes.

For me, though, Cody's words got in the way. His warning about anger and bitterness. Those were two things I'd been more afraid of than anything to face. Yet, as I sat there, the sun filtering through the stained glass window, I couldn't fight the sense of rage building inside of me.

Ten years ago, I'd been engaged to be married to the love of my life. My future was perfect, and the possibilities endless. Then, out of nowhere, the world shattered.

Joe shouldn't have died. He was one of the kindest, most compassionate, loving people on the planet. But because he made the choice to pick up a club sandwich with a side of fries and onion rings—I knew, because I'd asked for every detail—his future, our future, was cut short.

I was so angry with the man who'd attacked him. Terrance Grange. That evil, hate-eyed man now sat in prison, rotting for what he'd done. Through the years, I'd had all sorts of conversations with him in my mind where I forced myself to offer tears, hugs, and forgiveness. But now, I couldn't help but think the man deserved to be exactly where he was.

The thoughts sat in my heart like a stone through the final hymns and then the drive out to the graveyard.

The group gathered around Joe's grave. It was hot, and the air smelled like fresh grass. In the distance, the groundskeeper was mowing the lawn, which made it difficult to hear his mother as she read the eulogy.

Something about the imperfection made the situation bearable. Still, I gritted my teeth, wishing it could all be over. I only breathed easy once Joe's father spoke the final words and thanked the crowd for coming.

His mother turned to me. "Thank you for being a part of this. All of it." Her words seemed to encompass not only the memorial but also his life.

I nodded, holding her tight. His family paid their last respects and then headed out. They were hosting a dinner at the house, but I had declined the invitation.

The lawn mower had stopped, and birds chirped in the bright silence. I approached Joe's headstone. After sinking into the grass, I rested my head against it.

The limestone was warm in the heat. I closed my eyes and tried to imagine being back in his arms. But the time was too far out of reach, and finally, I got to my feet.

I stood in silence for what felt like years. Then I said, "I'm angry, Joe. I'm mad at the situation, but . . ." I closed my eyes. "I'm also mad at you."

There was nothing in me that had ever blamed Joe for what had happened. But now, disappointment nearly consumed me.

Why did you have to get involved?

If he wouldn't have gotten involved, he would still be here today. It had been a terrible risk. It had been irresponsible and had cost us everything.

He had been too wide eyed, too eager to help, and hadn't thought through the potential outcome. Still, the way that it had ended never could have occurred to him, or he would have made a different choice.

Would have, could have. None of that matters, in the end.

"It's not fair," I told him. "None of this is fair. There was so much that we were supposed to do, to be . . ." My voice echoed in the silence of the graveyard, and I stopped talking, worried someone would overhear. Then I pushed forward. "I have missed you every day since you've been gone, and I've got to tell you this sucks. I've watched my friends get married, have babies, and do all the things that we were supposed to do, and even though I have tried so hard to be happy for everyone, there are times that I'm not, and it makes me feel like the worst person in the world. There are so many things I thought we'd do, and instead, I've been out here struggling to do anything and failing at everything. My life is not what it was supposed to be, and . . ."

The deep letters of his name carved into the headstone blurred beneath my tears. Then, I looked around at the grass, the trees, the sky, as if Joe might suddenly appear to take me back to a time when the world was full of possibility. Instead, I rested my hand on top of the headstone.

"I love you, Joe," I whispered. "I loved you the first moment I saw you. But I can't keep hanging on. I have to let you go."

My mind ran through the moments we'd shared, the memories that had meant so much. The day we drove for ten hours, stopping at small towns across the state in search of the perfect ice cream cone. The ski trip where he waited until the last minute to confess he was scared of heights and couldn't ride the lift, so we spent the weekend in the hot tub instead. The winter nights in his first rental house in front of the fire, where we took turns reading to one another until we fell asleep.

"I'll never forget you," I told him.

The wind blew then, a slight breeze that brushed against my hair like a kiss.

I stood in silence for another moment, and finally, turned and walked away.

Chapter Thirty-Two

Over the next several days, Gillian left a handful of messages that ranged from angry to sympathetic, asking whether or not I intended to return to work. It was the final message that made my decision for me.

"You should be here to the end," she said. "I know things did not work out the way you wanted or the way I wanted, but sometimes, that's life. I would like you to help so that when I shutter the doors, you'll feel it was done in a way that honors your father's legacy."

My throat got tight, and quickly I erased the message.

But the next morning, I arrived right at nine-thirty. I was surprised to see the progress that had been made in just a few days. Signs had been posted announcing the impending closure, and several of the shelves were already empty. The majority of the merchandise had been moved up to the candy counter, and the sight of all of it was almost enough to make me turn and walk out the door.

Ashley rushed over to me, her wide eyes worried. "Emma, I'm so sorry. I heard what happened, and all I can say is you would have been the best owner ever. I can't believe it didn't work out."

"Well, that's the way it goes. I gave it my best shot, but in the end, things happen how they're going to happen, right?"

My voice was cool and stilted. To be honest, it had been a while since I'd spoken like that. It sounded like the type of blasé answer I used to give when people would express their condolences about Joe, and I was too afraid to give them a legitimate response for fear I'd burst into tears.

Keep it together. It's not her problem; it's yours.

"Still." Ashley shook her head. "I'm sorry."

"You've done a lot," I said, giving a pointed look around. "Feels like I've been gone longer than I have."

"Gillian's been here." Ashley pulled out the folder with the list of closing assignments. "She's been pushing through this stuff. We're supposed to spend the majority of our time on this list, because everything's supposed to be cleared out in two weeks."

"Two weeks?" I stepped closer to one of the signs and took the time to read it.

THANK YOU FOR YEARS OF LOYAL PATRONAGE. WE ARE PLEASED TO ANNOUNCE THE START OF A NEW CHAPTER IN OUR LIVES. THE SWEETERY WILL BE UNDER NEW OWNERSHIP BEGINNING AUGUST 1 AND RUN BY THE TALBACCIS FAMILY OF CHOCOLATES. BEST WISHES TO YOU ALL, AND THANK YOU AGAIN FOR YOUR PATRONAGE.

Wow. The sale of the store really was in full swing.

Once again, I almost turned and walked out the door.

Instead, the morning passed in a blur. When Gillian breezed in, I had to step into the back for a moment, because I found it hard to even look at her. Yes, I had failed, and as a result, she had every right to do what she wanted with the shop. Still, I didn't respect the decision. My father never would have encouraged her to sell the Sweetery to anyone other than me, especially since I still wanted to carry on his legacy.

"Emma, come on out when you get the chance," Gillian called back into the kitchen a few minutes later. "There's lots to do."

It was impressive that she could act like we were in the middle of a project together.

A huge part of me wanted to walk away and let her handle it herself. I would regret it, though. Like she'd said on the phone, I needed to see the sale through to the end, to make sure that she handled it in a way that left my father's reputation intact.

When the activity in the store hit a lull, Gillian gestured for me to join her at a table in the window, where she had been sorting through paperwork.

Sliding off her glasses, she said, "Do you have any additional news about the painting?"

"The police are looking into it." I glanced up at the blank spot on the wall, then looked at her. "I need to have all the necessary information to send their way, so I'm working on gathering up a couple of different leads."

The comment was a test. Something to see if Gillian would respond and implicate herself in having something to do with its disappearance.

Gillian wrinkled her brow, as best as the Botox would allow. "The police? That seems like a waste of resources. Besides, how could they get to the bottom of something that happened so long ago?"

Interesting. She did seem irritated the police were involved.

Irritated, or nervous?

"Cold case," I said. "They do that all the time."

"For murders." She gave a little laugh. "Not lost paintings."

We sat in silence. The conversation seemed to be over, so I got up to leave.

"Do the police have any leads?"

"No, not yet." I eyed her. "They're analyzing the note from Montee to prove it's authentic. Hopefully, that will convince them that the original did in fact belong to our family in the first place." Then, because that sounded a little too much like I was talking about us as a team, I added, "Me and my father."

Something I couldn't read flickered in her eyes. "Let me know how it turns out."

I was relieved when it was lunch, and I could step outside for some fresh air. Gillian had already stripped the shop of so many details, like the old photographs in the hallway that gave a pictorial glimpse into Starlight Cove's history. It was almost like she was looting the place. It was hard to believe it would be entirely empty in just a few short weeks. It hadn't been empty in over thirty years.

My phone buzzed as I headed down Main Street to grab a sandwich at Towboat. The number was blocked, which meant that it could be the police department. Eagerly, I picked it up.

"Emma? Dean Harrington."

"Hi, Dean," I said. "It's so good to hear your voice. It's been a minute."

Back in high school, Dean Harrington had been almost too good looking with his thick dark hair and haunted eyes, but he had always been a nice guy. He was older and had hung out with a tough crowd, and the whispers around town had said he'd fallen into drugs. It was a surprise when I'd first heard he'd joined the Starlight Cove police force, but rumor had it he'd turned his life around.

"Things good?" he asked.

We chatted for a couple of minutes; then Dean got down to business.

"So, I'm calling with some news," he said. "You got a minute?"

"Yeah." I took a seat on an empty bench. "Go ahead." I tried to sound nonchalant, rather than nervous.

"So, there wasn't much in the way of crime this week." We both chuckled, because around here, there wasn't much in the way of crime most weeks. Of course, that would be a different story if I could prove someone stole the painting. "So, we had some time on our hands to take a look at your note. One of our guys is trained on handwriting analysis, and he determined that, although it resembles K. L. Heathwood's penmanship, it's a well-crafted forgery. The letters are traced, which means that it could have been lifted off of anything that he wrote and pieced together. Henry doesn't feel the topic warrants further investigation, as there's no proof that the painting belonged to your family. I'm sorry, Emma. I'm sure you were hoping for better news."

I closed my eyes. "Thanks, Dean." There were so many other things I wanted to say, but that was all that would come out.

We hung up, and I kept my eyes closed, blocking out the sun and the traffic moving up and down the street. Instead of laughing and bike bells, I heard the whoosh of my heart.

My father had *faked* the note. Faked it. Why would he have done that? It wasn't like he was trying to impress anyone with his knowledge about art, especially not me. I was just a little kid. So, what was with the charade?

That type of deception was so far beyond the scope of who I believed him to be that I couldn't help but wonder if the things Gillian had said about him and their marriage could, in fact, be true.

You're blowing this out of proportion. Obviously, he was just playing pretend for you.

That made sense, actually. My father could have invented a fun game where he pretended Montee had gifted the finished painting to me, simply because he knew how much I'd loved his paintbrushes. Then, maybe the note had ended up getting filed when he died and became a piece of truth. That would be fine except that, like so many things lately, it had made me look like a fool.

I was tired of feeling like a fool, but I was the one letting it happen. It was time to start protecting myself.

Picking up my phone, I called the store.

"Ashley, I'm sorry to do this," I said when she answered. "I'm not coming back. I thought I could, but it's not going to work out. Do you mind passing the message along to Gillian?"

It probably seemed like a cowardly move to her, but to me, it felt brave. It was about time I accepted that things were not the way I wanted them to be and that if I wanted that to change, I needed to take the steps to change them. It was also time to accept the fact that the painting was long gone, right along with the perfect life it depicted. That moment was a slice of time, not meant to last forever.

It was well past time for me to say goodbye.

Chapter Thirty-Three

Gillian stopped by my house after work. She must have felt guilty about what had happened, because a visit from her was a rare occurrence. I considered not answering the door but figured it was easier to hear what she had to say.

"I brought you soup," she said, holding out a small bag. "It's chicken noodle."

That surprised me. I could not think of one moment in the past when Gillian had bothered to bring me soup.

"I'm not sick, Gillian." Taking it, I added, "Thank you, though."

She hovered in the doorway. Since she'd spent the day at the store, she wasn't wearing a flashy suit or dress but a pair of simple tan slacks and a lavender shirt. The casual clothes made her look nearly human or at the very least, approachable.

"Did you want to come in?" I asked, since she was still standing there.

"No. I'd just like to help." She lifted her chin. "What can I do to make this transition easier?"

The words were so clinical. To her, selling off my father's legacy was a transition. To me, it was a death, and I'd had too many of those.

"Nothing. I'm not coming back to the store," I said. "Don't try to talk me into it. You can celebrate your transition to Talbaccis. I'm not going to be there to pretend I support it, but I won't stand in your way. We've never had much of a relationship. I don't think we really need to keep pretending."

"Emma." She drew back in surprise.

"Sorry." I shrugged. "I'm just telling the truth."

Gillian pressed her lips together, her eyes bright in the light of the evening. "You know, Emma," she said, "letting go of the store has made me think a lot about the past and about . . . well, about us. I hope you know it was a tough decision, sending you to live with your grandmother."

I couldn't believe we were talking about this. Not now. I wanted to end the conversation and walk away, but for once, I wanted to let her know how I felt. Not because it would change anything but to let her know that her actions had hurt me, and I wasn't okay with that.

"It couldn't have been that tough," I said, with a little laugh. "Or you wouldn't have done it."

Gillian frowned. "It's not that simple, Emma."

"You know what wasn't simple?" The wood of the door felt rough beneath my hand. "Losing both you and my father at once. No matter how much I loved my grandmother, there was never a moment I stopped wishing you would come back. But now, Gillian? Now, I can't wait to see you walk away."

She looked stunned. Then, she opened her mouth as if to protest, and I held up my hand.

"Go."

Gillian lifted her chin. Then, she gave a tight smile and headed back to the car. The lightning bugs flashed in a sudden whirlwind of light, creating a surprisingly beautiful picture.

Part of me wanted to apologize to her, to call after her to come back. I couldn't, though. Because when it came to erasing a lifetime of hurt, a bowl of chicken soup and a couple of carefully chosen words could only do so much.

~

By Tuesday, I still hadn't heard from Charles Randolph, the artist who had crafted the frame for the painting. I wanted to learn more about his connection to the piece, but also I was curious to see how well he had known my father. Given how much of my family history was being erased with each nail stripped from the store, I wanted to preserve what still remained.

Belden Gallery was located only two blocks away from Jolene's studio. I considered dropping in, but I didn't want to risk bothering him. Instead, I called the gallery once again.

"Sorry, who?" he said, after hearing my name.

"Emma Laurent. I left a message while you were out." He was silent, so I added, "You knew my father. He used to own the Sweetery? I was hoping we could sit down and chat."

"Is there a purpose?" he asked.

"It's sentimental," I said, which was half true. "I don't know how often you get down to Main Street, but my stepmother is in the process of selling the candy shop. I'm trying to make sure that all of the important memories don't get overlooked."

"I see." He gave a little sigh. "The gallery's next to the Parker Lounge if you want to grab a drink there in an hour."

My pulse increased at the immediacy of the offer. "Great," I said quickly. "I'll be there."

Once we hung up, I picked up a photograph of my father and studied it for a moment. It was rare that I actually took the time to look at him. The photograph had been taken out on a dock, sometime in the early spring. He had a straight, long nose, and his hairline extended high into his forehead, giving his face an even longer appearance. The generous curve of his lower lip, always turning his face up into a smile, and the cheerful wrinkles by his eyes, made him look handsome and friendly.

In the picture, he wore a black T-shirt, some sort of overshirt, and a dual-colored windbreaker. I hadn't thought of the windbreakers in a while, but he'd had at least ten of them in different colors, blue with a red collar, green with a yellow collar, orange with a green collar. They were as snuggly as a parachute. I could still remember the soft crinkle the fabric made when I buried my face into his shoulder for a hug.

I didn't know exactly what I was trying to find by meeting with the artist. Or what I was trying to find these days, period. But everything in me said that chatting with this Charles guy was the right move.

Parker Lounge was a wood-paneled bar off a small steak house a few streets over from Main Street. It was upscale and played jazz on the weekends, but it had always seemed too old for me, so I never came in. Now, I breathed in the faded scent of cigars that lingered in the wallpaper and spotted a man in a large leather chair by a fire in the corner. It had to be Charles. I'd seen him before around town but had never had a reason to put the face to the name.

"Hi," I said, walking up to greet him. "A fire during the summer? That's fancy."

Charles was younger than I anticipated. Midfifties, maybe, with shaved black hair and small, round silver-rimmed spectacles. He was well dressed for his work at the gallery and wore a simple platinum band around one finger. The spicy aroma of a Manhattan lingered in the air.

"It's a good place to be. Would you like something to drink? The bartender will be back in a minute." He picked up his glass and swirled it, ice clinking, and gave me a sardonic grin. "Technically, they don't open until eleven, but they've given up on trying to follow the rules with me."

"Did you ever come here with my father?" I settled into the leather chair across from him. "It seems like his type of place."

"It was definitely his type of place." Charles took another sip. "We came here once or twice. It might have been where we met, actually. Oh, who am I kidding? I know exactly where we met. I've been at the gallery next door my entire career. Your father came in one afternoon, and he was one of the first to ever compliment my work. I appreciated that."

"I love hearing that," I said. "Do you have a picture of any of your work?"

He frowned. "Well, you could look at a picture, or you could consider the entire collection I have in the gallery. Two steps away."

"Oh," I said, embarrassed. "I haven't been."

"Story of my life." He took a long drink. "No one really cares. Trying to make a living as an artist is about as effective as trying to keep this glass full."

"It's not that I don't care," I said quickly. "I love art. I'm just afraid to go into galleries because I don't know anything about it, and I'm afraid I'll look foolish."

Charles gave me a surprised look. "Really?"

I shrugged. "Yeah."

We sat in silence for a moment. The waitress brought my drink, and I tried it, surprised at the sharpness of the alcohol so early in the morning. It was good, though, and made the situation seem cozy instead of awkward.

"Actually, I have seen some of your work," I said, the spice of the drink warming my tongue. "There's a painting that's hung in the Sweetery for years. I just discovered that you made the frame."

He sat back in his chair with a thud. "Yes. I did."

"It's beautiful," I said, hoping the praise would make him feel better. "I've been told you would not have painted the portrait, but I was hoping you know who did."

The fake fire crackled in the silence that followed.

"No," Charles said in a tone that was completely unconvincing. Before I could argue, he said, "Even if I did . . . some secrets aren't meant to be told, my dear." He swirled his drink, the ice tinkling in the glass. "I gave my word to your father, you see, and I don't break promises. Especially not to dead men. Did you know you look like him? I'm having a hard time looking at you without being pulled right back into that time."

The comment caught me off guard. The picture of my mother also jumped to mind. It was so strange that I could now think, *Yes, I might look like him, but I have my mother's eyes.*

Charles fidgeted with the platinum band on his finger. "It hurt to lose your father, you know. It took me to some dark times."

"I didn't realize you were that close," I said.

Charles squinted at me. "I would have liked to be much closer. It was not for lack of trying, my dear." He let out a sigh and sat back in his chair. "Emma, you should know that I loved your father. I used every trick in the book to try and make him love me back. He was still willing to be my friend, in spite of my antics, but your stepmother became jealous, so that was that."

"Wait." My shoulders tensed. "What do you mean, my stepmother became jealous?"

He rolled his eyes. "She had a problem with how much time he spent with me."

I finally pieced it together. "You're C," I said. "You wrote the love letter she found."

He took another drink. "You know about that? I'm touched."

My pulse quickened as I tried to process this. If Charles had sent love letters, Gillian had been wrong about my father betraying her. The hurt and the heartache were for nothing. Unless . . .

"*Were* you and my father involved?" I demanded.

"Of course not." He let out a small laugh. "He wasn't interested in men. And goodness, when Gillian found that letter, your father gave me such a stern talking to that I was nearly scared straight. It would have never worked out."

Then why did the letter say what it did?

"Gillian told me that letter talked about how much you loved my father's passion," I said. "And the importance of keeping his secret . . ."

Suddenly, it hit me.

"The painting," I said suddenly. "You were talking about the painting. You didn't just make the frame. You *were* the artist."

Charles finished his drink. "Perhaps too lofty of a term, but yes, I was . . ." He made a face. "The artist."

Of course. It's so obvious. But Gillian had been so convinced . . .

This news would mean everything to her. For so many years, she'd believed the man she'd loved with all her heart did not love her back. How ironic that her instincts had been right to dislike the painting, because in the end, it *had* been the thing that had pushed them apart, just not in the way she thought.

"Did you work off a photograph?" I asked, leaning forward. "Or the original?"

There was still a chance my father had taken a photograph of the original painting and, since I was in it, hired someone to make a copy.

"No, I did not work off a picture," he said, as if offended. "I copied the painting, stroke for stroke."

"You did?" I squeezed the arm of the chair. "Really?"

"Of course." Charles raised his eyebrows. "Do you know the identity of the original artist? Your father would not tell me, and I've had my suspicions."

"K. L.—"

"Heathwood." He smiled. "I knew it. I knew, deep down, once he became famous and I started to see his work everywhere. I knew that piece like the back of my hand. I sat for hours in the back of the chocolate shop in the midafternoon in the winter, watching the rays of sun fall against the windows, to better understand how he captured the light. Then, I would sneak off to the storage room where we had set up my studio and do the work, so that no one would see. It was a brilliant study, and really, invaluable training."

"Why did my father have you make the reproduction?" I asked.

"To protect it." Charles fiddled with his ring. "K. L. Heathwood was coming up at that time. The painting was quite extraordinary. Your father knew what he had, and he was so convinced of the value that he didn't want to risk anything happening to it."

"Do *you* know what happened to it?"

He peered at me. "You don't?"

It dawned on me that Charles was one of the only people in town, if not the only person in town, who knew my father had had the original. The tone in his voice and his body posture seemed completely sincere. Still, even if he hadn't known the identity of the artist, he'd known the painting was a valuable, important piece.

Could he have taken it? The idea felt like an outrageous accusation, given the situation, but so much of this had been a guessing game.

"It's kept under lock and key," I said, watching him closely.

His eyes lit up. "Oh, would you mind terribly if I came to see it? I'm sorry if that sounds bold, but you called me, and it was one of the greatest masterpieces I've ever seen."

No. It wasn't him, which was good news. I liked this guy, and I liked his affection for my father. It wasn't necessary to add him to the list of suspects, even though Gillian was the only person still on it.

"I've often wished to see it again," he said, cradling his empty glass in his hand. The glass was crystal, and the light from the fire filtered through it. "The chill of the outdoor evening contrasted with the warmth of the interior . . ." He gave a delighted shudder. "It was the work of a master. It's what made the painting so great. That's why your father wanted the duplicate to hang in the shop. He loved everything about it but knew the original was too valuable. And the time I spent with him as I recreated it, that was valuable to me as well."

"I'll show it to you one day." I took a final sip and got to my feet. "I really appreciate all the information, Charles. For what it's worth, that painting—your painting—has held my heart since I was a child."

His eyes lit up. "What a kindness to say such a thing." He sat back in his chair, looking delighted at the praise. "Now I'll spend the rest of the day dreaming about painting the impossible, thanks to you."

The maroon carpet was quiet beneath my feet, and I made it as far as the door when another thought struck me. Turning, I called, "Hey, Charles?" He squinted at me. "What did my father love most about the painting?"

His face broke into a smile. "The fact that it had everything that he loved deeply, all in one spot. Except whiskey, I suppose. But if you look behind the counter in the painting, you'll find an empty bottle."

Whiskey? There wasn't a whiskey bottle in the painting.

But sure enough, the moment I got home, I studied the painting and found a shadowy bottle tucked below the cash register. It was a small detail. Something where, if you didn't know to look for it, it never would have been seen.

Chapter Thirty-Four

This news was bigger than my anger at Gillian. The moment I was on my bike, I called her and briefed her on the meeting. For a moment, she tried to act like she didn't want to know but then listened in silence as I told her all about it.

"I asked him about his relationship with my father," I said. "Gillian, he said that he was attracted to him but that my father nearly scared him straight with a lecture. The love letter that you saw, the big secret it mentioned? That was the secret about the duplicate. He wasn't having an affair, with C or anyone else."

Within the silence on the other end, I thought I heard Gillian crying. "That's good to know, Emma," she said softly. "Thank you for telling me all this."

The relief in her voice was such that I was glad I'd shared the news. Part of me felt that she didn't deserve the truth, but on the other hand, her relationship with my father had meant everything to her. She deserved to know that the man she had loved so intensely had, in fact, loved her back.

I sloped down a hill toward my house and braked in surprise to see Lydia on the front porch, wringing her hands. Her face was red from crying.

"Jamal is missing." The words came out strangled. "Emma, I took a nap and when I woke up, he was gone. His backpack, most of his clothes—"

"The video game?" I demanded.

"Yes."

In another situation, we might have laughed. But now, as the light cast long shadows from the trees, I swallowed hard. "You're sure he's not at the park?"

Lydia's hair frizzed out around her head as if she'd been tugging on it, and she paced back and forth on the porch. "I've checked," she said. "I've checked everywhere. With Cody, Search and Rescue, the library, the park. No one has seen him."

I thought for a minute.

He couldn't have gotten far. There wasn't public transportation in town, but there were tons of people. He could have approached anyone to give them a song and dance, maybe even got into a stranger's car. The thought made me shudder.

"I'm calling Cody," I decided.

He picked up on the first ring.

"Jamal is missing," I blurted out. I ran him through all the places Lydia had looked, and Cody's tone went as serious as mine.

"I'll call the police and get Henry on it," he said. "Why don't you drive around and see if you can spot him? He should be easy to catch up with unless he stole someone's bike."

That was, unfortunately, a possibility. Few people locked up their bikes in Starlight Cove, because there wasn't the need. It would be easy for Jamal to swipe one. That would be just as dangerous as getting in a strange car, because the roads on the outskirts of town were narrow, and drivers didn't always look for bicyclists on the road.

"I'll get out there and start looking once I've made some calls," Cody said.

253

"Thanks. Talk soon." I hung up. Turning to Lydia, I said, "You're in no shape to drive. Let's take my car. If it doesn't work, I'll drive yours."

My grandmother's car had been parked in the garage for so long that I wasn't sure the battery would start, but we had to try.

The garage was next to the house, and its door hand operated. It lifted with a scream. I hoped we'd find Jamal crouched inside with the cobwebs, clutching his backpack and a box of chocolates. The garage was empty, though, but for the odor of old gasoline. Thank goodness my grandmother's old Chevrolet started with a thunderous roar.

"Cody's going to contact the police," I said as we pulled out. "We'll probably get a call here in a minute."

"No!" Lydia spoke so loudly that I swerved. "No police."

My blood went cold. The fact that she didn't want to talk to the police brought every suspicion I'd had about her to the forefront.

What is she hiding?

"Lydia," I said, my voice shaking. "Why don't you want to involve the police?"

Her face crumpled. "They'll think I'm a negligent mother. They'll put me on a list."

I exhaled slowly, feeling almost dizzy with relief. "No, they won't," I said gently. "They'll do everything they can to help."

Sliding on my sunglasses, I debated which road to drive down first. "We'll go down each street, one at a time, moving farther and farther back. Be on the lookout for playhouses or anything that he might try and hide in." Turning onto the first residential street, I said, "The police will help find him, Lydia. I know they will." My phone rang with an unidentified number. "That's them."

She sank lower in her seat as if trying to hide as I picked up.

"Emma, it's Dean Harrington." He sounded much more serious than the time we'd spoken about art and the forged note. "Cody Henderson reported a child missing. We have the units out. He's already supplied us with a photograph, but I'll need additional information.

It would also be a big help if you know the last thing he was wearing. Cody said you're with the child's mother?"

"Yes, hold on." I put the phone on speaker. "He needs to know the last thing he was wearing and some general information." Usually, I lacked the ability to drive and talk on the phone, but my fear had me in some weird underwater state that helped me to focus on talking, driving, looking for Jamal, and picking up on small nuances, like the fact that Lydia really did not want to talk to the police. She was hunched down in her seat, staring at the phone with dread.

"Ma'am?" Dean said. "Can I get your son's full name, please?"

Lydia looked at me with panic in her eyes. It hit me that she could have been in a state of emotional shock. Grabbing a water bottle out of my purse, I said, "Drink this. Hey, Dean, I think the mother is freaking out a little bit. Her son's name is Jamal Billings. He has dark hair and blue eyes and is probably about four and a half feet tall . . ."

"His last name is not Billings." Lydia put her hand over her eyes, wincing like she had a migraine.

I looked at her in confusion. "You said your last name was Billings."

Ignoring me, she took the phone off speaker and in a low tone, supplied Dean with the necessary information. My mind was racing. Why would she have given me a false last name? Once she hung up, I was about to demand an answer, but she burst into tears.

"They want an item of his clothing for Search and Rescue," she sobbed. "They're sending the dog out. Jamal loves that dog."

Heart pounding, I pulled into a driveway and turned around to head back to the house.

"What's going on, Lydia?" I said quietly. "Why don't I know your last name?"

"Because I used a fake name when I got here." She rubbed her forehead. "I was afraid my landlord would track me down. I didn't even think to tell you the truth until it was too late. You would have thought it was strange by then." She shook her head. "I'm sorry."

The air-conditioning in the old Chevy was not pumping out anything but hot air. I rolled down the windows, letting the wind whip my hair against my face. "That's why you didn't want to call the police? Because of your landlord?"

"It's complicated, Emma."

"Complicated in that you're wanted by the police and don't want to tell me?" I demanded, looking over at her.

"If my landlord filed a report, yes," she admitted. "Otherwise, no. Not at all."

We pulled into my driveway, and she rushed out to get one of Jamal's shirts. I sat and took deep breaths, trying to quiet the panic in my heart.

You already knew about the landlord. This is not news.

Still, the thing about her last name was strange. Something about it left a bad taste in my mouth, which probably wasn't fair.

But still.

She's a fraud and a grifter.

Lydia raced out of the house, clutching Jamal's sweatshirt close to her heart. The pain on her face was apparent as she got back in the car. "Here," she said, holding up the sweatshirt.

Immediately, I pushed aside the paranoid thoughts. Lydia had become a friend. She had helped find my mother. It was time to stop focusing on the bad and help her find her son.

"This town isn't that big," I said. "Hang on." I gunned the motor and took off toward Search and Rescue. "If anyone can find him, it'll be that dog."

Chapter Thirty-Five

Lydia and I were pacing the room at the Search and Rescue building when the call came that Jamal had been found. Lydia turned pale, and then silent tears streamed down her face. I walked over and gave her a hug, and she collapsed her head against my shoulder.

Ten minutes later, Jamal was escorted in by Captain Ahab and the volunteers who'd searched for him, drinking a red Gatorade. Captain Ahab strutted close to his side, licking his face each time he lowered the drink.

Lydia leapt to her feet. "Jamal."

It seemed that Jamal was doing his best to look brave, but the moment he saw his mother, he broke down in tears. Lydia pulled him tightly into her arms. I felt a pang, seeing the two of them together, and wondered for the hundredth time what would happen if I reached out to my mother.

Sheila rushed around handing out waters to the volunteers. She had been on duty when the call came in, and she had spent the last twenty minutes nervously painting her nails. The building reeked of acetone and frosted doughnuts. The black lab cozied up to her when she called him over for dog treats, pressing his nose against her hand and gobbling them up.

"He eats those treats like I eat chocolate." My laughter was bright with relief.

"You and me both, sister." Sheila's face fell. "Emma, speaking of chocolates . . . in the midst of all this, I forgot about the news I'd heard. The Sweetery is getting sold? What happened?"

It was a question I'd been asking myself again and again, each time the thought ran through my brain.

"I guess I didn't fight hard enough for it," I said, watching Lydia hold her son. "I was trying so hard to be good and fair. The truth of the matter, though, is that I don't have the first clue how to go after what I want."

"You wanted the store?" Sheila gave me a sympathetic look as she buried her hand in Captain Ahab's fur.

I could only hope her polish was quick drying.

"Yes." I nodded. "More than anything."

Lydia walked over with Jamal snuggled close. "Sheila, we can't thank you enough. I think we're going to head home." Her son shot her a warning look, and she said, "I mean, to Emma's house."

I sat on my knees so I could look Jamal in the eye. "We're going to go back and grill some burgers. Does that sound good to you?"

The way Jamal's dark eyes flashed, I could tell he had considered throwing attitude. He was either too tired or grateful to be back because he nodded instead.

"Cheeseburgers."

Affectionately, I ruffled his hair. "Cheeseburgers it is."

It didn't take long to stop by the store to grab the meat and get it started on the grill. Its smoky scent filled the yard, giving the long day the feeling of a normal, cozy summer night. In the kitchen, Lydia and I sliced tomatoes, onions, and lettuce while Jamal flipped through comic books. He was exhausted and dirty but had negotiated a bath after dinner, not before.

"They found him two miles away," Lydia said in a low tone. "Up in the bluffs. They said he'd hiked all that way by himself. It's so hot. He could have died up there." She pressed her hands against the counter, looking defeated. "I have to figure things out. I can't lose him . . ."

Her breath started coming quick, and I brought her a cold cloth. Shoulders heaving, she pressed it against her face.

"Everything will be okay. I promise you that."

"What if this is my punishment?" Her eyes looked haunted. "I could lose the one thing I care about the most."

"Punishment for what?" I said, confused.

There was a knock at the door. I knew it was Cody before I even opened it. Pulling the door open, I felt a grin stretch across my face at the sight of him holding a new soccer ball.

"Have you eaten?" I asked.

"No."

"We're having burgers," I said. "Hope that's okay. I'm fresh out of wild boar."

"Don't worry. There's already one strapped to the roof of my car." Strolling past me, he said to Jamal, "Hey, man. Let's go kick this ball around."

Jamal grunted like Cody, and the two of them headed out the back door.

~

The burgers were exactly what we needed to refuel and regroup. Jamal seemed to be showing off for Cody, which was fun to see. He ate two burgers, three pickles, and more chips than I could count. He also kept drinking the Gatorade that I pushed on him. He didn't seem to be showing any of the signs of heatstroke the Search and Rescue volunteers had lectured us on, once they'd given Jamal a thorough health check and declared him in good shape.

My phone was ringing as I carried the plates inside.

Kailyn.

"Hi," I said. "We've had some excitement around here today. Can I call you later?"

Her tone was hushed. "Where are you?"

"Home. Cody's here. We're having dinner with Lydia and Jamal."

"Okay." Kailyn sounded slightly panicked. "Is Lydia with you?"

"Everyone's outside." I rinsed off the plates, wiping off a smear of ketchup. "Do you—"

"Emma, this is Dean Harrington." A second voice came on the line. "I asked Kailyn to call you so it wouldn't raise any suspicion if you were with Lydia alone. You and Cody need to make an excuse to get out of there. Head to the store to pick up ice cream or something, okay?"

Slowly, I turned off the water and set down the plate. "Why?" My hands started to shake. "What's going on?"

Outside, Cody and Jamal chased each other around the yard as Lydia watched, laughing.

Grifter. Con artist.

"Is she a criminal or something?" I whispered.

"I heard your comment about the false last name," Dean said. "It struck me as odd, so I looked into it. Given the identity of her husband, I feel your personal safety could be at risk. We just want to bring her in for questioning."

"Who's her husband?" I said, completely confused.

"Terrance Grange."

I had to grip the edge of the counter to hold myself up. "No. That can't be right."

"Get out of there, Emma." Kailyn was practically in tears.

Blindly, I nodded, grabbing for my purse. I couldn't stay there a second longer.

Lydia's husband had killed my fiancé.

Chapter Thirty-Six

The shaking in my hands made it nearly impossible to hang on to my purse or put one foot in front of the other.

Why was she here, in my house?

Revenge.

The word invaded my mind. That couldn't be possible, though. Not once had she struck me as someone filled with anger, other than anger directed at herself. But maybe she was just good at hiding it. She'd had nothing but trouble ever since her husband was put behind bars. If Joe had never interfered, her husband wouldn't be in jail. Lydia wanted to blame someone, and I was the only one left.

The situation brought a picture of Joe to my mind. So kind, so pensive. He was such a good person that it made no sense that he was taken from the world so soon.

In fact, he never would have supported this type of ambush. He would have tried to talk to Lydia first, to understand what had happened and whether there had been some sort of mistake.

It was that type of thing that got him killed.

Besides, how could this be a mistake? Out of all the people in the world, Lydia just happened to end up in front of my store on a hot day, pretending to need a place to stay? It was not a coincidence. She had sought me out.

But for what? To steal? Maybe, but I didn't have anything to take. She hadn't tried to hurt me. If anything, she'd tried to help me. I had no idea what she was doing here and why she had hidden her true identity, and the uncertainty was more frightening than anything.

"Emma!" I nearly jumped as high as the ceiling as the screen door banged and her voice rang out. "Hey, the boys wanted us to—"

She walked into the kitchen and came to a sudden halt. "Oh, gosh. Are you sick?" She rushed forward and tried to touch my arm, but I jerked away.

"No, I . . ." The words wouldn't come.

The confusion on her face was so familiar. In a matter of a few weeks, she had become one of my closest friends. But everything had been based on a lie.

Get out . . .

"I got a text from Gillian that someone tried to break into the store," I said, since there was plenty of ice cream in the freezer, and Lydia knew it. "She wants me and Cody to come down to the store . . ."

"What? That doesn't sound like a good idea." She looked troubled. "It could be dangerous. I don't think you should get into all that."

"No, I have to," I managed to say. "I have to go."

Lydia's light-blue eyes fixed on mine. They were worried. Like she actually cared about me.

I felt sick to think it had been a setup the whole time.

Had the world really come to this? For years, Kailyn had been telling me to stop being such a sucker, and I'd ignored her. I refused to believe there was more bad than good in the world, but look where it had gotten me.

I was thirty-two years old, and my life was a mess. I didn't have a clue how to stand up for myself or go after what I wanted. In fact, I was such an easy target that the wife of my fiancé's killer had been living in my house for the past few weeks, and I'd been the one to open the doors to her.

"I am such a fool," I muttered.

Lydia's face went cautious, like she knew something was up. "Emma. What's really going on? Talk to me."

The screen door banged open, and Cody came barreling into the room. Kailyn must have texted him, because without a word, he grabbed me and pulled me out the front door, shielding me with his body, as if he thought Lydia might suddenly attack.

"Emma," she cried.

My legs took off running. Down the steps, across the yard, and into the street, where the police waited behind the enormous cluster of trees. One grabbed Cody and sheltered him, while the other did the same to me, pushing us to run farther down the block as fast as we could. The intensity of the situation left me waiting to feel a bullet slice through my back. Finally, safe behind a cop car, I slid down and put my head in my hands.

"Emma?" An officer sat in front of me, on his haunches. It was Dean. He looked the same as he did in high school, only a little older and a whole lot wiser. "Take deep breaths for me. Do you feel sick?"

I didn't feel sick. I felt sad. Intense sorrow coupled with an out-of-body feeling like I was watching this scene unfold from above, like something out of a dream or a movie. It was more of a shift in the light and the colors around me than anything concrete. The view of the trees seemed to fade from bright green and vibrant to a dull gray.

I managed to say, "Her husband killed Joe."

Right. It's that feeling.

Now I could place it. This same foggy feeling was the one that hit in those moments when I learned I'd lost someone I loved. My father and, years later, Joe.

"Sorry, I'm not . . ." The words faded out.

Dean signaled his partner, who fumbled in the car for a wool camping blanket and bottle of water. Cody pulled me into a tight hug. The sudden strength and warmth of his body, the safety I felt in his arms, made my eyes sting with tears.

He draped the blanket around me and handed me the water. "Drink this."

I put the bottle to my lips, barely feeling the warm water trickle into my mouth.

"We don't know what she planned to do," Dean said, his voice grim. "We will shortly."

"Where's Jamal?" I pressed my face into Cody's shoulder. "Is he in the middle of all this?"

"He's with one of the officers," Cody said. "They must have pulled him from the backyard. Man, that kid doesn't deserve all this. Neither do you."

Cody ran his hand over my hair. The move was intimate and protective.

The radio on Dean's belt crackled. He stepped to the side and picked up his cell phone.

"No, I don't feel comfortable with that," he said quickly. "Let me talk to her first."

I glanced up. "What's happened?"

Dean glanced at me but turned away, lowering his voice. But I caught the gist of it. Lydia was barricaded in the kitchen, and the police feared she could harm herself.

The idea of Jamal spending the rest of his life without his mother pushed me to my feet.

"Let me go in," I said. "I need to talk to her."

"Emma, no," Cody said. "It's too dangerous."

Dean nodded. "It's too big of a risk. Our team can handle the situation."

"You think that," I said. "But what if something happens? I can't live with that for the rest of my life."

I looked at Cody, half convinced he would tell me I'd risked enough. Instead, he squeezed my hand. "You sure you want to go in?"

The evening light was dull around me. I wasn't sure about anything. The only thing I knew was that there was a little boy in this scenario who'd already been through enough. He'd lost his father. He didn't need to lose his mother too.

Stepping forward, I nodded at Dean. "Tell me what I need to do."

Dean escorted me inside. Lydia was crouched in the corner of the kitchen, in the same spot my grandmother used to stand to drink her coffee. The moment she saw me, she burst into tears. She tried to move toward me, but Dean stepped between us.

"It's okay," I said. "Please. Let me talk to her."

Lydia was pale and wan. Her hands shook, and her eyes looked trapped. "I came here because I wanted to apologize," she told me. "Not because I wanted to trick you. You told me you didn't want to hear my story, that you wanted me to be safe." Tears spilled down her cheeks, and the anguish in her voice cut through me. "I didn't mean to lie to you."

I knew exactly the moment she meant. It was at the bed and breakfast that first day. Lydia had tried to tell me something, but she had started to cry, so I had stopped her. Still, enough time had passed that she could have told me.

"You should have told me at some point," I said quietly. "It's not like we haven't talked."

"Yes, but . . ." She sank into a chair at the kitchen table, looking lost. I stayed back, my hand on the kitchen counter. It unnerved me to have Dean hovering over us, especially since he had a gun.

"Please," I said, turning to him. "Let me just be with her."

Dean looked at me for a long moment. Then he took a few steps into the living room, close enough to help me but far enough away to give us some sense of space.

"That's the best I'm gonna do," he said.

Lydia drew her knees up to her chest. Her face was puffy, and there were deep circles under her eyes.

"I came here to apologize," she said after a moment. "To atone, I guess, after ten years, because I have always blamed myself for what happened to Joe. He saved my life, Emma. Did you know that?"

My breath caught.

Lydia was in the bar that night. She was the woman Joe had protected.

"I knew who my husband was long before I married him." She stared at a fixed point on the wall. "I was young and stupid, so I married him anyway. I should have put him behind bars long before for all the things he had done to me. That way, he wouldn't have had the opportunity to hurt anyone else, but I was too scared to stand up to him.

"That night at the bar . . . he was worse than he'd ever been, Emma. He thought I had flirted with the bartender and would not let it go. It was brewing and brewing, the alcohol and his rage turning him into a monster. Right before he lifted that bottle to me, he said he was going to kill me. I remember being down on the floor, on my knees and seeing stars, because he'd just punched me in the jaw. I watched the bottle go up, and all I could see was Jamal's little face, waiting for me to come home." She started to sob.

I moved to reach out and touch her arm, but Dean stepped forward and shook his head, which made her cry harder.

"You think I want to hurt you." Her wail echoed through the kitchen, and she stood up. "I would never hurt you. I came here to thank you, and to tell you it was all my fault. If it wasn't for me, Joe would still be alive."

I shivered and remembered the feel of the crisp fall air when he and I first met. The smell of movie popcorn. The look right before he kissed me. The memories rushed through me, and my eyes filled with tears.

Lydia stood in front of me shaking and sobbing. "Emma, I'm sorry."

I studied her as if from a distance. The idea of what her life must have been like was so clear and so frightening. She probably lived in fear each day that her ex-husband would achieve early parole. It was something I'd worried about as well, but it wasn't a threat to me in the same way it was to her.

Still, that did not mean I had to let her into my life. To bring that fear and heartache into my world when I'd dealt with it so many years ago. But no matter how hard I tried, I couldn't close my heart to her. It wasn't what Joe would have wanted, and it wasn't what I wanted.

In the past few weeks, Lydia and her son had become a part of my life. They were good people with good hearts. The fact that she made the effort to come here to make amends was not something I was willing to ignore.

Moving forward, I took her hands before Dean could stop me. "It was not your fault," I said quietly. Her body shook, and I held her hands tight. "You were the victim. You and Joe. It was not your fault what happened to him, and I'm here to tell you, he would have stepped in to protect you again and again. The fact that you have struggled with this for so long, the fact that you came here to try and make things right . . ." My words choked, and I had to blink hard to keep from breaking down in tears. "Lydia, they said you threatened to kill yourself. You can't do that. There are people here that love you and need you."

"It's just too much," she whispered, her eyes desperate. "It feels like too much."

"I know." I hugged her tight. "But I want you to get help and try to find a way to make it through. It's worth it. You're worth it."

I drew back and made her look me in the eye. "I promise you, you're worth it."

Tears ran down her cheeks, and she sank down into a kitchen chair, her shoulders heaving. I sat on my knees in front of her. "There have been so many times where I have been afraid that the world is a terrible place and the bad is winning. But Lydia, it's not. The fact that you came here to try and make things right proves that in the end, there are more people like you and Joe than there are like your husband."

"Ex-husband," she mumbled.

"Ex-husband," I clarified. For a split second, our eyes met, and I smiled. The moment vanished just as quickly, because there was nothing funny about the situation.

"I need help, Emma," she whispered. "Every day is still a struggle. I can't put Jamal through that. To make him live the life we've been living."

"I can help you," I said, but at the same time, I knew full well that she needed more than what I could offer.

"You've done enough." She wiped her eyes. "It's time for us to go home. It's been ten years since all this. As the time got closer and closer, I knew I needed to talk to you, to come here. I wanted to get closure, to thank you for the sacrifice that you made, that Joe made, and because I have to move on. It just so happened that the number in my bank account dwindled to zero, and I had to get out of town anyway, so I guess it was meant to be."

"Where will you go?" I said.

"I'll figure it out. I'll make things right with my old landlord. I have friends and a good psychiatrist who can help me get things back on track. It's time."

The words pained me, but I knew her plan was for the best. "I hope you'll come back."

"We will," she said. "Someday."

"Good." I pulled her into another hug, and my voice broke. "Next time, the two of you will stay with me."

Chapter Thirty-Seven

First thing the next morning, I went to pay a visit to my grandmother. It was early, so I wasn't sure if she would be up or not. If not, I planned to talk to the business office about the same issue that I had to address with her, that she would not be able to stay on at Morning Lark.

It made me sad, but at the same time, I was out of options. I'd checked the job boards, and there was nothing available where I could even apply. That is, unless I could somehow procure an engineering degree or complete medical school within the next five months, which did not seem likely.

I walked down to my grandmother's room. The hallway smelled like lilac powder, and I smiled, because that had to mean she was up. After knocking on her door, I pushed it open and stopped short. Gillian and my grandmother were sitting on the couch, drinking tea together and laughing.

The sight was absolutely baffling to me, as my grandmother had not had much of anything to say about Gillian since the day she'd dropped me off at her house. Every time I would try to get her opinion, my grandmother would wave her hand and change the topic. It was only later that I figured out it was because my grandmother preferred to operate under the "If you can't say anything nice" philosophy.

As a result, it had been my impression that the two did not like each other. Gillian, because she'd felt betrayed by my father, and my grandmother, because Gillian had walked away from her responsibility to me. The sight of them laughing and enjoying a visit did not match up with either of those ideas.

"Emma, I'm glad you're here." Gillian smiled at me. "It's quite perfect, actually."

The window was open, and a bird started to sing on the tree branch right outside the window, as if proving her point. I wondered if the bird would change its tune if it knew the reason I was there in the first place was because Gillian's decision had cost me my job and as a result, my grandmother's place at Morning Lark.

"Grab some tea, Emma," my grandmother said. "Join us."

My grandmother looked as happy and healthy as I'd seen her look in a while. Her hair was freshly done, this time with a silver-tinted rinse, and she wore a pale-blue day suit. It brought out the color in her eyes and made her cheeks look flushed and pretty.

Even though I would have preferred to walk out the door and return once Gillian had left, I poured myself a cup of tea and sat on the chair across from the couch. I couldn't imagine Gillian would choose to stick around much longer. I would simply have to wait her out.

"It's nice to have us all together." My grandmother looked at me. "Your father would have liked that."

My throat tightened at the sentiment.

"Family was incredibly important to him," Gillian said. "I always admired that about him, because I never really had much family. Even more so when I made the mistake of pulling away from the two of you."

I had been about to take a sip of my tea, but instead, I lowered it back down. "Sorry?"

Gillian's carefully made-up face resembled a pretty mask. Behind it, her eyes were pained. "Emma, the story you shared with me regarding the painter helped me in a way I can't even begin to describe. It might sound silly to you, but it was healing. I spent so many years thinking that your father was not in love with me, that I was not enough. To hear what that letter actually meant . . ." She put her hand to her mouth for a brief moment. Pulling it away, she turned to me. "The situation with the painting and the store has left me thinking a lot about your father, and a lot about the past. I came here this morning to speak with your grandmother about that, and we've had a nice conversation."

My grandmother reached over and took Gillian's hand. "Too many years passed with some pretty strong misconceptions."

"The one thing we settled on for certain was the fact that your father loved his family." Gillian looked at me. "That's where I made a big mistake." She let out a breath, and my grandmother nodded, as though encouraging her to continue. "Emma, over the years, I often saw you wonder why I didn't choose to raise you. I felt you thought it had something to do with you, and I should have addressed that."

"It's not necessary," I said, feeling more than a little uncomfortable.

"It is necessary," Gillian said. "The reason I didn't raise you was because I did not think your father would have wanted me to. We were not married for that long, and like I told you, he and I had agreed to divorce shortly before he died." She shared a shy look with my grandmother. "That would have been a big mistake."

"Your father loved Gillian," my grandmother said, as though baffled there had ever been a question about the matter. "The fact that those rumors caused such upset in the marriage . . ."

"Was well deserved," Gillian said quietly. "Because I never should have allowed anyone to see that letter."

"Who did you show it to?" I asked.

"Fanny Price." Gillian shook her head. "Lesson learned."

I drew back. "Mrs. Price spread those rumors?"

Gillian nodded. "We used to be very good friends, but when faced with the opportunity to gossip, the temptation was too strong."

The news disappointed me. One, because I'd always had a soft spot for Mrs. Price and two, because I knew she didn't have a mean bone in her body. Gillian was probably right that the temptation to share secrets was too much for someone like her to handle. Really, Mrs. Price probably saw the opportunity to gossip as a way to connect with other people. That was no excuse, however, especially when it had caused so much pain.

"Emma, the information you shared about your meeting with Charles, the things he said about the letter . . ." She shook her head. "I needed to hear those things. You don't know what that has done for my heart."

Even though I was still angry at Gillian, I was glad to hear the news had helped.

Letting out a deep breath, she turned to me. "Family was one of the most important things to your father, and I know I let you down. I've given it a lot of thought, and I've decided to withdraw my commitment to Talbaccis and to sell the store to you instead."

My heart started to pound. "What? No, they would sue you."

"I included a clause that gave me a thirty-day window to back out if any of the local businesses should choose to object to the sale. This morning, I spoke with Jenny at Chill Out. She is more than happy to voice the first objection."

Emotion tightened my chest. "But . . . I can't buy it. I don't have the money."

"The store is profitable," Gillian said. "We can set up a private payment plan. You'll pay me back in time."

"No." I shook my head, convinced the offer couldn't be true. "Gillian, you're planning to spend the winters in Florida. How will you afford to do that without the sale of the shop?"

"Well . . ." She smiled. "To be perfectly honest, there is a man I've been seeing, and it's become quite serious. That's another reason I wanted to talk to your grandmother today. He . . . well, he proposed."

She held up her hand and showed me a sparkling diamond ring. "I wanted to get her blessing. It looks like I'll be spending quite a bit of time here, after all."

The news was too much to process. I'd come here to tell my grandmother that she was going to have to move out of the living facility that she loved. If I owned the store, she would be able to live at Morning Lark as long as possible.

"What do you say?" Gillian asked, giving me a shy smile.

The old me would have hemmed and hawed and tried to talk her out of doing anything that would support me. Now, I simply gave an eager nod.

"I also hope . . ." She gave me a cautious look. "I hope that you and I could try and get to know one another again. I know I've made a lot of mistakes, but I still consider you a part of my family. Both of you." Her eyes misted with tears. "You're the family that I walked away from because I was afraid. I'm sorry for that."

My grandmother gave her a firm kiss on each cheek. "Welcome back."

I nodded. Then, for the first time in too many years to count, I leaned forward and hugged Gillian tight.

"Congratulations on the engagement," I said. "I'll be more than happy to build you a chocolate fountain to celebrate."

Then, for the first time in too many years to count, she hugged me back.

I didn't sleep that night. Instead, I sat out in the backyard, staring up at the stars. Millions of thoughts ran through my mind. Memories of my father, the pain of Gillian leaving, and the moments I had shared with Lydia and Jamal.

The night got colder the later that it got, and the ground became damp with a thick dew around my feet. Still I sat, pulling a blanket more tightly around me. The smell of citronella was strong in the air from the bug spray, and the scent of a late-night bonfire somewhere, perhaps down by the water, wafted up.

I thought about my time with Lydia and managed to put some things together. Like the fact that Lydia's lie about her last name is what had set Jamal off that one day. Cody had told me that his shirt in the group was printed with the name Billings, and he had to have been embarrassed, knowing that his last name wasn't correct but unable to explain to Cody what was wrong. The choices Lydia had made were not always the best ones, but they had come from a good place, and she had been a good friend.

The stars twinkled overhead as I considered the biggest gift of all she'd given me. The picture of my mother and the information on how to contact her, which now sat in my email. Lydia had tracked down both her phone number and her address, which was in Bruges. There had been so many moments I had considered picking up the phone and calling her, but I didn't know that it was the right decision.

I'd lived without a mother my entire life. Yet, I'd wanted to be with her so desperately. There was so much, I felt, that my mother could have given me. The fact that she chose not to be with me was something I had a hard time wrapping my mind around, especially when I watched my friends have children. The bond they shared with their child was one that caused almost a physical longing within me. That closeness. I'd had it for a nine-month period that I would never remember, at least on a conscious level, and after that, not at all.

It was only when I turned twelve and my emotions were in overdrive that I really longed for a mother. Someone to hold me when I felt the world was too much and someone to show me how to stand on my own two feet when I was ready to conquer. There were brief moments during this stage where I tried to reconnect again with Gillian, inviting her to school for Parents at Work Day and asking for her advice on what to wear to a school dance, but it was apparent she never really wanted to step in.

There were times she showed up at a school event but left early to report on a story, and every Christmas, I got my hopes up that she would buy me a present or at least stop by for Christmas dinner. That never happened. My grandmother had noticed my heartache during this phase and had tried to talk me out of chasing after something that was not meant to be.

"Gillian wants to forget life with your father," she'd said. "It's too painful to revisit those memories, and unfortunately, my dear, you were a big part of that time in her life."

The rationale was meant to serve as a comfort, but I had never believed it. I thought I was someone Gillian had only tolerated because she wanted to be with my father. Beyond that, I believed I didn't matter to her at all.

If only I'd known what she had been through. She'd only let me go because she believed that my father did not love her and that he would not have thought she was good enough to raise me. It was so ironic, because that misconception had led me to believe that I wasn't good enough either.

Losing Gillian had left an emptiness inside of me that nothing could fill. Not work, or chocolate, or helping other people, or any of the things that I had tried to distract myself with. There were moments when I had substituted that pain with missing my birth mother—or the idea of what my mother could have been—but at this point in my life, I was used to not having her around.

With that in mind, I wasn't sure that contacting her was the best idea. There was a chance she wouldn't want to talk to me, or even worse, that we would talk and that it wouldn't matter at all. The conversation might be light and chatty, where I told her about my life and she told me about hers and we promised to stay in touch. What would be the point of that?

To me, a mother was a person who would be present in my life. Like my grandmother had been. She had been there for every moment and each milestone. The hurts, heartbreaks, and disappointments, as well as the victories. It would take years to develop that type of relationship with someone who lived across the world, and even if we both wanted to make it work, the fact that we could not be in each other's lives except on a limited basis limited the emotional payoff that would come with the risk.

Risk and reward.

It felt good to think like a businesswoman again.

I felt a renewed sense of appreciation for Gillian and the significance that she was going to help me buy the store. Our relationship had been so strained for so long, based on mutual hurt and misunderstanding, but now, that had all changed. We had the chance to move forward into a new phase and get to know one another again, and it seemed like it was something we both wanted.

Pulling out my phone, I stared down at the picture of my mother.

I wanted to feel some sort of a connection with her as well. To see something there that would invite me in, but I didn't. Instead, I saw a stranger who I could pass on the street without giving it a second thought.

I looked up at the stars and closed my eyes. Finally, I shook my head.

It's not the time. Maybe it will be one day, but today is not that day.

My heart felt lighter at the thought. With a press of the button, I deleted the photo.

Chapter Thirty-Eight

The moment Gillian sold me the store was the happiest of my life. Her lawyer drew up some contracts, I signed off, and we celebrated in the kitchen with two chocolate-champagne stars. They were absolute perfection and something I decided to produce on a regular basis.

My phone rang as Gillian and I clinked stars. The number was unfamiliar. I wanted to answer in case it was Lydia. She and Jamal had started their trip back home, and she'd promised to call if she needed anything at all.

"Hello?" I said.

"Is this Emma?"

The voice on the other end was unfamiliar.

"Yes. Who is this, please?"

"Who is it?" Gillian whispered, nibbling at the champagne star. Then, she made an ecstatic face and gestured at it, as if to say *perfection*.

"It's William Masterson," the man on the other end said. "I bought the house you used to live in as a little girl, and we're currently doing some work on it."

"Oh, hi," I said, confused at the call. "How are you?"

The image of the diggers sitting in the edge of the yard flashed through my mind, followed by Mrs. Price and her flavored tea. Oh, goodness.

Mrs. Price.

I was on her list of emergency contacts. Had something happened? Even though she was the one who had started the rumors that had hurt Gillian, I had been close to her my entire life. In spite of everything, it would hurt me to see her in any type of pain or trouble.

"Well, I find myself in a rather odd position," Mr. Masterson said, and I braced myself for bad news.

Gillian frowned. "What happened?" she whispered.

"Don't know," I mouthed.

"My wife and I have found some things in the house that belonged to your father." He paused. "I think you should come over and take a look."

"Oh." Emotion welled through me. "Yes, I'd love to. When's a good time?" Covering the receiver, I told Gillian, "The people who bought our house are remodeling. They found some things that belonged to Dad."

Gillian's face brightened. "That's wonderful."

"Could you come now?" he said. "My wife and I are both home this morning."

"Yes. I'll be right there."

The second I hung up, Gillian said, "I'm coming too."

I smiled at her. "Well, of course."

Mr. Masterson waited at the front door with his wife at his side. They were both dressed in baggy clothes covered in dust and gave big smiles as we walked up the pathway leading to the house. It felt so strange to do that with Gillian by my side, like I was stepping back into time.

"Amanda Masterson." His wife stuck out her hand when we reached the front door. "I'm sure I look a fright." She wore a pair of demolition goggles around her neck. It was hard to tell if her close-cut blonde hair was streaked with gray or plaster, and her work clothes were indeed a mess, but her smile stretched from ear to ear. "We have been working on this place all summer, and today—"

"We tore down the wall in the library," her husband said. "Imagine our surprise when—"

"Don't tell them." She beckoned at us. "Just come. Please. Have a look."

The strangeness of the encounter was heightened by the sensation of walking through my old house. I hadn't been in it since it had been sold, and immediately, my memory went into overdrive. My father was everywhere. In the kitchen, dancing while he cooked in the kitchen. In the hallway, hanging up pictures of me. Standing by the main window, reporting on the weather, on an especially stormy night.

"This is a lot," I said, coming to a stop.

Gillian's eyes misted, and she took my hand. "It is."

I realized she was seeing the same playback, but with different memories.

The Mastersons walked in front of us, practically skipping down the hall. I wondered if they had found old photo albums or what, because they seemed so excited about it.

"Come on, you two," Mr. Masterson called back. "We can give you the tour later."

Gillian gave me a confused look. "This is starting to feel like a surprise party."

The two of us followed them, and they stopped right outside the room that used to be the library. In my memory, the shelves stretched to the ceiling on two sides and were filled with books. The fireplace was nestled between them, and the windows overlooked the small plot of trees outside.

It had been one of my favorite rooms in the house, because it was one of the few places where my father would actually sit down and relax. There were times he would fall asleep in the chair in front of the fire, and I would snuggle in at his feet, resting my head on his leg.

"So." Mr. Masterson clapped his hands together, turning to us. "We knocked down the wall that connected this room to the living room. We plan to widen the space to open the living room and kitchen, to let in more light—"

"They're not here to hear our remodel plans," his wife sang, tugging at his arm. "Let's show them, already."

"I'm building up to it." He wiped his hand across his forehead and gave us a rueful grin. "When we went to knock down the wall, we found something quite extraordinary. We found that it wasn't the only wall."

His wife gave a satisfied nod and stepped aside, letting us into the room. "There was a fake. Behind it, we found this."

The gasp that greeted the revelation might have been mine, or it might have been Gillian's. Because the wall had been torn down to reveal a second wall, and *The Girl with the Butterscotch Hair* hung in the center. The light from the window fell through the dust making it look like snow, and the sun's rays shined on the painting like a spotlight.

I had never seen anything so beautiful in my entire life.

"It's extraordinary," Gillian breathed. "The other one was lovely, but this . . ."

"It's something, isn't it?" Mr. Masterson rubbed his hands together.

"We've also seen the other one in the candy shop," his wife said. "Several times, because I can't stay away from your truffles. There certainly is a difference with this one, though, isn't there?"

"I took it down to wipe off the dust. I used a dry cloth so I'm sure it didn't hurt anything," Mr. Masterson said. "I also removed a small piece of paper that covered up a note written on the back. Emma, did you know that the artist bequeathed this painting to you?"

With the greatest care, Mr. Masterson picked up the painting and turned it over to reveal a handwritten inscription on the back. It was on the back of the painting, in the lower right-hand corner, in a rolling script.

"The girl with the Butterscotch Hair," 1992. Gifted to Gilroy Laurent with the understanding that it will pass down to the subject, Emma Laurent, with much affection.

—K. L. Heathwood

"I can't believe it," I breathed. "That's the note my father had in his files. It was analyzed, and they said it was a forgery. That he had traced the artist's words to create the note."

Gillian nodded, stepping closer to look. "He must have laid a sheet of paper right over the back of the painting. So, he did trace it, probably so he'd have it in his records. He couldn't very well take the painting to Kinko's to photocopy the back."

"He faked the signature too," I said. "He signed it from Montee to keep the secret safe, probably until he felt it was the right time to give me the real painting. Something he never got to do."

From the moment we'd walked into the library, my eyes had ached from trying to hold back tears. Now, the words made them spill freely down my cheeks.

"We know who K. L. Heathwood is." Mrs. Masterson touched the frame with affection. "We know the value of his work. We also know that technically, since we bought the house, the painting belongs to us." She took her husband's hand. "But, Emma, this painting belongs to you. We would not feel right about keeping it. Your father put it here to keep it safe, and we'd like to think in some small way, we had a hand in that."

"So please, take it," her husband said. "Before we come to our senses and change our minds."

The Mastersons watched me like it was Christmas morning. It certainly felt that way to me. Mrs. Masterson gave a small smile. "Everyone is going to say that we are such suckers."

"Maybe we are." Mr. Masterson shrugged. "But when it comes down to it, this feels like the right decision for us." He handed me the painting. "Here you are, Emma Laurent. With much affection."

I could barely breathe. I couldn't speak. Instead, I looked at Gillian and burst into happy tears.

Chapter Thirty-Nine

Since the painting was such a big deal, I wanted to celebrate the find with the people of Starlight Cove. The best way to do that, I decided, was in conjunction with the grand reopening of the Sweetery. Really, it had only been shut down for two days at the end of the week while Gillian and I closed out the final aspects of the deal. Still, I wanted to have a huge party to celebrate the fact that I was the owner and also to give people the opportunity to learn the story of the painting.

It was such an honor to think that such a famous artist had picked Starlight Cove to hide away in. It was also an honor to think that he'd completed such a beautiful work of art in our town, and about our town. In my opinion, it would make Starlight Cove even more attractive to tourists, especially those hungry for art history.

I half wished that I still had the information of the couple who had originally brought the origin of the painting to my attention, even if it was a fake. There was no doubt in my mind that they had truly loved the piece, as well as the idea of what it could have done for them. It would be nice for them to have the opportunity to see the real one, but maybe they would be back in town next year.

I set up the party for the following Friday night, hiring out a team of security. One of my good friends was a caterer, and even though she was booked through the summer, she promised to send some of her workers over to help me out, along with an impressive array of heavy hors d'oeuvres. The night of the party, the tables were dotted with red roses that complemented the gold-and-burgundy candy boxes that lined the walls.

The painting hung in the center of the candy shop, carefully covered to hide it from the curious glances of the tourists that strolled Main Street. Two beefy security guards stood at the front door, and one stood at the door that led into the kitchen. Outside the picture window of the candy shop, the evening light cast a golden hue. Inside, caterers set out trays of savory snacks and poured welcome drinks.

I looked around and let out a deep breath. The Sweetery had been put back together, and this time, the display cases were filled with our traditional chocolates as well as the handcrafted chocolate animal truffles I'd dreamed about making for the past twenty-five years.

The chocolate lab was probably my favorite. Its body was made from two dark chocolate truffles filled with milk chocolate ganache. The ears hung low and were accentuated with wide eyes and a pink fondant tongue that gave the dog a sweet, impish expression.

It made me think of the situation with Jamal. I missed him and Lydia and wished they could have been here to celebrate the night.

I rubbed my hands up and down my arms. The room was chilled with air-conditioning, but once my friends arrived, as well as the news crews Gillian had invited, it would get hot. My sleeveless black taffeta cocktail dress made me feel strong and feminine, or maybe it was that second round of hot yoga I'd attended, led by Cody.

The dark oak shelves lining the walls had been polished until they gleamed, and the burgundy-and-gold-striped candy boxes were once again perfectly arranged on the shelves. Cocktail tables had been brought in for the purpose of the party, so there were plenty of places for people to stand and chat.

Letting out a deep breath, I took a moment to marvel at the fact that somehow everything had worked out. There was nothing in this world I'd wanted more than the candy shop, and to think that I now had the honor to bring my father's legacy to life made getting out of bed in the morning a much more exciting prospect. There were so many things I planned to do, and I couldn't wait to get started.

"Hey," Kailyn called as the security guard let her in. She was carrying a large pink box. "I've got the cake!" She made her way to a marble table by the window and set down the box. Flipping her hair over her shoulder, she gave me a dimpled grin. "It's perfect."

I walked over to take a peek. "Oh, wow."

I'd tried to talk her out of a cake, because it seemed excessive. I'd always felt embarrassed on my birthday when people sang "Happy Birthday" to me, and I didn't see the need to get a cake tonight either. After all, we were standing in the middle of a candy shop, so wouldn't it be a little much?

Well, as it turned out, Kailyn was right. The cake was beautiful and just right for the occasion.

It was three tiered, iced in dark chocolate, and brushed with edible gold powder. The distinctive scent of vanilla cake added to the flavors of the room. The thing I loved about it the most, though, was that the cake shop had built the animal truffles from the painting in fondant and arranged them into adorable scenes on each layer. The cow, horse, and pigs frolicked by a red-frosting barn; the ducks and frogs played on a vivid blue lake; and the dog and cat were curled up beneath a moon-and-star scene. It was classic, whimsical, and absolutely perfect.

"I love it," I breathed.

"Well, I wanted the best," Kailyn said. "Especially considering the incredible VIP who's joining you tonight."

"Who?" I said, confused.

Her dimple deepened. "Oh, just the newest member of the Starlight Cove Chamber of Commerce Board of Directors."

"What?" I leapt up and down. "Really?"

"Yes! It happened a few days ago, but you've been a little busy." Her expression got serious. "I wanted to say thank you, though. For real. I was scared, and if you hadn't pushed me to go for it, this never would have happened. But we both took a leap, and now I'm on the board at the chamber, and you own a candy shop. I wanted to say thank you for being such a good friend, Emma, for pushing me to go for it."

"Some would say a best friend."

"Well, yeah." Kailyn surveyed the space and held up her hands. "I'll definitely be your best friend. Rumor has it you own a candy shop."

We both laughed, but the old joke actually made me sentimental. For the first time, I really *did* own the candy shop, something that was still a little hard to believe.

"How are you feeling about everything?" Kailyn asked, bustling around and getting the cake set up.

"Good." I nodded. "I was thinking about Lydia, actually, when you got here. I talked to her today." The telling purse of her lips made it clear that Kailyn was still suspicious, but with time, I knew she'd relax about it. Lydia had had some rotten luck, but she had a heart of gold. I only wanted the best for her.

"They're doing great." I rearranged one of the floral displays. "She's getting help to deal with her depression issues. It's going well, and she's feeling good about her relationship with Jamal."

"What's next for her?" Kailyn asked.

"I invited her to work for me," I said.

Kailyn's mouth dropped open. "She's coming back? Emma, I don't know if that's the best idea."

"No, she's not coming back," I reassured her. "Jamal needs to return to his school in the fall. She's going to work remotely, helping me to manage the e-commerce site I'm setting up for the store, as well as answer customer emails and things like that. She had a pretty big job before her life fell apart. I think I'm going to feel lucky to have her."

"Only you, Emma." Kailyn smiled at me. "Only you could turn that situation into lemonade."

"No." I spotted someone by the front door and smiled. "Not just me."

Cody Henderson stood outside with a group of friends we'd grown up with. I felt a tiny tug in my heart, seeing him. He'd started to become such a steady fixture in my life that the idea of getting involved with him no longer sounded frightening. It sounded like a lot of fun. I was only beginning to get to know him, but he had already managed to get me to talk through some of my feelings with Gillian and really had pushed me to be a stronger person.

"You ready to open the doors?" the security guy called, and I nodded, feeling that strange sense of relief I always got before a party, grateful that anyone had bothered to show up.

The security guard let them in, and Cody turned to look for me. Our eyes met, and he smiled. He walked right over and took my arm.

"You look pretty as a painting," he said, and I laughed.

Once that first group showed up, the rush of guests came steady and strong. I'd invited my close friends but also a handful of locals who I thought should be present, like the women from the women's chapter of the Starlight Cove Historical Society, Jolene and Charles, and of course, Gillian. The kisses, hugs, and handshakes went by in a blur, and the smell of chocolate and wine hung thick in the air.

Dawn and Kip walked in. I rushed over and gave them both big hugs. "You know that this all happened because of the two of you, right?" I said.

Dawn laughed. "Well, I had nothing to do with it. But if you insist, I'll go ahead and take a piece of chocolate as payment. Probably a few pieces for Kip too."

"Take as much as you want," I told her. "Take home boxes. You deserve it."

Finally, I spotted the one person I'd been waiting for. My grandmother walked into the Sweetery with her caretaker. She came to a sudden stop, probably at the familiar smell, and clasped her hands in delight. It had been years since she'd stepped foot in the place, and now she looked as happy as a little girl.

"Cody, come here," I said, gently pulling him out of a conversation. "There's someone I'd like you to meet."

My grandmother offered her hand with the grace of a grand dame. "So, you're the reason my Emma has been smiling again."

"No, ma'am," Cody said with a straight face. "I think it's because she's always hopped up on sugar."

My grandmother broke into peals of laughter. The two of them started chatting like old friends, and my heart warmed as I watched the scene. I didn't know where things were going to go with Cody, but I was more than ready to find out.

It looked like everyone had arrived, so I decided to take the stage and unveil the painting. The room seemed to spin as I weaved through the crowd, smiling at guests. The excitement of sharing the painting with everybody made my heart beat faster and my smile grow wide.

In a roped-off area in the back of the store, I'd commissioned a small platform with a podium, computer, and microphone, as well as a small screen on the wall next to the painting where I could project the PowerPoint Ms. Brandstein had sent me. The makeshift stage creaked under my heels as I stepped onto it. Eager silence filled the room as I looked around at the crowd of familiar faces.

"I must be the luckiest girl in the world to have you all here," I said, my voice thick with emotion. "As you all know, my stepmother, Gillian, has been generous enough to help me become the proud owner of the Sweetery." She stood to the side with a handsome man I'd seen around town, her brightly colored dress perfect for the eleven o'clock news. Earlier that day, she had filmed detailed B-roll to add to the story of the painting, including the information Ms. Brandstein had provided. At my words, she smiled and blew me a kiss. "Gillian, the fact that you have made this possible has changed my life. Words cannot describe what this place means to me . . ."

My eyes fell on my grandmother. She stood beneath a chandelier, her white hair lit and a sweet smile on her face. In that moment, she looked just like my father, and it was like he was in the room.

"The Sweetery meant everything to my father and now, to me. The fact that I will have the honor of running it never would have happened without your support. Gillian, I will be forever grateful."

The party guests broke into applause. Gillian waved them off. She blinked several times, and I could have sworn I saw her wipe away a tear.

Pointing up at the covered painting, I said, "You guys, my father took great pains to protect both the artist and this painting. When K. L. Heathwood first came to town, he suffered from the pressure of newfound fame, and he kept his identity a secret. My father knew the potential value of the painting, which is why he hired an artist to create a duplicate. He loved it and wanted to hang it in the candy shop for everyone to see, because he didn't want anything to happen to the original. Of course, I didn't know any of that, and that little mix-up made my life exciting for a while. Ultimately, it was the kindness of good neighbors that brought this painting back home." I nodded at the Mastersons, who smiled back.

"My father would be so pleased to know that *The Girl with the Butterscotch Hair* has finally been shared in the very place it was created." The excited murmur that passed through the crowd gave me a moment to regroup so that I didn't choke up. "It means a lot to me to be able to show the authentic version of the painting to you. So, I hope you enjoy this brief presentation about K. L. Heathwood and his work, followed by the opportunity to take a close and personal look at a masterpiece.

"Many of you might want to know what will happen next, like will it go to auction. I'm excited to announce I've decided not to sell the painting but to keep it." The words brought a small hush over the crowd. "It's what my father would have wanted, and based on the note on the back, it's what the artist would have wanted. However, I do plan to loan it out to the K. L. Heathwood Museum for six months, in exchange for restoration. It received some damage while hiding in the walls, although minimal. While it's away, I'll be working with a top-of-the-line security firm to set up a secure way to put it on display. Then, the painting will hang in this very spot, at its home in Starlight Cove, where it belongs. Without further ado, *The Girl with the Butterscotch Hair*."

I pulled the cloth off the painting, half-worried it would have disappeared again at some point during the night. But no, it sat on its throne on the wall like a princess. The party guests burst into applause, and I gazed up at it with affection.

Stepping away from the crowd, I surveyed the room and took a deep breath. It was so hard to believe I was sharing such a treasure surrounded by treasure of my own.

So much had changed, yet so much had stayed the same.

I felt a pair of eyes on me, and I turned.

Cody headed my way, carrying a small plate. It held a single chocolate truffle.

"What are you doing with that?" I asked.

"Being supportive." Giving me a rueful grin, he popped it into his mouth.

"What do you think?" I asked as he gave it a thoughtful chew.

"Hard to tell." His eyes sparkled. "Better have another to be sure. Probably some taffy too."

The caterer walked by with a tray of chocolates, and I fed Cody another truffle.

I rested my forehead against his chest, and he pulled me in close.

"Spending time with me might be good for you," I told him.

"It's going to be good for both of us," he promised, before giving me a kiss as sweet as chocolate.

ACKNOWLEDGMENTS

First, to my readers: thank you for investing your time in my work. Your interest and enthusiasm have made it such an incredible joy to share the stories and characters of Starlight Cove. Thank you for going on this journey with me.

Lake Union, thank you for sending me on this journey. From the beginning, I have been in awe of the immense talent that makes up this brilliant company: the editors, designers, and marketers, not to mention countless other team members who work so hard to champion the work of their authors. Danielle Marshall, thank you for believing in this project and making it possible. I am forever grateful. Alicia Clancy, thank you for your dedication to this series, your ability to lead me to the best book possible, and your commitment to making sure my books get read. It is truly a gift to work with you. Lindsay Guzzardo, I was delighted to work with you on this one and appreciated your guidance and insight. You helped make this book shine.

Brent Taylor, thank you for being the best agent in the world. Your support is endless and your enthusiasm inspiring. I am so proud to work with you and so thankful for the support of the team at Triada US.

Finally, thank you to my writer's group—Frankie Finley, Jennifer Mattox, and Stephanie Parkin—for your talent, your dedicated friendship, and the stories we've shared. I'm already looking forward to our next retreat. Mom, thank you for everything, but mainly for pushing me to achieve my dreams, no matter how out of reach they seemed. You are the best mom in the world. Finally, to my husband, Ryan. I will never forget the moment I first saw you. Thank you for spending this wonderful life with me, and thank you for our beautiful family. I love you.

ABOUT THE AUTHOR

Cynthia Ellingsen is the author of four contemporary novels—*The Winemaker's Secret* (a Starlight Cove novel), *The Lighthouse Keeper* (a Starlight Cove novel), *The Whole Package*, and *Marriage Matters*—as well as a middle-grade novel, *The Girls of Firefly Cabin*. She is a Michigan native and lives in Lexington, Kentucky, with her family. Connect with her at www.cynthiaellingsen.com.